DRAGON KEEPER

GARDEN OF THE PURPLE DRAGON

Carole Wilkinson was born in the UK but now lives in Melbourne, Australia, with her husband and daughter.

Books by Carole Wilkinson

DRAGONKEEPER

DRAGONKEEPER: GARDEN OF THE PURPLE DRAGON

DRAGONKEEPER: DRAGON MOON

CAROLE WILKINSON

DRAGON KEEPER

GARDEN OF THE PURPLE DRAGON

MACMILLAN CHILDREN'S BOOKS

First published in Australia 2005 by black dog books
First published in the UK 2007 by Macmillan Children's Books

This edition published 2008 by Macmillan Children's Books
a division of Macmillan Publishers Limited
20 New Wharf Road, London N1 9RR
Basingstoke and Oxford
www.panmacmillan.com

Associated companies throughout the world

ISBN: 978-0-330-44112-4

Typeset by Intype Libra Limited
Printed and bound in Great Britain by Mackays of Chatham plc, Kent

FOR
MARINUS WILLEM
DE VISSER

1875–1930

THE ULTIMATE SINO-DRACOLOGIST

CONTENTS

MING YANG LODGE

Touching
Heaven Tower

Princess Yangxin's Chambers

YELLOW RIVER

Late Spring Villa

Chamber of
Spreading
Clouds

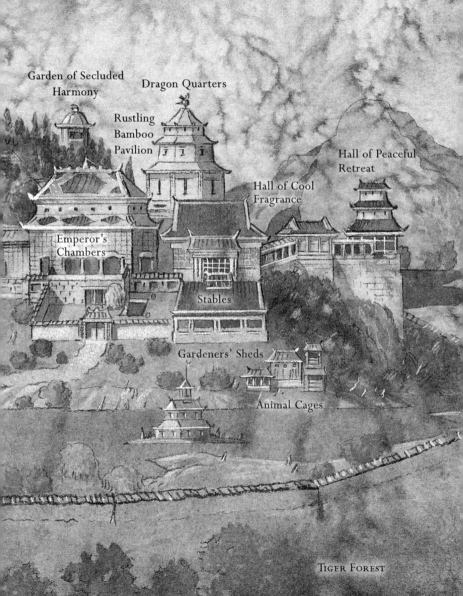

Garden of Secluded
Harmony

Dragon Quarters

Rustling
Bamboo
Pavilion

Hall of Peaceful
Retreat

Hall of Cool
Fragrance

Emperor's
Chambers

Stables

Gardeners' Sheds

Animal Cages

TIGER FOREST

Chinese Empire in the Han Dynasty

CHAPTER ONE

BLACK DRAGON POOL

The chatter of cascading water was the only sound that could be heard. It tumbled down a cliff and collected in a wide, dark pool. Beneath the surface, darker shadows circled – the slender, darting bodies of fish and larger oval shapes. Clumps of reeds grew among black rocks in the shallows. Further along the bank, delicate ferns pushed through a scatter of smooth black pebbles. One of the dark oval shapes drifted slowly to the surface. It was a turtle. A swirling current caught it and tugged it towards the rim of the pool. The turtle paddled its webbed feet to keep from being carried over the edge where water spilt out of the calm pool and hurried on its journey down the side of the mountain.

A dragonfly balanced on the surface of the pool. Its slender legs were blood-red. Its long thin body was a startling blue, like a splinter of sunlit sky that had fallen to earth. The insect had two pairs of delicate wings criss-crossed with black veins. Each wing was marked with an eyespot. It could have been a precious jewel dropped by a careless princess. The dragonfly's wings whirred and it took off. It buzzed to a reed, and then from the reed to a rock.

A shadow fell on the dragonfly. A bundle of reeds swooped through the air and landed on it with a thwack, squashing it flat. Ping picked up the dead dragonfly and put it in the leather pouch that hung from her belt, adding it to her collection of crushed caterpillars and flattened moths.

A breeze disturbed the reeds. There was a sharp chill in the air that meant winter wasn't far away. Ping gazed into the distance. She had been looking out at the same view for half a year, but she hadn't tired of it yet. It was a clear day and mountain peaks stretched before her like a crowd of giants. Pine forests covered the lower, gentler slopes. On the higher, steeper slopes there were only a few twisted pines perched like vultures wherever their roots could get a hold.

Among the dull green of the pines were a few trees tinted with the oranges and reds of autumn. Sunlight glinted off a distant lake. Ping sometimes felt like she was living in one of the paintings that hung in Huangling Palace. She had once believed that such landscapes existed only in the imagination of artists. Now she knew they were real.

Behind her the sheer cliffs of Tai Shan blotted out the sky. Ping preferred to look to the south, where the mountain peaks were smaller and softer and didn't bring back memories she would rather forget.

The peace of the afternoon was disturbed by a harsh squawk. Ping closed her eyes and sighed. The squawking grew louder, more persistent. It sounded like something was being strangled. She didn't hurry. She walked over to a stand of pine trees. They were small trees, less than twice Ping's height, gnarled and twisted. The squawking turned into a continuous screech.

She stood beneath a particular tree with her hands on her hips.

'Long Kai Duan,' she said crossly. 'I told you not to climb trees.'

A small creature was clinging upside down to one of the highest branches. It was covered in purple scales, the colour of violets in sunshine. Down its back was a row of sharp spines. Its tail was wrapped around the branch. It had large paws that seemed much too big for its body. Each paw had four sharp black talons that were all digging into the tree bark. The little creature turned its upside-down head towards Ping. Bright green eyes blinked anxiously. The creature's straight snout ended in a fat, pink nose with quivering nostrils. Its large mouth opened wide to let out another squawk, revealing sharp little teeth and a long, red tongue. It was a small dragon, not much bigger than a cat or a hare.

The bark under the creature's front talons came away from the branch. The little dragon's cry became more shrill. The talons on its back paws couldn't support its full weight. The dragon let go of the branch and was left dangling by its tail. It whimpered. Ping climbed on to a rock and reached up to the dragon. It clung on to her outstretched arm, digging its talons into her flesh.

'That hurts!' Ping said, but if the dragon understood, it took no notice.

Ping slipped on the rock's smooth surface and skidded down on her bottom, landing with a thud on the hard earth. The dragon let go of her arm, gave her a sharp nip on the nose and scuttled off.

Ping rubbed her nose. 'If that's your way of saying thank you, I'd rather you didn't bother.'

She examined the scratches on her arm. Both arms were covered with claw marks – some fresh, some healed to scars. She heard a splash. Kai had decided that tree climbing was too dangerous and had gone to swim in the pool. It was his favourite pastime, one that kept him happy for hours. He was a strong swimmer and as comfortable in the water as he was out of it, but Ping still watched him anxiously. She couldn't swim. And the times when she'd found herself in deep water she'd been terrified.

Ping had needed a place to bring up a small, purple dragon – a secluded place where no one would disturb them, where Kai could run around without being seen. She didn't have a lot of experience of the empire. She knew of only one place where no one ever went – Tai Shan, the sacred mountain that she had climbed with the young Emperor when he had sought the blessing of Heaven at the beginning of his reign. Only the Emperor and his shamans were allowed to climb past a certain point known as the Halfway to Heaven Gate. To do so without imperial permission was punishable by death.

The flight from Tai Shan to Ocean on the back of Long Danzi, Kai's father, had taken less than a day. It had taken her a week to walk back to Tai Shan. Carrying newly hatched Kai, she had climbed up the imperial path, passed beneath the Halfway to Heaven Gate and into the forbidden area. Then she left the path, cutting across the steep slopes. Liu Che, the young Emperor, had mentioned a pool to the west – Black Dragon Pool. It sounded grim, but with a dragon name it would be an auspicious place to raise Kai.

Black Dragon Pool wasn't as forbidding as it sounded. The cascade collected in a rocky depression where the steep slopes of Tai Shan levelled out briefly to form a small plateau. The water wasn't black; it was the rocks that gave the pool its colour. There was a grove of pine trees around one side of the pool and a narrow meadow on the other. The plateau was sunlit for most of the day. Ping had found roots, mushrooms and berries to add to the simple meals she made with grain and lentils. There were also fish in the stream.

By the time Kai had tired of the pool, the sun was an orange ball on the jagged horizon. The lake in the distance reflected the same colour, as if molten liquid from inside the sun had leaked on to the earth. Ping shaded her eyes to enjoy the spectacle while it lasted. Then she went back to stirring the pot of fish soup that she had prepared over a small fire. She felt guilty for catching the fish which swam up to her so innocently when she bathed in the shallows, but she needed more than roots and berries to eat. She had to conserve her small store of grain and lentils for winter. The turtles would have made a welcome change from fish, but Ping couldn't bring herself to kill them. Apart from the baby dragon, the turtles were her only companions.

A bleating sound reminded her that this wasn't quite true.

'Yes, you're a companion too,' she said to a she-goat tethered to a nearby tree. 'In fact, I get more sense out of you than Kai.'

Ping sat by the goat and milked her. She didn't have to call the dragon. He was there before she set the bowl of warm milk on the ground, slurping it up with his long tongue, his front paws in the bowl, milk splashed on his nose.

The goat bleated again.

'You also have better manners than he does,' Ping said.

She sat next to the fire, warming her hands. The baby dragon had grown. He was now ten times the size of the tiny creature that had hatched from the dragon stone into her lap. And he needed ten times as much food. When Kai had finished licking the bowl dry, he squawked plaintively.

'I've got something else for you,' Ping said.

She pulled the dragonfly from the pouch around her waist. Kai snatched it from her. Ping let go before he bit her fingers. His long snout snuffled around her pouch, looking for more.

'I wish you'd start catching your own meals,' Ping grumbled, giving him a caterpillar.

Kai swallowed it whole. Then he gobbled down the other five caterpillars in Ping's pouch. He sat back on his haunches and belched. Ping hoped that meant he was finally satisfied. After walking round in a circle three times on the edge of Ping's gown, the little dragon settled down. He was asleep almost immediately.

When the old green dragon had flown off to the Isle of the Blest, leaving her on the shores of Ocean with a dragon hatchling in her care, Ping had had no idea what to do next. Danzi had told her she was the Dragonkeeper and that she would know what to do. It was a heavy responsibility for a girl of ten-and-two years. She didn't want to stay on the beach. She didn't like Ocean. It was overwhelmingly huge. She felt insignificant enough as it was, without being dwarfed by the endless waters of Ocean.

The beach where Kai had hatched from the dragon stone was a long way from any town or village, but that didn't mean it was always deserted. Fishermen came to the shore to launch their flimsy bamboo and goat-hide boats, and Ping knew she had to keep away from people. If anyone saw Kai, the news of a baby dragon would soon spread from person to person, village to village. She didn't want that. Though Diao, the dragon hunter, was dead, there would be others who saw dragons only as creatures to chop up and sell. She'd already had to confront one of them – a necromancer. He'd captured her and Danzi, and had taken the dragon stone. He had powers beyond understanding that he used only for evil; he was a shape-changer too, like the old dragon. Ping felt a flash of pride. She'd managed to outwit him. She'd escaped with Danzi and the dragon stone.

Even a dragon as small as Kai was worth much gold to such greedy men. Also, if word of the dragon found its way to the Emperor's ears, he would send imperial guards to arrest her. As far as he was concerned, Ping had helped the only remaining imperial dragon escape. If he found out that she'd also kept secret the birth of a new dragon, he would be furious.

The sun disappeared behind a distant mountain. The sky darkened. Loneliness crept over Ping like a chill as it always did when she thought of Liu Che. They had had long conversations together, just the two of them. Although he was the Emperor, he was just ten-and-five years old. He had enjoyed spending time with her. Ping had led the lonely life of an ill-treated slave girl. Liu Che had lived the pampered life of an over-protected prince, but they had at least one thing in common – neither of them had ever had friends of their own age.

She reached out to spoon some fish soup into her bowl. With her gown pinned down by the sleeping dragon, she could only just reach the pot of bubbling liquid on the fire. Her soup spoon wasn't as roughly made as her bucket (which she'd carved from a log herself); it was a bronze ladle with an elegant curved handle that ended in a dragon's head. She had bought it in the village where she had gone to buy the goat and her store of grain and lentils. An iron ladle would have been much cheaper, but iron hurt dragons when it was nearby. When it touched them, it burned their flesh. Her knife was bronze as well.

Ping was relieved that Kai was asleep; there was no squawking; there were no talons digging into her. But evening was her least favourite time of the day. It was the time when she missed her friends the most. Liu Che wasn't the only friend she'd lost. She had enjoyed the young Emperor's company for just a short while, but Danzi and her pet rat Hua had been her companions throughout the perilous journey from the mountains in the west all the way to Ocean in the east. Danzi was a dragon of few words, but he was most talkative in the evenings. Other people thought of rats as dirty, ugly pests, but Hua had been Ping's saviour on many occasions. Before Hua had come into her life, Ping had had no one. She'd never had a family. Her parents had sold her as a slave to Master Lan when she was small.

Old friends and new, somehow she'd managed to lose

them all. She remembered the sounds that the old dragon made. They hadn't set her teeth on edge like the noises of the baby dragon. Danzi's sounds changed with his mood – the wind-chime sound of his conversation sounded melancholy, but meant he was happy; an urgent gonging meant he was impatient with her; the jingle of bells was the sound of his laughter. Then there was the gentle voice that she heard in her mind, translating his sounds into words. When Kai was still inside the dragon stone, she had been able to hear him as well, not in words but in raw emotions – sadness, happiness, fear. That ability had disappeared after he hatched. It had flown away with the old dragon. She kept waiting to hear words form in her mind, just as they had with Danzi, but there was nothing. Kai made all sorts of squawks and squeaks, but Ping had to guess what they meant.

She rinsed her bowl and filled it with water from a smaller pot on the fire. She sipped the hot water. (She'd long ago used up her small supply of tea leaves.) Her thoughts darkened with the sky. She tried not to think too much about Danzi and Hua. She wanted to believe that they were both happy and well – healed of their wounds and weariness by the magic waters of the Isle of the Blest, far across Ocean. But she couldn't convince herself this was true. At first she had spent hours staring off to the east in the hope of seeing the old dragon flapping back towards her, but as the months slipped by Ping had come to accept that he was never coming back. She wasn't even sure if she believed that the Isle of the Blest existed.

Sometimes when she remembered Danzi, it brought tears to her eyes. At other times, she felt frustration and anger bubble up inside her. She was grateful to the old dragon for freeing her from the misery of her life of slavery at Huangling Palace. She was thankful for all the knowledge he had given her about herb lore, about the constellations of stars, and how to concentrate her *qi* power. She owed everything to Danzi. She hadn't even known her own name until he came into her life.

At the same time, she was very angry with him. As they had travelled to Ocean, day after day, *li* after *li*, he had taught her much about the world, but the one thing he hadn't told her was how to raise a baby dragon. He hadn't even told her that the dragon stone she carried for him was an egg. Rather than telling her the names of birds and flowers, the mating habits of bears, why hadn't he spent every minute telling her everything he knew about dragon rearing? Instead he had given her just a few words of advice before he flew away from her and his dragon son – forever.

It made Ping furious when she thought about it. He had told her the baby dragon needed milk and she had found a goatherd willing to sell her a she-goat whose baby had died, but she didn't know how much milk Kai needed every day. It seemed he would go on drinking until he burst if she let him. Danzi had also told her that as Kai grew he needed to include insects in his diet, and later small birds, but he hadn't mentioned when and how many. She had started feeding him caterpillars and dragonflies when he was three months old because he was always squawking as if he was hungry.

Ping shivered. The fire had died down. It was dark. Her bowl of hot water had gone cold. The sleeping dragon's purple scales glowed faintly in the light from the slender moon. She carried him into the cave where they slept. Inside, a pile of dried grass and pine needles served as a bed. She put Kai on the bed and then lay next to him. Kai slept in a tight coil, with his nose under his back paws and the end of his tail drawn up through the centre. It looked as if someone had tied him in a knot. He wriggled closer to Ping until his spines stuck into her side.

At least the baby dragon slept well. Ping's nights were peaceful, but she often couldn't sleep. It wasn't the snoring near her ear that kept her awake, but the thoughts churning in her mind. Was Tai Shan the right place for them to live? Should she have stayed near Ocean? How would they get through the winter?

CHAPTER TWO

A BOWL, A BUCKET
AND A LADLE

Rain had been falling from a grey sky all morning. Ping stood at the mouth of the cave and watched the drops dimple the pool. Kai had eaten a small breakfast of worms, but it wasn't enough for him. The rain showed no signs of stopping, but sooner or later she would have to go out and milk the goat.

She sniffed. There was a bad smell in the air. She sniffed again. It was a sulphurous smell like rotten bird's egg mixed with long-dead fish – and far too familiar. Ping got up and soon found a large puddle of dark green liquid in a corner of the cave.

'Kai! I told you to go outside to pee. Even if it is raining!'

The little dragon hung his head. The spines along his back drooped. His scales dulled to the colour of plum juice.

'You're always wet from swimming in the pool, but you can't put up with a few drops of rain!'

Kai slunk away to the back of the cave and hid his head under his front paws.

'You'll have to wait for your milk until I've cleaned this up.'

Ping mopped up the dragon urine with some dry moss, but the smell lingered.

The weather showed no sign of improvement. The goat was standing outside with rain dripping from her. Ping didn't feel like getting soaking wet, so she brought the goat inside. She rested her cheek against the animal's damp coat as she milked her. The goat was a patient creature that caused no trouble and put up with the trials of life with a small dragon without complaint. She didn't protest when Kai nipped at her knees or jumped out from behind rocks to frighten her. And every day, without fail, she produced warm milk.

Ping filled a bowl. As usual the dragon was there in a flash, slurping up the milk as if he was starving. Sometimes there was a little left over for Ping to drink. Not this time. Kai lapped up every last drop.

The smell of wet goat only added to the stench in the cave, but Ping didn't have the heart to turn the animal out into the rain again. Her food supplies were dwindling. She should have been out collecting nuts, berries and mushrooms to add to her winter store, not sitting around doing nothing. She stared out through the drizzle. The nearest peaks were dull grey, the ones behind them pale grey, the furthest peaks were a faint outline almost blending into the mist. Perhaps she'd go out the next day.

Kai looked for something to amuse himself inside the cave. He dug up the pine-needle bed. He swung on the goat's tail. He chased beetles, but never managed to catch any. He soon got bored with the amusements available to him in the cave, and went over to annoy Ping. He climbed on to her lap and walked around in a circle, pricking her legs with his sharp talons until he was ready to settle down. But he wasn't sleepy. He scratched himself behind the ear, chewed on the end of the tie around Ping's waist and snuffled in her pouch for more insects. It might have been pleasant to have a cat or a puppy sitting on her lap on a cold day, but dragons were not cuddly. Although they were warm-blooded animals, their scales were cold to touch, and Kai had lots of sharp bits that stuck into Ping through her gown.

Ping didn't want to add smoke to the already foul air in the cave, so she didn't light a fire. For her midday meal she ate the nuts and berries that she had collected the day before. Kai ate the last of the insects that were in her pouch, then made a high-pitched whining sound that meant he was still hungry. Ping took no notice of him, so he snuffled around the cave until he discovered a large moth folded up in a crevice of rock at the back of the cave. He jumped up, trying to reach it, but his huge paws weighed him down like stones. He couldn't jump high enough, no matter how many times he tried. Ping could have got up and caught the moth for him, but the weather had left her as dull and lifeless as the sky.

It was cold in the cave. Kai's breath turned to mist. If he wanted to annoy Ping he could make it linger. The cave filled with a damp white fog, making it seem even colder.

The summer weather had softened Ping. It was only autumn, but she was shivering as if it was mid-winter. Her gown, though grubby and mended in several places, was still much thicker than the threadbare jacket she'd worn when she was a slave at Huangling. There she hadn't had a warm goatskin to sleep under at night. She'd slept in a draughty ox shed and Master Lan had forbidden her to light a fire for warmth. The memories made her shiver even more. She needed something warm inside her. She decided that she would light a fire after all.

She went out into the rain and quickly collected some damp wood. With her fire-making sticks, she soon made a flame in a tuft of dry grass, but the wet wood wouldn't burn. All she succeeded in doing was filling the cave with smoke.

The clatter of something metallic falling on rock came from the back of the cave. Kai had discovered her precious things hidden on a rock shelf that she'd thought was out of his reach. She hadn't realized how much he'd grown. He was standing on his back legs, rummaging through her belongings, knocking them off the shelf and on to the hard stone floor of the cave.

'Leave them, Kai!' she shouted. 'They're mine.'

There was nothing of interest for him, nothing to eat. He slunk off with his tail dragging on the ground and buried his head under the pine-needle bed. Ping didn't scold him again. There was no point. He never took any notice of anything she said.

She picked up her scattered things. Among them were precious gifts from friends. There was the bronze mirror that Danzi had given her and the white jade seal presented to her by the Emperor himself. One end of the slender rectangle of jade had characters cut into its flat surface. The other end was carved into the shape of a dragon. She ran her finger over the cool jade. One corner was chipped where Kai had knocked it to the cave floor. She collected the rest of her things – a comb and a dragon scale, which were also gifts from the old dragon. There were gold and copper coins, a jade pendant, a dish of seal ink, a bone needle and a length of red thread. There were several pieces of purple eggshell – all that remained of the dragon stone. There was also a large dried leaf folded in two. Finally, there was the square of bamboo with her name written on it, given to her by her parents. Some of her belongings were worth a lot of money, some were worthless, but Ping valued them all.

She had always worn the bamboo square around her neck, but Kai had snapped the string several weeks ago. She took a length of the red silk, threaded the bamboo square on to it and hung it around her neck again.

She held the jade seal in one hand and the bronze mirror

in the other. They were both symbols of the office of Dragon-keeper, but they each represented very different roles.

She inspected the mirror to make sure it wasn't damaged. On one side was an etched design – a full-grown dragon coiled around a knob that protruded from the centre. The dragon's paw was reaching out to the knob as if it was something precious, like a pearl. When Ping had accepted the mirror from Danzi, he had warned her that it was a commitment to him and his heirs – for life. Kai was his son, his only heir, and possibly the last living dragon. She had received the mirror gladly, proud to take on the role of Dragonkeeper, but without really understanding the responsibility that came with it, the lonely life she had chosen. The mirror had been carried by all of Danzi's true Dragonkeepers. It was hundreds of years old. She wasn't sure she deserved the honour. She had travelled with the dragon reluctantly at first. It had been her job to feed Danzi, who was held in captivity in Huangling Palace where she was a slave. She hadn't intended to help him escape. It was actually Danzi who had freed *her*. He had given her the task of carrying his dragon stone all the way to Ocean. She smiled, remembering how terrified she'd been at the prospect of leaving her miserable home. Ping turned the mirror over. The other side was supposed to be polished bronze. Instead it was dusty and criss-crossed with the silvery trail of a snail. She slipped it into her pouch. When it stopped raining, she would take it out to the pool and wash it.

The jade seal was the badge of the Imperial Dragon-keeper, whose job was to care for dragons owned by the Emperor. Ping should never have accepted the seal. Danzi would rather have died than be held in captivity again.

A crackling sound interrupted her thoughts. A small orange flame licked around the wood in the fireplace. Ping blew on the glowing coals and more flames sprouted. She hung a pot of water over the fire, adding a few red berries that gave it a pleasant flavour. Kai came over to the fire, giving her a wounded look as if she was the one who had done something wrong. He tripped over the woodpile and fell on his nose.

Ping laughed. 'Dragons are supposed to have excellent eyesight!'

She could never stay angry with him.

Kai sat by the fire. In the light of the flames his scales glinted like amethyst crystals. He squawked.

'And don't think you're getting anything to eat just because I've put on a pot of water. It's hours till dinner time.'

The dragon continued squawking and staring at the pot.

'I don't know why I bother talking to you. You don't understand a word I say.'

Ping lifted the pot off the fire with a stick and tilted it to pour the water into her bowl. Kai squawked again.

'You don't like hot water,' Ping said.

The air around the dragon distorted and shimmered. Suddenly there wasn't a small purple dragon sitting next to the fire but another pot exactly the same as the one she was holding. Ping spilt hot water on her hand, she was so surprised. A squawking sound came from the second pot. Ping wondered if she was starting to go mad. Strange things happened to people who lived by themselves. Or was it the endless diet of fish that was making her see things? Ping picked up the soup ladle and held it out to poke the pot. Before she could, the air shimmered again. Ping felt a wave of nausea as she watched the pot turn into another soup ladle with a dragon's head decoration, identical to the one in her hand.

'Kai, is that you?'

Ping's nausea increased as the second soup ladle turned into a bucket and then into a baby dragon.

'You can shape-change!'

The little dragon blinked his big green eyes at her and squawked again.

'That's wonderful! What a clever dragon you are.'

She went to the back of the cave and cupped the sleeping moth in her hands. It fluttered its wings frantically, leaving dusty grey powder on her palms. Ping held the struggling insect out to Kai.

'You've earned a reward.'

The dragon's jaws snapped over the moth – and the ends of Ping's fingers.

'Good boy, Kai.'

*

She kept the fire going all day. Towards evening the rain stopped. When Kai was asleep, Ping fetched the old dragon's scale from its place at the back of the cave and went outside. The moon had risen early and the sky glittered with stars. In daylight the dragon's scale was a faded grey, but in the moonlight it had a greenish glow. She rubbed her fingers over its rough surface. She wished she could tell Danzi that Kai was showing signs of learning dragonish skills at last. She felt a flicker of hope. If he could shape-change, it meant they could move among people. They could go to a market and buy food to see them through the cold months. Perhaps one day Kai would grow into a proper dragon.

CHAPTER THREE

THE RED PHOENIX

Let muddy water stand still and it will gradually clear.

The dragon's paw reached out to her. His talons were huge and sharp and could have easily ripped her open, but they touched her hand as delicately as a butterfly.

'I don't know what you mean, Danzi,' Ping said.

Ping knows.

'I don't.'

Do.

The dragon opened his wings. They were not torn or scarred, but completely healed. The membrane of the wings was divided into segments by long thin bones, just like a bat's wings. The full moon came out from behind a cloud. Moonbeams collected in the dragon's body until it glowed luminous green.

'Don't leave me alone, Danzi.'

Must go.

She tried to run towards the dragon, but her feet wouldn't move. She looked down. The rest of the earth was as dry as a sun-bleached bone, but her feet were in a puddle of sticky mud. She couldn't pull them out.

The dragon lifted off the ground.

'Please don't leave me,' she wailed. 'Help me get on to your back.'

The even way is often the rough track.

The beautiful moonbeam-dragon flapped up into the night sky. The more Ping tried to drag her feet out of the grasping mud, the further they sank. The dragon shrank to a small dot of light and then she lost him among the stars. A wind blew up whipping leaves and small stones into the air. One of the stones hit her sharply on the nose. It stung, but the ache in her heart hurt much more.

Ping woke up to find a small purple dragon nipping her nose.

'Kai, I wish you'd find a less painful way to wake me,' she said as she sat up.

The despair of the dream was still with her. She didn't dream of Danzi often, but when she did the dreams were heartbreaking. He seemed to be trying to tell her something, but she could never understand his message. It took a few minutes for her to summon the strength to face the day.

The excitement of finding out that Kai could shape-change soon wore off. Ping's stomach was constantly churning with the sick feeling she got whenever she saw the dragon transform. She tried not to watch, but it was hard to avoid as he changed from one thing to another when she was least expecting it.

Kai shape-changed into whatever he laid his eyes on. One minute he was a bush, the next a turtle, then he was a bowl. Ping tried to encourage him to stay in one shape, rewarding him with treats of tufty brown caterpillars. They were Kai's favourite food, but Ping didn't like collecting them because they squirted sticky green stuff at her when she picked them off leaves. As usual Kai didn't understand a word Ping said. He ate the caterpillars and then changed into something else. Ping's optimism faded. Walking around with a bowl that turned into a bush or a bucket before people's eyes would cause just as much fuss as carrying a baby dragon.

Ping knew that dragons could live for thousands of years if they maintained good health. That was one thing that Danzi *had* told her. After five times a hundred years a dragon grew horns, after a thousand it grew wings. Perhaps it took hundreds of years for them to learn their dragon skills. Even if Ping lived to be a hundred, Kai would still be a very young dragon. He might still need looking after.

A question had been forming at the back of Ping's mind ever since the dragon was hatched. Who would look after Kai when she died? One day she would have to find some-one to take her place. She could teach them everything she knew about dragons – but would anyone want to take on such a task?

Ping scanned the surface of the pond. There wasn't a dragonfly in sight. She had searched the nearby bushes and hadn't found a single caterpillar. She hadn't bothered to go out looking for moths the night before. Now she had no insects for Kai's breakfast.

Kai was swimming in the pool as he did every fine day. When he walked, he was clumsy and awkward, always tripping over rocks or fallen branches. In the water he moved quickly and gracefully, diving towards rocks on the bottom of the pond and gliding away from them at the last second.

'I'll be glad when you can catch your own insects,' she said when he next came up for air.

Ping peered into the dark waters. She could see large water beetles, striped with black and yellow, diving among the reeds. She had collected the larvae of these creatures for Kai to eat, but it wasn't the season for them now. The beetles were big. Three or four of them would make a good meal for the little dragon.

'Why don't you catch them instead of just chasing them?' Ping grumbled.

Since he took no notice of this suggestion, she decided to catch them herself. She fetched the fishing net that she had woven from thin, flexible twigs and dipped it into the pond. It only took her a few minutes to catch five beetles.

'Try these, Kai,' she said. 'They look like they'll make a tasty meal.'

Kai pulled himself out of the pond. He sniffed at the beetles that were squirming in the net.

'That's all you're getting this morning,' Ping said.

Kai squawked.

'All right, I'll squash them for you,' Ping said.

She emptied the beetles out on to a flat rock and crushed them with the stone she used to pound grain. Kai sniffed them again. He licked at the yellow stuff oozing from the squashed beetle shells. Then he picked one of them up in his mouth. He crunched the shell and then spat it out again.

Ping sighed. 'If you don't like them, you'll have to make do with milk.'

Ping went over to where the goat was tethered. She knelt down and rested her cheek against her flank. The goat continued to crop the grass.

'I wish Kai was as easy to feed as you are,' she said.

Kai started making noises again. Not the complaining squawks he made when he was hungry. Not the noise he made when he wanted Ping to play with him. It was a hoarse coughing sound. Ping turned and saw that the dragon was retching. She ran over to him.

'What's wrong, Kai?'

Ping patted him on the back, which was not easy to do to a creature with sharp spines from head to tail. He didn't seem to be able to take a breath. Ping thought that he must have been choking, that he had swallowed something and it was caught in his throat. She banged harder on his back. He still didn't breathe. Then with one last retch, he vomited into Ping's lap. In among the unpleasant milky mix of dragonfly legs and caterpillar skin was a squashed water beetle.

Kai made a plaintive sound and lay down. His eyes looked dull. His tongue was no longer bright red. His scales had turned the colour of a bruise. She brought the bowl of milk over to him, but he wouldn't drink. Ping carried him into the cave and laid him on the bed of pine needles. She gently rubbed the little dragon's stomach.

'I'm sorry, Kai,' she said. 'I shouldn't have given you the beetles to eat.'

Ping felt ashamed. When she had first introduced insects into Kai's diet she had given him tiny little tastes at first. Then if there was no bad reaction after a day, she gave him a little more, increasing the amount over a week until she was sure that the insect wasn't poisonous. She had grown careless. She could have killed him.

Ping didn't have any breakfast herself. It didn't seem fair to eat when Kai couldn't. She sat by him all day, stroking his stomach. At last, late in the night, he stopped groaning and went to sleep.

Kai ate a little the next morning. By mid-afternoon he was back to his usual tricks, annoying the goat, messing up the bed and demanding food every hour. As Ping put a freshly squashed dragonfly in her pouch, her hand brushed the mirror. She remembered her promise to clean it. She took it over to the pool. The sun warmed her face. She had a feeling that there wouldn't be many more warm days before winter set in. She glanced around, but couldn't see Kai.

'Where are you, Kai?' she said.

He had been quiet for too long. It was always a sign that he was up to mischief. There was a branch under one of the pine trees that hadn't been there before.

'I want you to stay close to the cave,' she said to the branch.

It didn't respond.

'Just until I'm sure you're completely well.'

There was a squawk behind her. She turned to find the little dragon sitting at her heels. She had been talking to a tree branch. One big disadvantage of Kai's new-found shape-changing powers was that even when he was under her nose, she couldn't always find him. It would take a while for him to get the hang of this new skill, just like a child learning to walk. She had to be patient.

The mirror fitted into the palm of her hand. She dipped a corner of her gown in the pool and wiped the mirror clean. She could see her reflection. Her hair was knotted and there were leaves tangled in it. Her face was dirty and scratched. There was a scab on her nose. And she was thinner. She had been so busy taking care of the baby dragon, she had forgotten to take care of herself.

Ping remembered when Danzi had made her bathe and comb her hair. The memory brought a smile to her face, but a pain to her heart. Memories of the old dragon always had that effect on her. He would have disapproved if he saw her hair in such a state. She went back into the cave to get her comb. It was a beautiful thing made of ebony inlaid with mother-of-pearl. She started to comb her hair.

As she combed, she stared out at the endless sky. She noticed a black spot in the distance towards the east. She rubbed her eyes but the spot didn't go away – it grew bigger. As she looked, it took shape. It was a bird flying towards Tai Shan. It continued to grow in size as it flew closer and closer until it was right above her. It was a big bird. At first she thought it was a trick of the sunlight, but the bird appeared to be bright red. It flapped down and landed in a pine tree.

It was like no bird Ping had ever seen. It had three long tail feathers that curled at the ends. On its head was an upright crest. It folded its large wings. The bird *was* red, the colour of ripe berries. It was a red phoenix. As Ping stared at it, she could also see that there was a hump on the bird's back. She couldn't make out what it was. It wasn't covered in red feathers like the rest of the bird. It was grey. A rock beneath the tree let out a terrified squawk and turned back into a baby dragon. Kai ran to Ping, leaping up on to her and wrapping himself around her neck. He buried his nose under her hair and wound the tip of his tail around her ear. Ping tried to unwind the little dragon, but he was clamped like a shellfish on a rock.

'I can't breathe, Kai,' she spluttered.

As Ping staggered about trying to free herself, she could see the bird, unaware of the fuss it had caused, preening its startling tail feathers. Each one was as long as Ping's arm and ended in a rainbow-coloured eyespot.

The grey shape on the phoenix's back shifted. It broke away from the bird's body and moved quickly down the tree trunk. Whatever it was, it was alive – and heading straight for Ping. She wished she had something to hide behind, but there was nothing. She reached for the soup ladle, it was the only thing close by that she could use to protect herself. The grey blur ran straight toward her. She tried to hit it with the ladle, but it was too quick. It clambered up her gown as if it was going to attack the little dragon. Kai squawked with terror, leapt to the ground and ran to the pond. He dived into the water.

Ping tried to pull the grey thing off her. She thought it was going to take her by the throat, but instead it crawled inside her gown. She screamed, got hold of the creature and flung it away. It landed neatly on four feet. Ping saw for the first time what it was. It was a rat, but it was no ordinary rat. It was very large and it was staring at her with bright blue eyes. In the sunlight its fur had a bluish sheen, like embroidered satin. It also had a chunk missing from one ear.

Ping stared at the rat. She had known another rat with a piece missing from its ear.

'Is that . . .' Ping could hardly bring herself to say it. 'Is that you, Hua?'

She sat down, stunned.

The rat scuttled on to her lap, looked up at her and squeaked. Ping stared at the rat. She reached out and cautiously stroked its warm fur.

'It is you, Hua!' Ping said. 'You're healed and you've grown and . . .' she stared at the rat's blue eyes, his huge yellow teeth, 'and you've changed.'

She hugged Hua to her, examined his bluish fur and then hugged him again. The smile on her face kept growing. 'I'm so glad to see you.'

The rat gently nibbled her ear.

The red phoenix finished preening its feathers, flapped its wings and took off. Ping watched until it was no more than a black dot in the sky again. It seemed that Hua had come to stay.

Ping could find no trace of the wounds Hua had suffered. He was completely healed. The Isle of the Blest did exist after all.

'Kai,' she called out. 'Come and meet Hua.'

She looked around. Her smile shrank and then disappeared completely. Kai had dived into the pool – and he hadn't come up again.

CHAPTER FOUR

A DRAGON FRIEND

Ping peered anxiously into Black Dragon Pool. She could see nothing.

'Kai! Where are you? If you're hiding from me, you're going to be in trouble.'

She searched the reeds, looking for any rocks or fallen branches that weren't there before. She'd seen Kai dive into the water after Hua had startled him. He had to have come up for air by now. Could he have resurfaced when she wasn't looking? Or was he still underwater?

Ping lifted the hem of her gown above her knees, tucked it into her belt and stepped into the pond. The water was icy. She peered into the dark depths, but could see only fish and waterweed. She waded up to her waist. Kai was as at home in the water as the fish. Could he have been washed over the rim? Fear gripped her heart. Surely he couldn't have drowned? Her feet slipped on the slimy rocks. She splashed and spluttered and managed to regain her footing.

The passing time was marked by her heartbeat pounding in her ears, getting faster and louder the longer Kai was gone. He had been underwater for at least ten-and-five minutes. What sort of Dragonkeeper was she? All she'd had to do was take care of one small dragon. She hadn't watched over him carefully enough.

She remembered the terror of being underwater. She'd nearly drowned when peasants had tried to sacrifice her to the dragon god that they believed lived in their lake. She remembered her panic when she'd taken a breath and sucked in, not air, but water. Panic was rising in her throat again, threatening to burst out in a wild scream. She swallowed it down. Danzi had saved her then. She had to save Kai.

She took a deep breath and plunged into the water. She opened her eyes, but all her stumbling had stirred up the mud and she couldn't see anything. She reached down into the murky water but her hands only found slimy rocks. She came to the surface, gulping in air.

Ping collapsed on to a rock, her legs too wobbly to support her. She pushed aside the Dragonkeeper's mirror. Tears spilled down her face.

Hua jumped on to the rock and tilted the mirror with his nose until it caught the sun's rays. A beam of bright light reflected into the pool.

Something floated to the surface. Something purple,

spiky and lifeless. It turned around and around slowly, caught in an eddy in the middle of the pool. It was the body of the little dragon. Poor Kai. He should have lived for thousands of years, not a few months. Tears blurred her vision. She fell to her knees. The dragon's body made another slow turn until its head was facing Ping. Two big green eyes blinked open. A red mouth opened wide and a squawk came out.

Ping leapt to her feet. 'Kai!'

The little dragon paddled his big feet and easily escaped the pull of the water. But he wouldn't come to her. He was staring at Hua.

Ping waded towards him. 'It's OK,' she said. 'This is Hua. He won't hurt you. He's a dragon friend.'

Ping eventually managed to coax the little dragon out of the pool. He kept close to her, staring anxiously at the rat. Hua seemed to understand perfectly that Kai was afraid of him, and kept his distance. Ping, wet and shivering, tried to light a fire. The wood was dry enough, but her hands were trembling at the thought of what might have happened. She couldn't make them rub a stick back and forth fast enough to make a spark. Hua came over to the fireplace and reared up on his back legs. Kai squawked in alarm. The rat's fur seemed to stand on end and it looked blue, though there was no sunlight shining on it. He looked even bigger. Then a small glob of saliva shot out of his mouth. When the spitball hit the wood, it exploded with a loud pop and a flash of flame. The flame only lasted for a second or two, but it was enough for the wood to catch fire. Hua then sat down on his four feet, his fur flattened and dull. Ping couldn't believe her eyes. Kai blinked in surprise, but moved closer to the warmth of the fire.

'Hua,' said Ping. 'What a remarkable rat you've become.'

Ping put a pot of water on the fire and started to cook some of the lentils and grain that she had been saving for emergencies. After so many shocks and surprises, she needed something to eat.

Ping realized she should have known that dragons could stay underwater for a long time. Danzi had survived underwater. She remembered him telling her that, if there wasn't enough food to last them through winter, dragons could spend the coldest months hibernating in deep pools. Kai was only learning how to be a dragon. She had learned something too. Kai responded to the flash of light reflected in the mirror just like a dog responded to its master's whistle. Danzi had told her that the mirror could be used as a signal to dragons, but she hadn't thought of it in connection with Kai. If it hadn't been for Hua, she might never have realized it. She flashed the mirror several times and Kai always came to her. She gave him dragonflies and an extra bowl of milk. He sat by the fire munching the insects, unaware of the scare he'd given her.

Ping shared her food with Hua. She noticed how his claws

were more dexterous than before. He could move his toes independently and pick things up with his front feet as easily as Ping could with her hands.

'If only you could talk, Hua,' she said.

The last time she had seen Hua he was close to death. His small body had been crushed by a blow from the dragon hunter's club. Danzi had taken him to the Isle of the Blest to heal him with the water of life. If the rat could talk, he would be able to tell her what had happened to Danzi. Hua squeaked, but the story of his adventures over Ocean remained untold.

Ping sighed. She had companions, three of them now, but the only sounds she ever got from them were squeaks, squawks and bleats. She thought about the conversations she'd had with Liu Che – about dragons and flowers and the colour of robes. She longed to hear a human voice other than her own. Even memories of happy times with a family would have eased her loneliness, but she had none. When she was a slave at Huangling Palace, she had always been too busy or too tired to think about her family. But on Tai Shan the nights were long and the faceless shapes of her father and mother often found their way into her thoughts.

CHAPTER FIVE

A TRICKLE OF BLOOD

A week after the unexpected arrival of Hua, Ping woke to find a cooking pot sitting next to her ear, whining plaintively. It changed into a bucket and then a rock, whimpering all the time. She turned over. A small fire was glowing in the fireplace. Next to it was a pile of mushrooms for her breakfast. Every morning Hua lit the fire and went out foraging, not only for himself, but also for her and Kai. He would be off collecting insects for Kai now. Ping stretched, enjoying the luxury of not having to do everything herself.

She put on her gown, socks and shoes and went out to milk the goat. Kai sat at the mouth of the cave, his scales drooping. A freezing fog had settled over the mountain. Ping looked around for the goat. She should have been tethered to the nearest tree. Ping's mind was still fuzzy with sleep. Perhaps Hua had moved the goat to a spot with more grass. She searched around but the mist made it difficult. Ping shivered but not from the cold. She had a feeling inside that something was wrong. She walked to the edge of the plateau. The goat was nowhere to be found. Ping couldn't even call her, because she'd never bothered to give her a name. The back of her neck prickled. She turned quickly but even if someone was there, she wouldn't have been able to see them through the fog.

Ping walked towards the grove of pine trees. The feeling inside her formed into a hard mass, like a stone inside her stomach. There was someone hiding in the pine trees, she was sure of it.

The boughs interlaced above her shut out the light. Her feet moved soundlessly on the thick carpet of pine needles. There was no birdsong, no whirr of insects, no rustle of grass. It was as if she were walking in a room hung with thick wall hangings that blocked out all sound. She was sure she wasn't alone. She crept forward. Then she heard a faint scraping sound. A snake slithered through the pine needles just in front of her. It was a big one, with bands of black and orange. It lifted its head and looked towards her. It was long past the season for snakes. She wished she'd brought her knife, so that she could kill it. Ping wanted to go back to the safety of the cave, but her feet wouldn't move. The snake slithered off into the fog. Ping kept walking. The trees began to thin. The ground became rocky and started to slope away steeply. It wasn't safe to walk any further. The feeling that she was being watched increased. Her foot stumbled against something. Not a rock, something heavy but soft. She had found the goat. It was lying at her feet. A trickle of blood ran from its lifeless body.

An animal must have attacked the goat. A wild cat perhaps? Had she startled it, just as it was about to eat its victim? Ping bent down to examine the goat's body. Ping was struggling to understand what had happened. Its head was thrust back and there was a red gaping wound across its throat. But it wasn't the ragged wound of an animal attack. Its throat had been neatly cut with a sharp blade. The goat was still warm. It couldn't have been dead for more than a few minutes.

CHAPTER SIX

BLINDFOLD

Ping ran back through the pine trees, her heart pounding. Kai wasn't sitting at the mouth of the cave where she'd left him. She looked around, but the fog was like a blindfold. She called his name and ran into the cave. The little dragon was digging up the bed, scattering pine needles everywhere. Ping rushed to him. He lowered his head, ready for a scolding, but she scooped him up and hugged him, not noticing the spines sticking into her.

'We're going to find somewhere else to live,' she said, trying to sound calm.

She packed the cooking utensils into her leather bag, shoving them in any way they would fit. She collected her precious things and the meagre food store. Then they left the cave. Kai didn't resist. Though she'd tried to hide it, he could sense her fear.

'It's all right,' Ping said. 'I'll look after you.'

She hoped she sounded convincing.

Ping hurried away from the cave towards the imperial path that led beneath the Halfway to Heaven Gate. She kept expecting the goat's killer to loom in front of her at any moment. Hua was at her heels. She broke into a run.

She reached the imperial path out of breath. She would have preferred to use the smaller animal tracks that only she knew, but they would have been too hard to follow in the fog. Sometimes they zigzagged back the way they had come, sometimes they led to unexpected precipices. They were too dangerous. The imperial path was the only safe way down the mountain. But she felt uncomfortable on it, exposed, though no one could possibly see her through the fog.

The path plunged steeply down the mountainside and soon turned into steep steps cut into the rock. Ping looked back to convince herself that no one was following her and tripped, falling down six steps. She picked herself up, checked that Kai was all right and set off again. She forced herself to take the steps more slowly. The little dragon was making high-pitched, peeping sounds that made Ping's head hurt. She couldn't think. She didn't have any idea where she was going. She glimpsed human shapes out of the corner of her eye, but when she turned they were just twisted pine trees or rocks looming out of the mist. But the feeling that someone was close by didn't leave her.

She made a sudden turn on to a narrow track that led off to the west. It had been made by sheep or goats, but hadn't been used for some time and grass was overtaking it. She followed it wherever it wanted to lead her.

The track might be dangerous, but that could be in her favour. No one could cut her off – if there was anyone there, they would have to be behind her. She turned on to a different path and then on to another, hoping that she wasn't going to end up back where she started. She was glad of the fog to hide in. When she came to a rocky outcrop, she crouched behind a boulder, holding Kai's jaws shut. She waited, her ears straining for the slightest noise. Hua was listening too. There was no sound. She waited longer, until she was sure there was no one following her.

She kept going over and over the events of the morning, trying to think of why someone had killed the goat. She could only come up with one answer. Someone had wanted to frighten her. Questions crowded her head. Where would they sleep? What would they eat? How could she get another goat?

Her gown clung to her skin, wet and heavy. The cold penetrated her bones. Kai whimpered. She held him close, hoping that some of his body heat would find its way through his scales and warm her. She had planned to walk until sunset, but she was already exhausted.

Each step was an effort. Her legs ached from the unaccustomed walking. Her arms hurt from carrying Kai. Her head was throbbing from trying to work out what she should do.

She put Kai down. 'Walk in front of me where I can see you.'

The little dragon was too frightened to wander off. He wanted to keep as close to Ping as possible. Every now and again he suddenly stopped and shape-changed into something – a large leaf, a rabbit, a pile of dung – and Ping tripped over him. She showed him how to walk behind her, holding the hem of her gown in his mouth so they didn't lose each other.

Ping began to think that leaving Black Dragon Pool had been a mistake. Perhaps she'd over-reacted. She tried to think of other explanations. A hungry mountain hermit might have come across the goat, but she'd disturbed him before he had the chance to carry the dead animal away. A goatherd could have seen the goat and thought that Ping had stolen one of his flock. A shaman might have climbed up the sacred mountain to give an offering to Heaven, seen the smoke from her fire and decided to punish her for venturing on to the forbidden slopes of Tai Shan. None of her theories made her feel any easier.

She stumbled on through the fog. When she walked into a boulder, she realized that she had left the track and was up to her knees in wet grass. The path wasn't the only thing she'd lost. Kai was no longer holding on to the hem of her gown.

'Where are you, Kai?' she called and then tripped over

him where he had stopped in the long grass. He whimpered miserably. Hua was sheltered between Kai's feet.

A flash of anger did nothing to warm her numb body. She was angry with the nameless person who had forced her from Black Dragon Pool. Angry that she was so powerless. Then Ping was vaguely aware of a sensation she hadn't felt for a long time. Something was drawing her, as if an invisible thread were tied to her and someone at the other end was pulling it. It encouraged her. She picked up Kai, and followed the thread.

An hour later, a dark, squarish shape loomed out of the fog. It was a hut. This was what had been drawing her. Somehow she had known that the hut was there. She also knew that there was no one inside. Ping lifted the latch and entered.

The hut was small, just one room. The only light came through a hole in the ceiling designed to let out smoke from a fire-place in the middle of the room. A straw mattress hung over the rafters. Ping found a neat stack of chopped wood, a basket containing folded sheepskins and a chest packed with food. Compared to the chilly cave they'd left behind, the hut was luxurious.

Hua climbed up into the rafters and found a large selection of insects for Kai. Ping ate salted meat, dried fruit and nuts from the food chest. After she'd eaten, she pulled down the straw mattress and made a bed on the floor. Kai didn't need any encouragement. He was curled up under the sheepskins in moments. Ping crawled in alongside him.

She had almost forgotten about her second sight. Living a simple life at Black Dragon Pool, she'd had no need for it. When she really wanted to find something she could concentrate her mind and somehow she was drawn to it. That's what had led her to the hut. Anger could rouse her second sight unbidden, but she had started to learn how to summon it at will. Her second sight also gave her warning of danger — a sense of dread, like the hard mass she had felt in her stomach when the goat was killed.

Ping felt as warm as a baked taro root. The delicious, almost forgotten, taste of orchard-grown nuts and fruit lingered in her mouth. The hut was a perfect place to spend the winter.

CHAPTER SEVEN

A SHEPHERD'S HUT

When Ping woke the next morning, she got up and opened the window shutters. Daylight flooded in. She'd slept late. The food chest was open. Nuts and dried beans were scattered on the floor. Several dried plums had distinctly dragonish teeth marks in them. Kai was squawking miserably. He didn't like the shepherd's food. He was hungry.

The door opened a crack. Hua came in carrying three moths which he put next to the large mushroom that he'd already collected.

'Look. Hua has brought us breakfast.'

Ping lit a little fire and cooked the mushroom in the coals. The moths didn't satisfy the hungry dragon. Hua seemed to understand that Kai would need more food now that they didn't have a goat to provide milk. He scurried off again and a little while later returned with a bird's egg in his mouth.

'Hua! You know what I want even before I do!' she exclaimed.

The rat put the egg down in front of the dragon. Kai sniffed it and rolled it around with his nose. Then squawked unhappily at Ping.

Ping laughed. 'Give it to me, Hua.'

Hua brought the egg over to her. She looked into the rat's bright blue eyes. She could see a glimmer of understanding that was missing even in the eyes of some people she had known. There would be useful knowledge inside the rat's furry little head, she was sure of that.

'If only I knew what you were thinking,' Ping said.

She broke the egg into a bowl and Kai ate it raw.

Perhaps Danzi had sent the rat to help her. He might not have had the strength to fly all the way back from the Isle of the Blest. She tried to picture the old dragon healed and happy on the Isle of the Blest, sitting in the sunlight, eating peaches of immortality, sipping on the water of life. Whatever the reason, she was glad Hua had returned.

After breakfast they went outside. The walls of the hut were constructed from saplings and bark. The roof was made of neatly woven bundles of grass held in place with rocks. It was well built and Ping was sure it would keep out wind and rain. Around the side of the hut, under the shelter of the eaves, was a spade and more neatly stacked chopped wood. From the way the sheepskins and food store had been carefully packed away, she suspected the hut belonged to a shepherd who had taken his flock back to his village for the winter.

The hut was built on a narrow terrace that had been cut into the hillside. The shepherd had chosen the position well. A meadow for grazing sheep sloped gently down the hill in front of the hut. From the door there was a lovely view of two mountain peaks. In the narrow space between the peaks, Ping could see the plain reaching to the horizon. She could just make out a small village. Perhaps that was where the shepherd lived.

Behind the hut was a steep hill. Behind that was another hill, steeper and higher than the first. The peaks of Tai Shan were beyond that. It was good to have the dark mountain at a comfortable distance, not looming over her every move as it had done at Black Dragon Pool. They had walked a long way.

The few clouds kept their distance from the sun and Ping was enjoying its warmth. Her fear had disappeared with the fog.

'I'm sure the shepherd won't be returning till spring,' Ping said to Hua. 'We can spend winter here. But we have to be much more careful than we were before.'

She went back inside and put out her little fire. 'There might be someone in the village keen-sighted enough to see the smoke. We'll have to leave lighting a fire until after dark.'

She picked up her bucket. 'Come on, Hua. Let's go and explore. We need to find water.'

Kai squawked plaintively when she set off.

'You can come too, but I'm not carrying you.'

The little dragon followed her.

In summer, the meadow would be studded with flowers, but this morning it was covered with small snails, coaxed from their hiding places by overnight rain. Kai liked snails. Ping collected some for him.

She could see no sign of a pool or stream. To the west of the hut, an outcrop of large rectangular rocks scarred the smooth green slope. It looked as if a piece of the mountain had broken off a long time ago, and tumbled all the way down to this slope, where it had lodged and become part of the landscape.

'Perhaps there's a stream over there,' she said to Hua.

The rocks were taller than Ping. A path led through them to a flat rock platform. In the middle was a hole that was full of water.

Ping smiled. 'I knew the shepherd wouldn't have built his hut far from water.'

The pool was much smaller than Black Dragon Pool, less than a *chang* across. It was more like a well, but formed by nature, not dug by men. There was no waterfall tumbling into it, no stream rushing to fill it, just a still pool. Whether the well was filled by rain or from an underground source, Ping couldn't tell. A mesh of slimy waterweed floating on the surface made it impossible to see how deep the water was. Ping pushed aside the weed and cupped some of the water in her hands. It had a greenish look to it. She tasted it. It wasn't as sweet as the water in Black Dragon Pool, but if it was good enough for the shepherd, it was certainly good enough for her. She dipped her bucket in.

Kai came up to the edge of the pool and sniffed the water. Then he dived in and disappeared beneath the surface.

'I wish he wouldn't do that,' Ping said to Hua.

After the experience at Black Dragon Pool, Ping knew there was no reason to worry. The little dragon always surfaced again – eventually.

'Dragons can stay underwater for weeks,' she told Hua, as she peered uneasily through the weed. 'I don't know how they do it. They must be able to breathe water like fish do.'

Ping found herself holding her breath, as if she was the one underwater, relying on just the small amount of air she could hold in her lungs. She finally had to take a breath. Perhaps food would entice Kai out of the water. She took the snails out of her pouch and set them down on the rock, wiping her slimy hand on the hem of her gown. The snails slowly emerged from their shells and started to crawl away.

'Where are you, Kai?' Ping called. 'You'd better hurry, your meal is escaping.'

She remembered the mirror. She pulled it out of her pouch and angled it so that it caught the rays of the sun. The mirror flashed. A few moments later Kai resurfaced. Ping took a deep breath. The little dragon pulled himself up out of the water. He had green weed draped over his head and a happy expression on his face. The water seemed to revitalize him. He shook himself, showering Ping with drops of water, and went over to the snails. He looked at her expectantly.

'You're supposed to crack them open yourself,' Ping complained as she squashed the snails with a stone. 'What would you do without me?'

Kai snuffled through the broken shells to find the snail meat. Ping scratched the little dragon's head. There were a number of places he liked to be scratched – in his left armpit, between the pads of his paws, in the wrinkles around his nose. He liked to be scratched almost anywhere except under the chin, which was strange because the soft spot under his chin was where Danzi had liked to be scratched. Kai's favourite tickle spot was around the bumps on his head where his horns would eventually grow hundreds of years from now. Thinking about the little dragon's future made her anxious. She hoped things would get easier as he grew, but she couldn't be sure. Kai nipped her fingers, which was his way of saying he'd had enough scratching. He went back to licking out the crushed snail shells to make sure he hadn't missed any flesh. Ping smiled as the dragon chased a piece of shell among the rocks with his long red tongue.

As she walked back to the hut, she thought about the invisible thread that had drawn her to this place. Danzi had explained to her that second sight developed after spending time with a dragon.

'I'd forgotten so many things Danzi told me,' Ping said. 'I'd forgotten about my second sight and my *qi* power. I don't even know if I can still summon it.'

Qi was the life force that flowed through all living things. The old dragon had taught her how to harness the *qi* within her so that she had the strength to fend off attackers much stronger than herself. She could also make the concentrated energy shoot from her fingertips. It had taken many weeks of practice to master this skill.

'It's been so long since I practised the *qi* exercises,' Ping said to Hua. 'If we hadn't left Black Dragon Pool, I might have completely forgotten about Danzi's teachings.'

Every event under Heaven has its reason – or so the old dragon had told her.

She stood on the grassy slope outside the shepherd's hut and faced the lowering sun. She took deep breaths just as Danzi had instructed her, breathing in the sunlit air. Morning sunlight was richest in *qi*, but the orange afternoon light would do. Then she began the exercises the dragon had taught her – slow twisting movements of the arms and legs. She hadn't forgotten them, but she was rusty. She couldn't balance on one leg without wobbling. There were exercises for the mind as well to help clear away all thoughts. She resolved to use the winter months to practise the exercises and regain her skills.

'And if I have to practise *my* skills,' she said to Kai. 'You have to practise *yours*. We have to go down on to the plain and buy another goat. And we won't be able to do that until you can stay in one shape for at least an hour.'

Kai blinked back at her. Ping couldn't tell whether he understood.

'You have to earn your supper tonight,' she said. 'You have to shape-change into something and stay that way for at least a minute.'

He scratched his ear.

Ping had been wondering if it was easier for him to shape-change into simple objects. She picked up the little dragon and set him down in front of a rock.

'Change into that,' she said.

The little dragon looked at the rock and changed into an identical rock. Ping was delighted.

'Good boy, Kai,' she said. 'Now stay like that for a minute and . . .'

Before she could finish, he had popped back into his dragon shape and was squawking at her again.

She pointed at the rock. 'No, stay like that.'

Kai turned into a rock again.

'That's it!'

The dragon didn't stay in the rock shape for very long, but at least he wasn't turning into everything in sight.

'That was good, Kai,' Ping said, though she wasn't entirely sure the dragon had understood what she was saying. He only seemed to turn into things that he could actually see, and there was nothing much else in sight but rocks.

Hua came back from his search for food. He stopped in front of the rock-shaped Kai. The rock turned into another rat, identical to Hua. The two rats sniffed each other suspiciously for a moment or two before one of them transformed into a dragon.

'I'll see if I can find you some insects,' Ping said to Kai. 'Just in case you did it on purpose.'

The following morning, after another comfortable night's sleep in the shepherd's hut, Ping got up early to practise her *qi*-concentrating exercises as the sun rose. The little dragon was busy eating his breakfast. Hua had gathered a number of fat worms and an impressive collection of moths for him.

Ping faced the rising sun and began her exercises, focusing on each move, breathing in the cool morning air and the golden sunlight rich in *qi*. After she had completed the sequence of exercises, she sat down to practise concentrating her thoughts. Kai had finished his breakfast. He came and sat in front of Ping and turned into a cooking pot. The cooking pot belched.

'I'm going to count backwards from five hundreds,' Ping said. 'Let's see if you can stay in that shape while I do that.'

Ping couldn't count backwards without closing her eyes, but whenever she opened one eye to check on the dragon, he was still sitting in front of her in his pot shape. She finished her counting and then began another exercise. She stared at the distant mountain and imagined following the path of a beetle on it. Kai stayed in his pot shape.

'That's good, Kai,' she said when she'd finished. 'You can turn into your proper shape now. I want to clean your ears.'

He remained in the shape of a pot.

Grass seeds sometimes got stuck in the dragon's ears, causing them to produce dark, smelly wax. Ping found a small twig and chewed the end to make a soft brush that she could poke into his ears, but Kai was still in the shape of a cooking pot.

'That's enough shape-changing for today, Kai.'

The pot didn't move.

For the rest of the day, no matter how much she coaxed him or tempted him with a plate of squashed snails, Kai still wouldn't change into his proper shape. Ping thought that if she didn't take any notice he might get bored with the game, so she busied herself around the hut, but every time she looked at him out of the corner of her eye, he was still a pot.

She wondered if he understood more than she had thought. Perhaps he knew she was going to clean out his ears.

'OK,' she said. 'I'm not going to clean your ears. I'll never clean your ears ever again. Let them get smelly. I don't mind.'

It was no good. He remained a pot. By late afternoon, she was starting to get worried. She reached out to pick him up. Though she could see a pot, her hands closed around a small scaly body. It was an uncomfortable sensation that made her feel dizzy and see specks of light in front of her eyes. She had to wait a few moments for the dizziness to pass, and then she carried Kai inside.

'Please, Kai, turn back into a dragon. Is it because you haven't got any milk? Is that the problem?'

The pot didn't reply.

'If that's it, we'll go in search of a goat tomorrow. You've learned how to stay in one shape for a long time, so we can go to a village.'

The pot didn't move.

'Tomorrow,' Ping said anxiously. 'First thing. We'll go out and find a goat or a sheep.'

Despite the comfort and warmth of the shepherd's bed, Ping didn't get much sleep that night. The pot at the end of the bed wasn't having any trouble sleeping – she could hear it snoring.

'Perhaps he's stuck,' she thought to herself. 'Shape-changing must be very hard to do. He might not be able to change back.'

The next morning, Kai was still in his pot shape. The cicadas Hua brought for Kai's breakfast were left untouched. The pot was making a miserable whining sound and Ping was convinced he couldn't change back.

There was no one she could turn to for help. Even if she went in search of a herbalist or physician, she could hardly tell them her dragon was stuck in a pot shape. They would think she was mad.

'What can I do, Hua?'

The rat blinked. He couldn't help her either.

Ping carried the pot to the well, hoping the chance of a swim might entice Kai to change back. It didn't.

She was a terrible Dragonkeeper. The day before, she'd been congratulating herself on her skills. But what was the point of finding a pleasant place to spend the winter if she didn't have any idea how to help Kai when there was something wrong with him? If only he would speak to her with his mind like Danzi used to.

She didn't practise her *qi*-concentrating exercises. She was too worried.

'What use could I have for my *qi* power up here on the mountain anyway?' she asked the rat.

'Perhaps I could kill snails and caterpillars without having to get up,' she said.

Her second sight had been most useful when it had warned her that the dragon hunter was nearby. In that way, it had never let her down. She shuddered at the memory of Diao, the man who had hunted them across the country, who had tried to kill Danzi and take the dragon stone.

'At least I won't be needing my second sight for that anymore,' she told Hua.

The words were barely out of her mouth when she felt heaviness in the pit of her stomach. Her heart pounded. She stood up and looked around expecting Diao to emerge from behind a rock.

'It's impossible,' she told herself. 'He's dead.'

When the dragon hunter had confronted her on one of the peaks of Tai Shan, she had sent out a bolt of *qi* power which had knocked him back so that he lost his footing. She had seen the dragon hunter tumble over the edge. She had heard his bones snap when he landed below. But she hadn't seen his body. What if he'd survived? What if his bones had mended? The feeling of foreboding made her want to run and hide. She sniffed the air. It was crisp and clean. The air wasn't tainted by the sickening smell of uncured hides that always accompanied the dragon hunter, but the lump in her stomach was unmistakable.

The sun went behind a cloud. It was only a small cloud, but it covered the sun completely. The foreboding grew stronger. The hairs on the back of Ping's neck prickled. Her blood turned to ice. She spun round.

There was a man standing between two rocks. He was wearing a dark, hooded cloak. He was perfectly still, as if he'd been there for some time. He pushed back his hood. Ping stared at the face and all hope drained from her. The man had a bald head and a short beard of orange-coloured bristles. He wore a patch over one eye. On his right cheek was a dark mark. It wasn't Diao. It was the necromancer.

CHAPTER EIGHT

DEEP GREEN

'Where's that doddering old dragon?'

The necromancer's voice was harsh and rasping, like a blade scraping across a stone. Ping had been longing to hear another human voice for months, but this was the one voice she had never wanted to hear again. She stared at the necromancer in disbelief. It had never occurred to her that he would be able to track her down.

The mark on his cheek was a tattoo of a monstrous animal with bared teeth and skulls hanging from its mane. Around his waist hung dreadful weapons – a long sword with a curved blade, a saw-toothed knife, a hatchet, a thin double-edged dagger. Their cutting edges were sharp and shiny.

'It doesn't matter how feeble it is,' the necromancer continued. 'As long as it's still breathing.'

He was talking as if the old dragon was no threat, but his eyes were darting around, keeping an eye out for Danzi.

'And where's the little one?'

Ping glanced at the cooking pot sitting on the edge of the well. 'I don't know what you mean.' She prayed that Kai didn't choose that moment to change back to his proper shape.

'I saw it with my own eyes when I was spying on you up on Tai Shan. That dragon stone cost me a lot – in effort and gold – and you stole it from me. Anything that hatched out of it is mine. It won't fetch as much money as the big one, but it'll still be worth a bit. Once I get it to Wucheng, I'll butcher it. Fresh dragon parts are worth a fortune.'

Ping felt anger bubble inside her like water coming to the boil.

Wucheng was the town where sorcerers and magicians purchased ingredients for their spells and potions. The most prized component was the heart of the dragon.

Both Diao and the necromancer had held the dragon stone in their greedy hands. She had stolen it back from the necromancer while he slept. When he came after her, she and Hua had fought him and escaped, leaving him struggling on a muddy river bank.

His mouth twisted into an ugly grimace, exposing stained and chipped teeth. Ping realized it was supposed to be a smile.

'You got a nasty shock when you found your goat dead, didn't you?' he cackled. 'I enjoyed watching you run like a startled rabbit.'

He would have been a laughing stock in Wucheng when word got around that a young girl had got the better of him. Ping was glad she'd shamed him.

He moved so close that Ping could smell his foul breath. The ugly smile on the necromancer's face turned into a snarl.

'I need that dragon and its whelp. And I can't wait any longer.'

He pulled a heavy sword from his belt and dug the point into Ping's cheek. She felt its sharp point break the skin and blood trickle down her neck.

'Tell me where the old dragon is and I won't kill you.'

'He's gone far away where you'll never reach him. He's flown to the Isle of the Blest and he's taken the baby with him.'

She summoned her *qi*. Even though she was out of practice, the hatred she felt for the necromancer enabled her to focus it easily. She thrust out her left arm and his sword dropped from his hand.

'Don't waste my time with your pathetic tricks,' he sneered. 'They're no match for my powers.'

He raised his hand and Ping felt herself being lifted into the air by an invisible force. She tried to focus her mind. Just summoning that one burst of *qi* had exhausted her. The *qi* blow had startled the necromancer, but it hadn't hurt him. He sensed Ping's weakness. He allowed her to drop down to the ground, the ugly smile back on his face. Ping backed away from him, trying to make her mind do her bidding, to think of a plan, to refocus her *qi*.

The necromancer picked up his sword. Ping's hatred was replaced by fear. He was right. Her powers were pitiful. He would defeat her easily.

Hua appeared on top of one of the rocks. His bright blue eyes glared at the necromancer. His fur stood on end, gleaming bluish in the sunlight. He looked huge and unearthly. The confidence drained from the necromancer's face like water through a strainer. But he only hesitated for a moment. He grabbed the neck of Ping's gown and raised his sword ready to strike her. Hua launched a spitball. It hit the necromancer with a small explosion and a flash of flame. He let go of Ping and beat out the smouldering patch on his cloak. Hua launched another spitball. The necromancer yelped with pain as it hit him on the head. Ping could smell burning flesh. She jumped back, out of his reach. It was only then that she realized she was on the lip of the well. She tumbled backwards. As she fell, she saw the necromancer lunge towards Hua with his sword. The rat was quicker. Sparks flew as the sword clanged on the rock.

Ping hit the water. She sank under the surface, reaching with her feet to touch the bottom. She couldn't find it. The well was deep. She heard a muffled scream of pain. She peered up through the greenish water and could see the dark shape of the necromancer and flashes of flame. Ping paddled her arms, trying to stop herself from sinking. She had to get back to the surface and save Kai. Her arms were as heavy as iron bars. Her gown billowed up around her head.

Then something hit the surface of the water and plunged towards her in a cloud of bubbles. When the bubbles cleared, Ping saw that it was a cooking pot. The pot was twisting and distorting. Kai was finally changing back into his dragon shape. His hard little body slammed into her. Ping was running out of air. Panic gave her strength and she kicked her legs and paddled her arms. She slowly started to rise again. Ping resurfaced and just had time to gulp a mouthful of air before she felt something pull her beneath the water again. She turned to see the little dragon with the hem of her gown in his mouth. He was dragging her down. In the water he was stronger than she was. She struggled against him, but she'd used up all her reserves of energy. He kept pulling her down, down, down. The well was deeper than she had ever imagined. Kai dragged her into its depths, until there wasn't enough light to see him through the dark green water.

'Don't, Kai.' She shouted the words in her mind, even though there was no way he could hear them. 'I can't stay underwater like you.' Her voice in her head sounded hopeless. 'Kai, I'm drowning.'

Ping had to have air. Immediately. Kai was above her now, pushing her down with his large paws. She used her last *shu* of strength to try and resist him. Her feeble efforts were useless. She gave herself up to the waters. She opened her mouth and breathed in the dark water. At least Kai could hide in the depths. He might be saved from the necro-mancer. The thought calmed her. Then she heard a faint voice in her head.

'Ping.'

Someone was calling her name.

'Ping.'

It wasn't a voice she had ever heard before. She thought it might be her ancestors calling her up to Heaven, but the voice sounded high and excited, like a child's. Kai pushed her sideways with his big paws. She banged her head on a rock archway.

Then she was coughing up water and breathing air again.

It was pitch dark. Ping struggled to make sense of what had happened. Her body was still floating in cold water, but her head was in air. She sucked in the air gratefully. It was dank and stale. She reached out into the darkness. Something nipped her fingers. It was Kai. Ping felt around. He was on a rock shelf. She hauled herself up on to it. It was like lifting a sack of stones.

A sound like high notes played on a silver flute echoed on rock surfaces.

'Ping,' said the voice in her mind. 'Ping.'

Her fumbling hands found a small dragon shape. She hugged it to her even though the talons and the spines stuck into her skin. She didn't mind. A few minutes ago she had been convinced she would die and Kai would be left to fend for himself. Just the fact that they were both together and alive was a miracle.

Kai nibbled her ear. She heard the tinkling flute notes again. They were coming from the dragon.

'Ping,' the voice in her mind repeated.

Her body was numb with cold, but her brain was starting to work again. A realization hit her like a slap on the face. The voice in her head. It was Kai's.

'You saved me, Kai,' she said.

'Ping.'

She felt around her. The underwater cavern was small, narrow enough so that she could reach both sides with outstretched arms, not even high enough for her to stand up in. Kai must have found this underwater pocket of air when he dived earlier. He had jumped into the water to push her down to the safety of the underwater cave. He had said his first word and it was her name.

Sitting in the damp darkness, everything became clear to her, like a spider's web hung with dew in the morning sun. It wasn't Kai's fault that she hadn't heard his voice. It was her fault. She had never spoken to him with her mind before. All these months she had been chatting and chiding with her mouth, she hadn't once thought of speaking to him with her mind. Not until she thought she was drowning, when she couldn't open her mouth because she was surrounded by water. Not until she was forced to, had she spoken to him with her mind as she'd done with Danzi. She had somehow been expecting Kai to start the communication, not realizing that she needed to teach him. How stupid she'd been! Babies didn't wake up one day and know how to speak. Their mothers talked to them every day, teaching them language slowly, word by word. Ping was ashamed of herself. Her concern had been all for herself — her loneliness, the weight of her responsibilities, the sacrifices she'd made to care for the dragon. It wasn't until she thought she was dying and leaving the little dragon alone in the world that she had cared enough to speak to Kai with her heart.

She had always thought of her relationship with the baby dragon as a one-way thing. She'd had to do all the work with no reward. Kai didn't teach her the way Danzi had. She had been too slow-witted to realize the truth. She was the most important thing in the world for Kai. And equally, he was the most important thing in the world for her. He was her reason for living, her life's work. If he died, she would have no reason to go on. Why had she never realized this before? Caring for him wasn't a burden. It was a pleasure, a privilege. And it certainly wasn't a one-way relationship. Kai was very young, but he had already saved her life. He had rescued her from the necromancer. The little dragon nipped her fingers.

Even though it was pitch dark, she closed her eyes. It helped her concentrate. The necromancer would assume she had drowned. He would search the shepherd's hut for Kai but when he didn't find him, he would leave.

'We'll wait,' she told Kai without opening her mouth. 'We'll wait here until he's gone.'

'Ping,' the little dragon said, and he curled up on the ledge beside her with his head in her lap.

In the damp darkness it was impossible to measure time. Ping couldn't tell whether minutes or hours had passed, but she felt stronger. She closed her ears and eyes and turned off her bodily senses one by one, until her second sight was the only thing that linked her to the world. There was no hard mass in her stomach. The necromancer had gone, she was sure of it.

'Come on, Kai,' she said, sounding the words in her head. 'We're going back up, but I can't do it without you. You'll have to lead the way.'

Ping couldn't see Kai, but she heard him plop into the water. It was as if she'd been previously speaking to him in a barbarian language and had only just started speaking his native tongue. She lowered herself into the water.

She felt Kai place his tail in the palm of her hand. She held on to it and took a deep breath.

'Swim, Kai,' she said, though she didn't say the words aloud.

'Ping,' said the voice in her head.

She felt the water around her move. She kept her eyes closed, concentrating on not breathing, on kicking as hard as she could. The journey up through the well seemed long, much longer than the journey down. Her lungs felt like they would burst. She opened her eyes. The water still stretched above her, but it had changed from black to dark green. Kai was moving through the water, as sleek as a fish.

Finally Ping broke through the surface, gasping in the sunlit air that filled her hungry lungs but blinded her eyes. She pulled herself out of the well, still breathing hard. She leapt to her feet, bracing herself for an attack, summoning her *qi* power. Her eyes grew accustomed to the light. It was late afternoon and there was no sign of the necromancer, no trace of his contaminating presence. Kai climbed out of the well and shook himself like a wet dog. Hua appeared with drops of blood around his mouth.

Ping picked up Hua and went straight to the hut. The necromancer had been inside – the sheepskins were thrown on the floor, the food chest upended – but the mess looked like frustrated anger rather than a proper search. Still, Ping had to be very careful – the necromancer was a shape-changer. But she had one advantage over him. Her second sight. She would have to pay much more attention to it.

Ping shivered. 'It will soon be dark enough to light a fire and have some supper,' she said.

Kai made a tinkling flute sound.

As Ping sat by the fire and ate a hot meal, she was grateful for these simple comforts. She would never take her good fortune for granted again. There was one thing she had to do, though, before winter set in. Kai needed a daily supply of milk. She had to find another goat. She decided to go down the mountain to the nearest village the next day and buy one. She resolved to start collecting nuts and berries for her winter store. She would practise her *qi* exercises every day without fail. She now spoke to Kai in her mind, but when it was bedtime she told him stories. She repeated important words aloud, so that he would gradually come to understand spoken words better. It would be important for him to be able to know what people were saying when they were out in the world. He liked her simple stories about shepherds tending sheep, about a clever rat, and about a slave girl who lived on a lonely mountain.

When Kai was asleep, Ping sat by the fire and thought of ways she could repay the shepherd for the use of his hut. She would carve a bowl for him. She would mend his summer trousers and tunic, which were full of holes. She would wash his sheepskin rugs that smelt like they were still attached to sheep. When they left in spring, she would leave the little hut spotless.

She got up at dawn ready to make the journey down the mountain. Before she set out, she did her *qi* exercises on the grassy slope outside the hut, breathing in the *qi* from the rising sun, feeling it warm her skin. Kai kept interrupting her.

'Ping, Ping.'

He was excited about the trip down the mountainside.

'Sssh, Kai,' she said. 'We'll be leaving soon.'

Ping closed her eyes so that she could concentrate and block out any other interruptions.

'Ping. Ping! PING!'

'Kai, I told you to wait.'

Ping opened her eyes. The golden sunlight was reflecting on metal. There were swords and spears – many of them. There were also red leather caps and vests, and wooden shields. It took her mind a few moments to make sense of these unfamiliar things. It was a section of imperial guards, ten of them. They had crept up the hillside without making a sound. Kai had taken the shape of a rock. The guards formed a ring around her, their spears all pointed in her direction. Ping couldn't understand why her second sight hadn't warned her.

'It is a serious crime to trespass on the sacred slopes of Tai Shan,' the captain said.

One of the soldiers peered at Ping. 'I know who this is,' he said. 'It's the sorceress from Huangling.'

'The one who escaped with the imperial dragon?' the captain asked.

The guard nodded and looked around nervously, as if he expected a dragon to jump out and attack them. The captain stood up straight.

'In the name of the Great Emperor, Son of Heaven, Commander of the Armies, Wisest Among Us, I arrest you for the crimes of deserting an imperial post, stealing the last imperial dragon and trespassing on the sacred slopes of Tai Shan,' he said. 'Before the eight Immortals, between the five sacred mountains, under the sun and moon, I arrest you and take you to bow down before your Emperor, and confess your crimes.'

A blur of blue fur attached itself to the nearest man. The guard yelped as Hua bit his arm, and blood poured from it. Another guard lunged at Hua, hitting him with the hilt of his sword. Hua let go of the guard's arm and slumped to the ground.

'No,' Ping shouted. 'Don't kill him! He's a special rat, a sorceress's rat. The Emperor will want to examine him.'

Ping looked around anxiously for Kai. The rock had disappeared. All she could see was a spade leaning against the hut wall. Her mind wasn't working as fast as it should be. She thought the spade was around the other side of the hut. She heard a short, sharp flute note over and over again. It was Kai. He was afraid.

'Ping,' said a frightened voice in her head.

The spade turned into a soup ladle. The guards were all staring at Ping, so they didn't see the shape-change. Two of them moved towards her. She thrust out her arm, sending out a bolt of *qi* power. The invisible force knocked the nearest guard off his feet. The guards raised their shields. Ping sent out another *qi* bolt, but the soldiers' shields deflected it. Two guards grabbed Ping by the arms.

They brought Ping's belongings outside and studied

them. The captain looked at the two identical soup ladles with a puzzled frown. He reached out to pick one up. Ping held her breath and waited for a small dragon to appear. The air around the ladle shifted slightly as the captain tried to grasp it. His hand turned rigid. The colour drained from his face. His eyes glazed over. He opened his mouth to say something. The words remained unspoken. He fell to the ground with a heavy thud and lay as stiff as a spear. The guards stared at their leader's inert body, unsure what to do. One of them bent close to his chest.

'He's still breathing,' he said.

The guards all turned fearfully to Ping. She felt nine spears digging into her through her gown. She could hear an anxious 'Ping, Ping, Ping' in her head. There were so many iron weapons. Though they weren't close to Kai, they were still causing him pain.

'Don't try any more sorcery or we'll stick you,' one of the guards said.

He waved his spear towards her things. 'Pick them up.'

Ping collected up her cooking bowls and the other ladle, and put them in her bag. She turned her back on the guards as she picked up the ladle that was Kai, shielding him from the iron. As she reached out to the ladle her hands grasped a dragon-shape. The sensation of seeing one thing and feeling something completely different made her feel dizzy. Specks of light drifted in front of her eyes and there was a ringing in her ears. She glanced at the unconscious captain.

It obviously had a more drastic effect on other people. Kai wrapped his tail around her arm. To the guards it looked as if she had a ladle hooked over her arm.

'Good boy, Kai.'

Some of the guards searched the hut.

'There's no dragon in there,' one of them said.

Ping felt the spears jab into her. 'Let's go then.'

She slung the bag over her shoulder. The guards pushed her forward with the points of their spears. As they marched her down the sloping meadow, Ping turned to look at the shepherd's hut. It looked so comfortable and welcoming her heart ached to be leaving it. All her peace and safety had evaporated like mist in the morning sun.

CHAPTER NINE

A ROUGH JOURNEY

The wagon slowed. The leather cover was laced shut, so Ping couldn't see what was happening. She could hear the low mumble of the guards' conversation. It must be evening, she thought to herself. We're stopping for the night at a village. That's what had happened on the three previous nights. She imagined the scene outside the wagon. The entire village would be gathered to catch a glimpse of the prisoner who was being escorted by the imperial guards. A disappointed mumble would pass through the crowd when they saw that it was only a young girl. One of the guards would whisper to someone.

'Sorceress,' he would say, and the word would hiss through the crowd like water spilt on a hot stove.

The imperial guards had marched Ping to the foot of Tai Shan, where a two-wheeled wagon was waiting, harnessed to a patient ox. It was made for transporting sacks of grain and vegetables, not people, and didn't look sturdy enough to withstand bumping along a rocky mountain path. The guards had bound her hands and feet and pushed her into the wagon. The roof of the wagon was so low that Ping couldn't sit up straight beneath it.

At least they hadn't discovered Kai. Ping heard long, low notes. She looked down at the baby dragon in her lap.

'Ping, Ping, Ping,' Kai said.

It was like an accusation. Why had they left their pleasant mountain home? Why had she allowed them to be captured? What were those horrible metal things that made him feel bad? There was nothing she could say to reassure him. With her hands tied, she couldn't even stroke him. She didn't complain when he nipped her fingers.

The guards hadn't been searching for Ping. That was why her second sight hadn't told her they were near. They'd meant her no harm. She didn't know why they'd been wandering around Tai Shan. They'd all heard about the 'dragon sorceress', but once she was tied up, they weren't so afraid of her. Hua was another matter. She'd heard them muttering about the unusual colouring of his fur in the sunlight, his exceptional size – and the fireballs he spat out. They would have put an end to this unnatural creature with a spear, but knew that Ping was right. The Emperor would want him brought back alive. They had tied the rat up so that he couldn't escape, muzzled him with a leather thong so that he couldn't launch any spitballs. After what had happened to their captain, they were all wary of the soup ladle, and no one dared take it from her.

Kai had been terrified and she had comforted him as best she could with her hands tied. She knew her reassurances that everything would be all right were not very convincing. One thing she had been able to do as they bumped along in the wagon was tell him stories. She always spoke to him with her mind not her mouth, but his vocabulary still hadn't increased. The only word he said was 'Ping'.

The little dragon whimpered.

'At least they haven't found you,' she said.

It wasn't much consolation.

Ping didn't have to tell Kai to shape-change whenever the guards threw back the leather cover. It was his natural instinct when he was in danger. She'd been able to carry the ladle-shaped Kai with her whenever she was allowed out of the wagon. These times were few and far between. The guards had kept her shut inside the covered wagon day and night, allowing her only a few minutes each day to get out and stretch her legs.

They fed her reasonably well, but stood with spears digging into her as she ate. She heard them grumbling about their ration of gruel. Ping's meals on Tai Shan had been small and simple, and the goat-meat gruel was a welcome change from fish, but Kai couldn't eat it. She'd hoped that Hua would be able to help her, but he was trussed up like a chicken ready for roasting and couldn't escape.

Ping knew Liu Che would be furious. He had given her the position of Imperial Dragonkeeper. It was a great honour – and she had rejected it. He had treated her as a friend, confided in her. He had allowed her to call him by his personal name. No one else had that privilege but his closest family members. In return she had helped the last imperial dragon to escape. That was a crime punishable by death.

She had managed to collect a few worms and a snail or two in the brief times that she was allowed out. Kai had found some grubs in the rotten vegetables still in the bottom of the wagon. Ping had fished weevils out of her gruel for him, but he was still very hungry. And every time the guards came near, their iron blades made him weak and sick.

Ping tried to think, though her mind was as weary as her body. The Emperor would be in Chang'an at this time of year. It would take the ox weeks to plod all the way to the capital city. Even if they travelled by river, it would be a slow journey as oarsmen would have to row against the strong current. She had to come up with a plan of escape quickly or Kai would starve to death.

When the wagon came to a halt, Ping heard footsteps approach.

'Kai,' she said. 'It's time to shape-change.'

The little dragon wrapped his tail around her arm and

changed into a soup ladle. The leather flap was thrown back. Ping blinked and shaded her eyes. Her eyes grew accustomed to the light and she saw that they were not in a village, but in a courtyard with high walls on all sides. Large wooden gates were closing behind them. The gate was decorated with paintings of red bats and blue cranes – the symbols of good luck and long life. Her captors were talking to the guards at the gate, pointing at her.

'We caught the dragon sorceress,' one of them boasted. 'She tried to cast spells on us. Did you hear what happened to our captain?'

The wagon started to move again. This time the guards didn't retie the leather flap. They passed under another gateway. This one had three large characters painted on it in gold.

The wagon made its way across a many-arched, curved bridge, which crossed a wide lake. A steep rocky island rose up out of the water. On top of the island was a pavilion. On the opposite shore of the lake, willow trees bent sadly, their boughs dipping into the water, falling leaves drifting down like tears.

This wasn't the wild beauty of nature like on Tai Shan; every tree, flower and rock had been carefully placed. It was a huge garden. On the other side of the lake, the narrow road started to rise. The garden spread up the slopes of a small hill. The wagon passed a cluster of maple trees, their leaves just starting to turn red. Ping had seen these trees before. The road meandered between flower beds to a beautiful building halfway up the hill. Ping knew where she was. It was Ming Yang, the imperial hunting lodge where she had met the Emperor.

When the wagon reached Ming Yang Lodge, a nervous guard untied Ping's hands and feet. The others pointed their spears at her as she stiffly climbed down. She stared up at Ming Yang Lodge. It looked different. The roofs were no longer black. Gleaming yellow tiles had replaced the gloomy black ones. The Emperor had gone ahead with his plan to change the imperial colour. Ping smiled – even though there were spear tips sticking in her back. She had suggested that Liu Che change the imperial colour from black to yellow.

The lodge seemed quiet. Two serving women hurried by, glancing fearfully at Ping, but there wasn't the bustle of servants and ministers that there had been the last time Ping was there. The smell of cooking wafted from the direction of the kitchens. She could smell garlic, ginger and plum sauce. Her stomach rumbled. They were the fragrant aromas of an imperial banquet. Her heart thudded. It could only mean one thing. The Emperor was at Ming Yang Lodge. She had thought she would have weeks to work out what she would say to Liu Che, how she would plead for her life. Now she had no time at all to think about it.

Ping felt a strange mixture of excitement and dread at the thought of seeing him again. In the brief time she had spent at Ming Yang before, she had enjoyed his company very much. Besides being the Emperor, he was also the only person she'd ever known who was close to her own age. The only boy. There had been young men working at Huangling Palace from time to time – sour-faced, scowling stable hands and gardeners – but they had all avoided her as if she was an ugly spider. The handsome young Emperor, despite his exalted position, had smiled at her and treated her with respect. He had taken notice of what she had to say, even though she was just a slave girl. She longed to renew her friendship with him, but she knew that would not happen. She had seen the look on Liu Che's face as she had flown away with Danzi.

The guards didn't take Ping before the Emperor or to the pretty chamber where she had slept on her previous visit to Ming Yang Lodge. Instead they led her to a new building some distance from the lodge, hastily constructed of bamboo canes, roughly thatched with untidy bundles of twigs. Ping could hear strange sounds coming from it. Animal sounds – growls and screeches. Inside were bamboo cages. One contained a large black cat as big as a tiger. Another contained two sad-eyed monkeys. The guards kept away from the cage containing the black cat. One of them touched a deep scratch on his arm.

'I'll be glad when it's released into the Tiger Forest,' he muttered.

Ping remembered how Liu Che had decided to turn the

Tiger Forest that lay beyond the gardens to the south into a wild animal reserve for creatures from all over the empire.

'Where's my rat?' she asked.

They ignored her and led her to an empty cage. The guard reached out to take the ladle from her arm.

'Don't touch it!' Ping shouted.

But he took no notice. As he touched the ladle, a strange expression passed over his face before he collapsed to the floor and lay like a plank of wood. The other guards opened the door of the cage and shoved her in. A pile of dirty straw and a bucket were the only furnishings. They locked the door and left her with the animals. Any hopes Ping had that the Emperor might forgive her disappeared.

Ping shut her eyes as the ladle on her arm turned into a small dragon.

'Hungry,' said the sad voice in her head.

A few days earlier, nothing would have made her happier than hearing Kai say another word. But now she had much more serious concerns. She had to keep them both alive.

Ping sank into the straw. It smelt of horse manure.

'Good boy, Kai,' she said, scratching him around the bumps on his head, trying to sound pleased. 'You did well today.'

The little dragon whimpered. Her cheerful words didn't fool him at all.

Her own feelings were unimportant now. Kai was her first priority. He was thin and his scales were dull. He lay in the straw making soft, low sounds that only made her feel worse. She would have preferred it if he'd bitten her.

Sometime later, a guard came in and without a word pushed a bowl of gruel through the bars of her cage. Kai tried to eat the gruel but it just made him sick. He wasn't able to digest meat yet. Ping ate a mouthful of the gruel, but she couldn't bring herself to eat much with the hungry dragon watching her.

Ping had been imprisoned before. She had been cornered by strong enemies armed with weapons. She had always been able to think of a way to escape. But Danzi was with her then. Now she was on her own. She didn't even have Hua to help her. There seemed no way she could escape.

She lay down in the straw and curled around the little dragon to comfort him.

Eventually he went to sleep, but Ping lay awake. She could only think of one way to feed Kai. She remembered the day he had hatched from the dragon stone. He had needed milk then and there was none. Danzi had cut his chest and fed the baby with his own blood. She would have to do the same. She lay awake the whole night thinking of how she could get her hands on something sharp enough to cut her flesh.

CHAPTER TEN

THE LONGEVITY COUNCIL

Early morning light filtered through the bamboo walls. Ping had hoped that she would dream of Danzi and he would tell her what to do. But she hadn't slept at all. She remembered the old dragon's soft voice, the way his mouth sometimes looked like he was smiling, how he would point out things of interest with one of his talons.

'Hungry, hungry, hungry,' said a miserable dragon voice in her mind.

Ping stroked the little dragon, ashamed that his second word only proved how much she had failed in her role as Dragonkeeper.

She felt around for something sharp. She broke off a long splinter from one of the bamboo canes and dug it into her arm, but it only scratched her. What she needed was a blade or a piece of broken pottery or a thorn from a rose bush. She wished the guards hadn't taken her bag and her knife.

Then Ping realized she had the thing she needed at hand. The very same tool that Danzi had used to cut his flesh — a dragon's talon. She sat Kai on her lap and held his left forepaw in her hand. Unlike cats, dragons didn't tuck their claws away when they weren't using them. They were always out, as Ping knew only too well. Kai's talons were small, but very sharp. They had often made her bleed.

Ping examined the inside of her arm. Just beneath her skin, she could see the blue lines of the vessels that transported blood around her body. She chose the largest one, in the crook of her elbow, and placed the talon against the tender skin. She dug the talon deep into her arm, clamping her teeth together so that she didn't cry out. Blood ran from the wound and she caught it in her cupped hand.

'Here, Kai,' she said. 'Drink this.'

The little dragon blinked at her uncertainly.

'It's OK, it doesn't hurt,' she lied. 'It will make you strong.'

He lapped at the pool of blood, cautiously at first, but then faster. He drank until the wound started to congeal.

There was nothing Ping could use to bandage the cut. She felt dizzy. She lay down in the straw and slept.

Ping woke when the outer door was thrown open. It was full daylight. She just had time to hide Kai under her gown before an imperial guard came and stood in front of her cage. Her eyes focused on misshapen toes bulging through holes in a pair of shabby slippers.

'Ah ha!' said a cheerful voice.

She looked up. It wasn't a guard at all, but a fat man wearing the gown and ribbons of an imperial minister. He was out of breath.

'So!' he said. 'This is the terrifying sorceress I've been hearing so much about.'

Ping tried to stand up, but the cage started to spin, so she settled for getting to her knees.

The man was nothing like the slim, stern-faced government ministers she had seen before. He had a big smile on his face and bright, twinkling eyes beneath eyebrows that reminded Ping of Kai's favourite tufty caterpillars. His ears were the longest she'd ever seen. His beard was tangled and he had a mouth that couldn't help smiling, even when he was trying hard to be serious.

'I am Dong Fang Suo,' he said. 'The Imperial Magician.'

'A magician?' Ping said.

Dong Fang Suo chuckled to himself as if he had just remembered something very funny. 'Not the sort of magician who turns people into toads,' he laughed. 'I am a scientist. We have met before.'

Ping looked at the jolly old man. His ministerial cap was askew. His gown was creased except where it was stretched tight over his large, round belly. His ribbons of office were twisted in a knot. She didn't recognize him at all.

'I was among the scientists summoned by the Emperor that memorable day when you escaped with the imperial dragon.' Dong Fang Suo laughed.

'I don't remember you,' said Ping.

'My position was much humbler then. His Imperial Majesty has since honoured me with a higher position.' He sucked air into his chest and stood a little straighter. 'I am now His Imperial Majesty's Privy Counsellor, Imperial Magician, *and* Head of the Longevity Council.'

Ping tried to look impressed though she had no idea what the Longevity Council was.

Dong Fang Suo looked at Ping.

'I remember *you*,' he chuckled. 'And your dragon. You must tell me about your adventures – when we have time.'

He waved one of the guards over to unlock the cage door. Ping stood up. She was relieved to see a soup ladle lying in the straw and not a small purple dragon.

'Where is my rat?' Ping asked.

The Imperial Magician's smile narrowed slightly. 'It is being held . . . elsewhere.'

'You're not going to hurt him, are you?'

Dong Fang Suo ignored her question. 'Your presence is awaited in the Chamber of Spreading Clouds.'

Ping got to her feet, steadying herself on the bars of the cage.

'You look a little pale,' Dong Fang Suo said cheerfully.

'We've been shut in a wagon for three days, then thrown into prison,' Ping replied.

'We?' asked the Imperial Magician.

'I mean I,' Ping stammered. 'I can't think straight. I need some fresh air.'

It wasn't the first time Ping had been inside the Chamber of Spreading Clouds. The silk wall hangings, the dragons painted on the ceiling rafters, the carved shutters were just as beautiful as she remembered. Dong Fang Suo led Ping to the centre of the room. Imperial guards were positioned all around the chamber. Every guard had his eyes fixed on her and a spear pointed in her direction. The captain of the guards stepped forward and pushed her to her knees. He was the one who had fallen into a swoon on Tai Shan. In spite of the rough way he treated her, Ping was glad to see he had recovered.

Ping's heart was beating faster than usual. She took some deep breaths to control it. She waited for the Emperor to appear, but he didn't. Instead, four ministers entered the room and formed a circle around her, examining her just as they might have examined the black cat or the monkeys. They wore the winged headdresses of imperial ministers, but in every other respect they were nothing like any government ministers she had seen before. One had a beard divided into five plaits with dead flowers woven through them; another was very small, no higher than Ping's waist, with a tiger's tail tied around his waist; the third was bare-foot and his hair hung past his shoulders in matted clumps as if he had never combed it; the last one carried a carved staff and appeared to be blind. The ministers began questioning her.

'Where did the dragon go?' asked the tiny minister. 'Do you expect him to return?'

'He flew away to a place where people like you can't bother him,' Ping replied. 'And I don't think he has the strength to return.'

'After he was wounded, did you keep any of the dragon's blood?' inquired the blind minister.

'No!'

'What gives you magic powers?' asked the barefoot one.

'Why did the guards become entranced?' asked the one with the flowers in his beard.

'I don't have any magic powers. I'm not a sorceress,' she said truthfully. 'And I don't know why the guards fainted,' she added – less truthfully.

They whispered to each other and then left the chamber.

'Who are those men?' Ping asked Dong Fang Suo.

'They are the other members of the Longevity Council,' the Imperial Magician replied. 'His Imperial Majesty has given the council the task of discovering a way to make him live an exceptionally long life, so that the empire can benefit from his rule for many generations.'

'The last time I was in the Chamber of Spreading Clouds,

the Emperor had gathered scientists and alchemists together to make an elixir that would keep him young forever,' Ping said. 'Didn't they succeed?'

It had seemed to Ping like the whim of a spoilt boy at the time.

'They concluded that such an elixir was impossible. The Emperor sent them away and formed the Longevity Council.'

Dong Fang Suo told the guards to take her back to her prison. On the way back to the animal cages, they passed by the gardeners' sheds. There were heaps of leaves and dead plants that would be spread on the garden beds when they had rotted down. Ping pretended to stumble over a rake and fell to her knees.

She scrabbled among the pile of leaves. The guards jabbed her with their spears, but she ignored them, collecting the worms that she found among the rotting plants.

'Get up!' one of the guards shouted.

Ping stuffed the worms into her pouch and got to her feet again.

The guards were whispering about her, debating whether she was going to eat the worms or use them in a spell. They hurried her back to her cage.

Among the sounds of the garden – the birds, the hum of insects, the rustle of leaves – Ping could hear another faint sound. She stopped to listen. It sounded like someone crying. The guards jabbed her with their spears.

She waited until the guards had locked the cage door and

taken up their post outside, then she pulled the worms from her pouch.

'I have something for you, Kai,' she said.

The little dragon ate the worms hungrily. She reopened the wound on her arm and gave him another drink of her blood, wondering how many more times she could do so without risking her life. She felt herself drifting off to sleep when two unsmiling guards came to the cage door.

'Dong Fang Suo says you're allowed to walk in the garden,' one of them said. He had a short beard and squinty eyes.

The other guard was younger and was unsuccessfully trying to grow a moustache. He glared at Ping. He clearly didn't approve of the prisoner having such freedom.

Two seasons had passed since Ping had walked in the gardens of Ming Yang Lodge. It had been in the full bloom of spring then. Now autumn was colouring the leaves of the trees. The fan-shaped leaves of the gingko trees were turning yellow. A few fallen leaves swirled around her feet in a gentle breeze. Maples, ashes and other trees whose names Ping didn't know were turning orange and red. Dogwood trees and holly bushes bore red berries. The tiny white flowers of the sweet olive tree filled the air with fragrance. A grove of cypress trees stood apart from all this autumn colour, dark and green as ever.

Ping knelt down to take a closer look at the wilting

chrysanthemums, though she was really more interested in the fruit that had fallen from a crab-apple tree. She picked through the bruised fruit and found snails and slugs.

'I'd like to visit the Garden of Secluded Harmony,' she said to the guards as she stood up.

They looked at each other.

'I'm not sure about that,' said the bearded guard.

'Did Minister Dong say I couldn't go there?'

She could see him going through his orders in his head.

'Not exactly.'

'I just want to admire the view,' Ping said.

The guards both gripped their spears firmly.

'Just remember we're watching you,' said the guard with the unsuccessful moustache.

Ping followed the path up the hill as it curved between strangely shaped rocks that twisted and contorted as if they were in pain. She knew each rock had been carefully chosen for its resemblance to a lion or a dragon and placed in the garden to be admired like statues.

The Garden of Secluded Harmony was at the top of the hill. As she approached, Ping knew it had changed before she reached it. A tower soared up from the top of the hill.

'What's that?' Ping asked.

'It's called the Touching Heaven Tower,' one of the guards replied. 'The Emperor ordered it to be constructed. Stone-masons have only just finished building it.'

Ping walked faster up the path. She could hear faint music

– clear ringing notes – that grew louder as she climbed. At last the hill flattened out and the Garden of Secluded Harmony was spread before her. She remembered the morning she had walked around it with the Emperor, crossing the Precious Jade Lake on the zigzag bridge, peering into the lake's depths looking for turtles, sitting in the Watching Magnolia Buds Open Pavilion. Ping remembered the exact spot where the Emperor had insisted she call him by his personal name. A wave of sadness wiped away her happy memories, like an ocean wave washing footprints from a beach. Danzi had been with them that day.

There were no daffodils now, no magnolia flowers, no cherry blossoms. Autumn flowers were in bloom – anemones, day lilies, wind flowers. But even if the daffodils and magnolias had been in flower, they wouldn't have held her attention.

The last time she had been in the Garden of Secluded Harmony, there had been a small pavilion halfway across the zigzag bridge. The pavilion had disappeared and in its place stood the tower. In the imperial capital of Chang'an, the gate towers were four storeys high. This tower was more than twice that height. It was built of large blocks of stone that were alternately painted red and white, like a board for playing draughts. The cornerstones were painted with swirling cloud patterns. A wooden pavilion with carved eaves and balconies was perched on top of the stone tower. How anyone could climb up to reach it, Ping had no idea. A yellow-tiled roof, like a miniature version of the lodge roofs, topped the structure. Bells hung from the edges of the balconies, under the eaves and from the corners of the roof. They were the source of the music she had heard. The lower bells were large and made a deep ringing sound. The bells under the eaves were smaller and had a higher chime. Those hanging from the corners of the roof were smaller still and made just a faint tinkle. Each breath of wind created a different melody – pretty but sad. On the top of the tower, a statue of an Immortal glittered in the sunlight.

'Is that gold?' asked Ping.

'Yes,' said the guard in a hushed voice. 'Solid gold.'

Ping shaded her eyes so that she could see the details in the sunlight. The Immortal's hands were raised above his head. In them he held a green jade dish.

'But why did the Emperor build this tower?'

'To catch the pure dew of Heaven that drips from the stars,' the bearded guard replied, proud of his knowledge.

Not to be outdone, the other guard continued. 'The Longevity Council believes that if the Emperor drinks star dew every day, he will live for a thousand years.'

'Is it your job to collect the dew?' Ping asked.

The guards looked horrified.

'No! Not us,' exclaimed the guard with the failing moustache. 'Spilling even a drop is punishable by death. That's a shaman's job.'

Ping gazed up at the tower. She wondered how the

shaman could climb up it to get the dew without risking plunging to his death, but she didn't ask the guards. Now she had them at their ease, she had another question, one she'd been wanting to ask ever since she'd arrived.

'Is the Emperor at Ming Yang Lodge?'

'No,' they replied together. 'His Imperial Majesty is in Chang'an.'

Ping didn't know whether to be disappointed or relieved.

As she walked back from the Garden of Secluded Harmony, Ping saw a plant whose leaves she knew would help heal her wounded arm. It grew along a path that led to a dense ring of bamboo plants. The bamboo canes were three times Ping's height and grew so close together that it was impossible to find a way through them. She could hear a soft sound coming from behind the bamboo. It sounded like the crying she had heard before.

Ping found a place where the bamboo canes were not quite as dense. Pretending to be interested in the healing plant, she peered through. She could see a small square pavilion that was walled in on all but one side. Ping could just make out a dim figure inside. It was a woman. Her head was bent low. She was sobbing softly. It was the sound of someone who had completely given up hope of happiness. It was the saddest sound Ping had ever heard. The bamboo canes formed a living prison. It seemed that she wasn't the only prisoner at Ming Yang Lodge.

The woman's hands lay palm up on the bench beside her. Small ornaments hung from her ears and trembled as she sobbed. She allowed the tears to drip from her face. There were so many tears her pale blue silk gown must have been soaked. From her fine clothing she looked like a woman of position and wealth. How could someone so privileged be so unhappy?

The guards realized what Ping was doing.

'You shouldn't be spying on the Princess!' one of them hissed, prodding her until she went back to the path.

As they led her away, Ping looked back at the weeping woman with new curiosity.

The guards suddenly froze in their tracks, looks of terror on their faces.

'What is the prisoner doing wandering around the gardens?' said a voice.

Both guards fell to their knees and bowed their heads to the ground.

Ping knew who it was without having to turn her head. It was Liu Che – the Emperor.

· CHAPTER ELEVEN ·

THE PRINCESS
WHO COULDN'T SMILE

Liu Che was standing with his hands clasped behind his back. He wasn't wearing the yellow ceremonial gown that he had worn the last time Ping had seen him, but a dark blue satin one embroidered with gold. Over the gown, he wore a fur-trimmed sleeveless coat. He looked weary. Three government ministers, several servants and a number of imperial guards were hurrying along the path. As usual they were having trouble keeping up with him.

The Emperor's expression was grim, just as it had been when Ping first met him. Despite this, she felt a bubble of hope form inside her. Surely he would understand that she'd only done what she thought was right. She sank to her knees and lowered her head till her forehead touched the stone path.

'It's good to see you again, Your Imperial Majesty,' Ping said.

'Don't speak to His Imperial Majesty!' one of the guards said, kicking her.

'I will permit the prisoner to answer my questions,' the Emperor said.

Ping saw his feet move towards her.

'You allowed my dragon to escape,' he said bluntly.

It wasn't actually a question, but Ping replied anyway.

'Yes, Your Imperial Majesty. I felt it was my only choice. Danzi was wounded. He wouldn't have lived long in captivity.'

'You deserted your imperial post.'

'Yes.'

She lifted her head so that she could see him.

The guards started to move towards her, but the Emperor raised his hand to stop them. Liu Che had changed. He was no longer a boy, but a young man. He had grown several inches. His hair was pulled into a tight knot on the back of his head and he wore a flat, square headdress with black beads hanging from the corners. Ping was suddenly aware of her crumpled gown, her untidy hair, her dirty fingernails. She wished she looked better. The Emperor didn't return her gaze. He watched a snail crawl out of her pouch. There was a look of anger and distaste on his face, but Ping was so happy to see him she couldn't stop her mouth from smiling. Her thoughts formed into words and escaped from her mouth. 'You look older.'

He scowled at her. 'That is no compliment.'

His smooth skin was the colour of hazelnuts. His mouth, though stern, had a pleasant shape. The small scar that cut through his right eyebrow was the only imperfection. The Emperor looked into her eyes and Ping's smile faded. His dark eyes were as cold as stones in winter.

Ping had hoped that once he saw her, Liu Che would remember their friendship and forgive her. There was no hint of warmth in him, only anger.

'So where is my dragon?' the Emperor demanded.

Dong Fang Suo came puffing up the path and stood panting behind the Emperor.

'Danzi flew across Ocean to the Isle of the Blest with Hua,' Ping replied. 'I don't know if he survived the journey.'

'Your rat went to the Isle of the Blest?' the Imperial Magician asked.

The Emperor was about to reprove the Imperial Magician for interrupting, but then he stopped and turned back to Ping.

'Did he?'

'Yes, Your Imperial Majesty.'

'This is the same rat that we have now?' the Imperial Magician continued. 'The one with the blue eyes?'

Ping nodded.

Everyone knew about the Isle of the Blest, the magical place that was supposed to lie over Ocean. Stories told of trees that bore giant peaches of immortality and the fungus of everlasting life. There was also a stream of jade water –

the water of life. Some people had set out in flimsy boats to find the magical island. No one had ever returned. This was Ping's only hope now. As long as the Emperor thought she had knowledge of the Isle of the Blest, he might keep her alive.

'Unfortunately the rat escaped while the Longevity Council were examining it, Your Imperial Majesty,' the Imperial Magician confessed.

Ping's heart leapt. Hua was free.

'Do you know where it is?' the Emperor asked Ping.

She could honestly say that she had no idea where Hua was.

'I want the rat found,' the Emperor commanded.

Dong Fang Suo bowed. 'Whatever Your Imperial Majesty commands,' he said.

One of the other ministers stepped forward and kneeled before the Emperor.

'The punishment for stealing an imperial dragon is death, Your Imperial Majesty,' he said. 'Is it your wish that the prisoner be executed?'

The Emperor's face turned hard again.

'Not yet.'

He turned and walked away.

The guards prodded Ping with their spears and marched her back to her prison.

Kai popped back into his dragon shape as soon as the guards left. She gave him the few snails and slugs that she had collected for him. He ate them, but continued to make low, sad sounds. She sat down in the straw and let him drink a little more of her blood.

Ping had saved a sharp piece of bone that she'd found in her gruel. She stayed up most of the night trying to saw through one of the bamboo canes of her prison with it. If she could remove just one cane they could escape and she and Kai could take their chances in the Tiger Forest. The only other choice was to reveal Kai to the Emperor. Once that was done, there would be no turning back. The little dragon would be kept in captivity for the rest of his life. That wasn't what Danzi had wanted. Though he had been in captivity at Huangling for many years, he had spent many hundreds of years free.

The next morning, Ping was allowed to walk in the garden again, but the same pair of imperial guards were always a few steps behind her, spears at the ready in case she attempted any sorcery. She didn't want to go to the Garden of Secluded Harmony again. The looming tower spoiled the design of the walled garden. She was too weak to walk that far anyway.

Dong Fang Suo appeared suddenly from behind a tree just as she was squashing a large slug. He was the only person who didn't seem to be afraid of her. Before he had a chance to say anything, Ping asked a question of her own.

'Who is the woman imprisoned in the bamboo grove?' she asked.

'That is the Emperor's sister, Princess Yangxin,' Dong Fang Suo replied. 'But she is not imprisoned.'

'Then why is she so unhappy?'

The Imperial Magician looked around to make sure the guards couldn't hear.

'Her father arranged a marriage for her with the Duke of Yan. Politically it was an excellent marriage. In the past, disputes with the State of Yan cost the lives of many imperial soldiers. There were rumours that the Duke might even join with the barbarians on the other side of the Great Wall. That would be a great threat to the empire. The marriage brought peace with Yan.'

The Imperial Magician continued to smile even though the story was very serious.

'Unfortunately the marriage was not as desirable for the Princess. Her husband is an old man, rather coarse in his eating habits, who already has six wives. Her Imperial Highness has spent several years in lands within arrow range of barbarian invaders.'

'She must have been very lonely,' Ping said. 'But she's here now, so the Duke must have allowed her to visit her brother.'

The Imperial Magician turned in the direction of the pavilion.

'No one has seen her smile for six years.'

His own smile shrank to a small curve like a piece of orange rind. That seemed to be as close as he could get to a frown.

He asked her questions about Danzi. Did she expect him to return? Had he spoken of other dragons? What magical powers did he have? Half an hour later, he hurried off just as unexpectedly, halfway through a sentence.

The rest of the day dragged by as Ping listened to the miserable screeches of the monkeys and the soft padding of the black cat. Then Dong Fang Suo appeared on the other side of her cage and continued their conversation where he had left off as if he had merely paused for thought, rather than disappeared for half a day. Ping tried to answer the Imperial Magician's questions, but needed all of her concentration just to stay awake.

The next day, Ping knew that she couldn't bleed herself again without collapsing. The guards came to take her for her daily walk.

'I'm going to take you out into the garden today,' she told Kai. She turned her back on the guards as Kai wrapped his tail around her arm and took on the shape of the soup ladle.

'Why do you want to take that with you?' asked the guard with the thin moustache.

'So that I can drink from a stream,' she said. 'If I get thirsty.'

The guards weren't quite so afraid of their pale, quiet prisoner now. They looked at each other and shrugged.

They led her to a quiet part of the garden. No one else seemed to go there, not even the gardeners, who had neglected the fallen leaves, leaving them to pile in corners. Out of sight of their captain, the guards sat on one of the stone benches and played a game with pebbles.

The breeze carried the faint sound of crying. Ping wanted to get another glimpse of the weeping Princess, but she didn't have the strength to walk that far. She was just thinking that she would have to reveal Kai to the Emperor, when she noticed one of the piles of leaves shifting. She thought loss of blood was making her see things. A rat's head appeared among the leaves. Ping clamped her hand over her mouth to stop a cry of pleasure escaping. She glanced at the guards, who were still lounging on the stone bench.

'Hua!' she whispered. 'I've been so worried about you.'

She picked up the rat and examined him. A patch of fur had been neatly shaved off him and several of his whiskers were missing.

'What have they done to you?'

Dong Fang Suo suddenly popped out from behind a twisted rock. Hua dived back under the pile of leaves.

'And the dragon's speech?' the Imperial Magician asked.

He carried on his conversation from the previous day as if he'd just paused to order his thoughts. Ping felt so weak, she was worried she might fall into a faint. She focused on the magician's misshapen slippers.

'Were you the only one who could understand it?'

'I have only met one other person who could understand dragon speech,' Ping replied. 'That was Wang Cao, the herbalist. Unfortunately a dragon hunter killed him. But he wasn't a true Dragonkeeper. He didn't have second sight.'

'Did you always understand Danzi?' he asked.

'No, understanding only seems to come when the Dragonkeeper has been in the company of a dragon for some time.'

Dong Fang Suo nodded his head. 'The same as the second sight,' he said.

'Yes.'

The Imperial Magician thought about this for quite a long time. Then he spoke again. 'Come with me, Ping. The Longevity Council is waiting.'

The Imperial Magician led Ping to the Chamber of Spreading Clouds. Ping slowly followed him. Two carved chairs with cushions on them had been placed at one end of the chamber. The other four members of the Longevity Council were gathered there. A nervous-looking imperial guard came in carrying a cloth bundle. He placed it on a low table and gingerly opened out the corners. The bundle contained all her belongings – her gold coins, her jade pendant, the dragon-stone shards, the dragon scale, the large leaf folded in half. Her comb, sewing needle and thread were also there. Her cooking things were there, as well as her hand-carved bucket and a soup ladle that was identical to the one hanging over Ping's arm. The only things that weren't there were the Dragonkeeper's mirror, which she kept in a secret pocket sewn inside her gown, and the imperial seal, which was in her pouch.

The strange men of the Longevity Council inspected her belongings. They peered at her simple cooking utensils as if they might hold deep secrets. But they didn't touch anything. They poked at her belongings with sticks — except for the blind minister, who sniffed each item.

Everyone in the room suddenly collapsed to their knees and bowed their heads to the floor. The Emperor entered, sweeping into the room in his formal yellow satin gown woven through with soaring golden dragons. Ping was feeling faint, so she was relieved to sink to her knees. A young woman was with the Emperor, her hand resting lightly on his arm. It was the weeping woman from the pavilion, Princess Yangxin. She was as slender as a sapling and took such tiny steps that she seemed to glide, like a swan on a still pool. Her gown was made of lilac silk gauze, which was so light it floated around her. Her sleeves were so deep they nearly reached the floor.

The Emperor escorted the Princess to one of the carved chairs. He took her hand to lend her support as she lowered herself gracefully on to it. A lady-in-waiting arranged the Princess's gown around her. The Emperor smiled fondly at the Princess. Ping felt a pang of sadness. Perhaps he would smile at her again if he knew about Kai.

The Emperor gave permission for everyone to get to their feet. Ping stayed on her knees. She could see the Princess's face for the first time. Her eyes glistened. They were dark and moist as if about to overflow with tears. Her lips were painted red, but her mouth was downturned. Her face was as pale as moonlight. She was the most beautiful woman Ping had ever seen. But she was also the saddest. It wasn't just her sorrowful face. A shroud of miserable sadness cloaked her just as the folds of her gorgeous gown did.

The Emperor didn't sit. Without glancing in Ping's direction, he went over to the low table and studied the things laid out on it. Ping felt very uncomfortable. Her whole life was spread out on that table, all her hopes and secrets were there in full view for anyone who took the trouble to interpret the items. He reached out to pick up something.

'I advise you not to touch the items, Your Imperial Majesty,' Dong Fang Suo said.

'Why not?' asked the Emperor.

'There is some sort of enchantment on the sorceress's things.' The Imperial Magician's smile looked dangerously close to fading. 'Two imperial guards who touched her belongings immediately fell to the ground in a faint. One of them woke after a few days, the other is still unconscious. Physicians have been unable to rouse him. Let someone else pick up the items for you, Your Imperial Majesty.'

The Imperial Magician moved to pick up an object for the Emperor, but changed his mind and waved a servant over to do it instead. The terrified servant reached towards Ping's comb with a trembling hand, but snatched his fingers back before they touched it.

The Emperor let out an impatient sigh. He picked up the comb and the jade pendant. He looked at all the items and then picked up one of the pieces of dragon stone. He held it up to the light.

'Is this a piece of the stone that the dragon hunter tried to take from you on Tai Shan?'

Ping nodded. Liu Che had witnessed her battle with Diao from a distance. He had seen her defeat the dragon hunter, and then watched as she picked up the dragon stone and escaped on the old dragon's back.

'What happened to it?' he asked.

'I dropped it,' Ping replied. 'It broke.'

He put down the shard.

'You no longer have the seal of the Imperial Dragon-keeper,' the Emperor said angrily.

'Yes I do,' Ping said, pulling the white jade seal from her pouch.

Liu Che waved Dong Fang Suo to take it from her. The Imperial Magician wiped off the caterpillar innards and insect legs that were stuck to it and put it in the Emperor's hand. The Emperor examined the seal, rubbing the chipped corner with his thumb. Ping wished she'd taken greater care of it. He put the seal on the table with the other things and reached towards the folded leaf. He opened it out. Ping's cheeks burned. Inside was the pressed magnolia petal on which the Emperor had shown her how to use the Dragon-keeper's seal. Ping had kept it as a souvenir of that happy time. He turned the brittle petal over. It was a fragile thing and would have crumbled if handled roughly, but he put it back between the folds of the leaf undamaged.

The Emperor turned to Ping.

'Your possessions are puzzling,' he said.

He picked up the soup ladle on the table and examined its dragon-head handle. Then he looked at the ladle on Ping's arm.

'My spies tell me you have been living on Tai Shan in a cave.'

He moved over to stand in front of her as he spoke.

'Why did you find the need to have two such expensive bronze soup ladles?'

With the Emperor standing so close, Ping couldn't think of an answer. He reached out to take the ladle from her arm.

'Don't touch it, Liu Che!' Ping cried, jumping to her feet and holding back the Emperor's hand.

There was a sound like a brief, sharp wind, as every single person in the hall gasped in astonishment. Ping had dared to touch the Emperor . . . and to call him by his personal name. Most people weren't even allowed to hear the imperial name, let alone speak it. But before the guards had a chance to drag her away, the soup ladle on Ping's arm started to shimmer. Its colour began to change from dull bronze to purple. The gasps turned to cries of real fear. There before the eyes of twice-ten or more witnesses the soup ladle turned into a small dragon.

The ladies-in-waiting screamed. A servant dropped a wine jar. The ministers and guards jumped back in astonishment – except for Dong Fang Suo, who chuckled heartily to himself, as if he'd just solved a puzzle that had been eluding him. The servants stared at the baby dragon. The Princess leaned forward in her chair to get a closer look. The Emperor stood with his mouth open, looking more like a startled boy than an Emperor.

Kai blinked and made a high sound like a single shrill note on a flute repeated again and again. He was terrified. He'd never had so many people staring at him before. He turned into a bucket, then a pot plant, then back into a dragon again. There were groans of discomfort from those who had continued to watch the shape-changing. One of the Princess's maids was sick.

Then Ping heard different sounds, high-pitched but tuneful. It took a moment for Ping to realize that the sounds weren't the dragon's. They were coming from Princess Yangxin. When the small dragon reappeared, the melody broke out again. The Princess was laughing. The guards and servants stared from the dragon to the Princess, not sure which was the most miraculous. Not only had a dragon materialized in front of them, but also the Princess, who hadn't smiled in years, was laughing. Dong Fang Suo laughed with her. It was infectious. The ministers and servants began to chuckle. Ping smiled too.

Kai saw the Emperor's smiling face. His sounds changed to happy flute notes.

'His name is Kai, Your Imperial Majesty. Long Kai Duan,' Ping explained. 'I didn't know it the last time I was here at Ming Yang, but the dragon stone was an egg. When we reached Ocean, Kai hatched out of it.'

The little dragon ran over to the Emperor, making excited noises, like someone blowing the highest possible notes on a flute. The Emperor looked down at the purple creature at his feet. He shook his head in amazement.

'Hello, Kai,' the Emperor said. 'My name is Liu Che.'

'Lu . . . Lu,' said the dragon voice inside Ping's head, trying to pronounce the unfamiliar name. 'Lu-lu!'

Ping was very glad no one else could hear.

The Emperor laughed as Kai sat on his gold-embroidered shoes.

'This is a most auspicious day,' he announced. 'Heaven has chosen to deliver a gift to me. Where is the scribe? Let him record that on the ninth day of the ninth month of the first year of my reign, a new imperial dragon appeared at Ming Yang Lodge.'

CHAPTER TWELVE

THE AUSPICIOUS SPARROW

Ping and Kai were moved out of the animal cage and into a chamber in Ming Yang Lodge. It was just as lovely as the one that Ping had stayed in the last time she was at Ming Yang, but this time it was Kai who slept in the comfortable bed. Ping was expected to sleep on a straw mattress on the floor.

A cook came to ask what the dragon ate. Ping gave him a long list of insects. The cook went away with a perplexed look, never having been asked to serve such things before. Not long after, a servant arrived and presented Kai with a platter of worms, snails and caterpillars, artfully arranged and decorated with butterfly wings. There was also a large bowl of milk. It was three times the size of the meals he'd had on Tai Shan, but he ate it all, including the decorations. Ping thought that for the first time in his short life he'd had enough to eat. When Kai had finished eating, the servant brought Ping a small bowl of gruel.

They were allowed to walk in the gardens whenever they wished, but some things hadn't changed. The pair of imperial guards was never far behind them. Ping tried not to let Kai out of her sight, but it was hard to keep up with him. He was enjoying his freedom. On Tai Shan, Ping had never let him go far. Worried that he might trip over his big feet and fall down a cliff, she had only allowed him to play in the restricted space around the pool. Now he could run around wherever he pleased.

Ping walked slowly up Ming Yang hill. It would take her a while to recover her full strength. She couldn't keep up with Kai. She had last seen him heading towards the Garden of Secluded Harmony. When she came to the Watching Magnolia Buds Open Pavilion she sat down to rest. She heard footsteps and the high sweet notes of a flute. The Emperor was walking towards the pavilion with a happy dragon at his feet.

'Ping,' Kai's voice said in her mind. 'Not hungry, Ping.'

Ping lowered herself to her knees and bowed down before the Emperor.

'Lu-lu,' said the little dragon excitedly. He had taken to imperial life as if he were born to it.

The Emperor didn't say anything. Ping remained on her knees, wondering what he would think of the name Kai had for him. A pair of worn slippers came into view alongside the Emperor's embroidered shoes. They had holes cut in them to accommodate the lumps on the feet inside. Ping could hear the panting breath of the Imperial Magician.

'It seems that there is another crime to add to your list of charges,' the Emperor said. 'The theft of an imperial dragon egg.'

Ping could tell from his tone that Liu Che was no longer angry with her. She smiled into the path and then sat back on her heels.

'Yes, Your Imperial Majesty.' Out of the corner of her eye, she saw Kai wander into a flower bed, trampling yellow autumn crocuses before he lifted his back leg and peed on a plant pot.

'Pee,' he said proudly. That was a new word.

'Why did you commit this crime?' the Imperial Magician asked.

The foul smell of dragon urine drifted over the garden.

'Pong,' said Kai. Another new word.

'It was what Danzi wanted me to do,' Ping replied. 'He didn't want his son to live in captivity.'

'Pee pong,' said the dragon. 'Pong, Ping.'

Dong Fang Suo's straggly ribbons of office were fluttering in the breeze. They caught the little dragon's attention. He ran over and tried to catch them in his mouth.

'So you chose to hide the young dragon from His Imperial Majesty?' the Imperial Magician said.

Ping nodded.

Kai's teeth snapped around one of the ribbons. He tugged at it, growling as he did.

'Stop that, Kai,' said Ping. 'Don't annoy Dong Fang Suo.'

'Fat-so,' said Kai.

'You didn't trust me to care for the dragon, Ping?'

It was the Emperor who spoke this time. Ping felt her cheeks burn.

'It was Danzi's wish.'

'Do you expect Danzi to return?' the Emperor asked, ignoring the tussle between his dragon and his Imperial Magician.

The Imperial Magician pulled the other end of the ribbon. It ripped, leaving a length dangling from the dragon's mouth. Dong Fang Suo staggered backwards, his belly jiggling.

'Fatso, Fatso, Fatso,' said Kai.

Ping lowered her forehead to the path again, so that the Emperor couldn't see her smile.

'Did you hear my question, Ping?' the Emperor asked.

'Yes. I'm sorry, Your Imperial Majesty,' Ping stammered, 'but Kai keeps distracting me.'

'Do you understand his sounds as you did with the old dragon?'

'Yes,' Ping said.

'What is he saying?'

'Pee pee pong,' said Kai.

'Nothing that makes any sense, Your Imperial Majesty,' said Ping. 'It's just baby talk.'

'Get up, Ping,' the Emperor ordered. 'I can't hear what you're saying when you're talking into the path.'

Ping stood up.

'I have been speaking with the Longevity Council,' he said. 'They think it is most fortunate that the young dragon has arrived at this time. They see it as a unique opportunity to learn more about dragons.'

'Since dragons live for hundreds, possibly thousands of years,' Dong Fang Suo said, 'the council believes that dragons might be important in His Imperial Majesty's search for longevity. We are looking forward to studying the dragon to discover what gives them such long life.'

Ping was about to ask how they were going to study Kai, when Dong Fang gasped in surprise.

'Look!' he said. 'Your Imperial Majesty, a green sparrow! The most auspicious bird.'

He was pointing at a tree. Ping and the Emperor both peered at it, but couldn't see a bird. The leaves rustled.

'I see it!' exclaimed Liu Che.

Ping stared at the tree, but still couldn't see a bird.

'There, on the lower branch.'

Ping finally located the bird. It was just like an ordinary sparrow, except that it was green. Not bright green, but a rather drab colour flecked with brown. It blended almost invisibly with the leaves that were starting to turn brown around the edges. The Emperor and the Imperial Magician were very excited by the dull little bird.

'I have never seen such a bird before!' the Emperor said.

'I have lived four times as long as Your Imperial Majesty and this is only the second time I have glimpsed one!' the Imperial Magician said. 'This is a true sign that Heaven is smiling on your reign.'

Ping thought the bird was rather dowdy and unremarkable compared to the red phoenix she'd seen on Tai Shan, but she kept this to herself.

The Emperor smiled. Ping was glad to see him happy.

'Good,' he said. 'I have been hoping for an auspicious omen.'

The bird fluttered to another tree and disappeared among the leaves. Ping wondered why there weren't more birds with green feathers. It was the perfect concealment for them.

The Emperor turned to Ping. His smile didn't fade. 'I have decided not to have you beheaded.'

'Your Imperial Majesty is very kind.'

'I didn't have a choice,' he said bluntly. 'The court's knowledge of dragons has greatly diminished thanks to my family's neglect. You know more about dragons than anyone.'

He sat on a stone bench. 'I am still angry with you for allowing my other dragon to escape, though.'

'I'm sorry, Your Imperial Majesty.'

'But you made my sister laugh. I'm grateful for that.' His voice softened when he spoke of his sister.

'Thank you, Your Imperial Majesty. But it was Kai who made her laugh, not me.'

'Don't contradict me, Ping, or I might change my mind. You brought him here. I like having a dragon around.'

'He likes you, Your Imperial Majesty,' Ping replied. 'He's wary of others, but he took to you straightaway.'

The Emperor gestured for Ping to sit on the bench next to him. Kai was trying to sit on the hem of his gown. 'You can call me Liu Che again, Ping,' the Emperor said.

'Lu-lu,' Kai agreed.

'Thank you,' Ping said. 'I shouldn't have hidden Kai from you. It only put him at more risk.'

'You must trust in me to take good care of Kai.'

'I will.'

They sat in silence while Kai scampered after some autumn leaves. It was the comfortable silence of friends.

'I missed our conversations, Ping,' Liu Che said. 'I'm looking forward to renewing our friendship.'

'So am I,' Ping whispered.

'Do you remember when we first met? You called me an annoying boy.'

Ping blushed at the memory. This time when Liu Che looked at her, his eyes were full of warmth and affection. She hadn't felt so happy for a long time. In fact, she thought she had probably never felt so happy.

'I am reinstating you to the position of Imperial Dragon-keeper,' the Emperor said.

Ping couldn't speak for a moment.

'As a member of the imperial staff, you will eat in the Hall of Cool Fragrance with the ministers and myself.'

'Thank you, Liu Che,' she whispered.

'You will need a new gown as well.'

Ping looked down at her grubby gown.

'Tell me about your rat, Ping,' he said. 'How has he changed since returning from the Isle of the Blest?'

Ping saw no point in keeping secrets from the Emperor any longer. She told him all about Hua's new skills. The Emperor was very interested. She didn't tell him that the rat visited her every night.

'I have sent six men off to Ocean to sail east until they find the Isle of the Blest,' the Emperor told her enthusiastically. 'I must have some of the water of life. If it can transform a rat in such a way, imagine how it will transform an Emperor!'

'Liu Che, there is something I must tell you,' she said. 'While I was on Tai Shan, I was attacked by a necromancer. He killed my goat. He was looking for Danzi.'

The Emperor looked puzzled. 'A necromancer?'

'He was the one who captured Danzi and was going to kill him and sell his body parts in the town of Wucheng. He got hold of the dragon stone, but I stole it back from him. He wants to get his revenge.'

The Emperor frowned. 'Do you know anything about this, Dong Fang Suo?'

The Imperial Magician shook his head. 'I have heard of people who can conjure up the dead and meddle with dark magic,' he replied.

The Emperor turned to Dong Fang Suo with a frown. 'Why have you never told me of such men?'

'Your Imperial Majesty, I—'

'We must commence a search for this necromancer,' Liu Che interrupted. He glared at the Imperial Magician. 'Call for the captain of the guard. Immediately!'

Ping was pleased the Emperor was taking her concerns so seriously.

Dong Fang Suo opened his mouth to make some objection, but was interrupted by a sudden shrill cheeping from behind a chrysanthemum bush. Everyone turned to see where the noise was coming from, but it stopped abruptly. Kai appeared out of the bushes looking very pleased with himself. Ping's heart sank. His cheeks were stuffed full, green feathers were poking out of his mouth.

'Kai!' Ping shouted, jumping up from the bench and rushing over to the dragon.

She thumped him on his back. Kai swallowed. It was too late. His long, red tongue licked his lips. He had eaten the auspicious green sparrow.

'You're a bad dragon!' Ping scolded.

Kai belched loudly. He didn't look at all sorry.

Ping glanced back at Liu Che. Surely it was a bad omen

if the auspicious green sparrow was eaten. Neither Dong nor the Emperor seemed to think so. They were both laughing.

'He must be hungry,' the Emperor said. 'We must give him more to eat.'

Ping watched Kai closely for the rest of the day. She remembered what had happened when he had eaten the water beetles. She was worried he was too young to start eating birds. But there didn't seem to be any ill effects.

'I suppose it's all right for you to eat birds,' Ping said, examining the little dragon's droppings, which he was in the habit of leaving all over Ming Yang Lodge.

'Birdie good,' said Kai.

• CHAPTER THIRTEEN •

READING LESSONS

Ping knew that Liu Che's grandfather had disliked dragons so much that he moved them to Huangling Palace so that he could forget they existed. His father had planned to sell the imperial dragons to a dragon hunter. She was pleased that Liu Che's attitude to dragons was the exact opposite. He wanted to see Kai every day. In fact, he seemed determined to make up for his ancestors' neglect. He appointed five members of his staff to tend to the baby dragon's needs and gave them all special titles. The Dragon Attendant's job was to follow Kai around, wipe up puddles of urine, collect droppings and carry Kai on an embroidered satin cushion if he didn't feel like walking. The Dragon Cook prepared six dragon meals a day. There was also the Grand Hunter of Birds whose job it was to catch swallows. The Sheep Constable took care of a small herd of sheep that provided milk for the dragon (Kai had decided he didn't like goats' milk any more). The Grand Officer of Ducks looked after a flock of ducks whose eggs were solely for Kai.

The Emperor was so delighted with his new dragon that he decided to name the garden surrounding Ming Yang Lodge after him.

'From now on it will be known as the Garden of the Purple Dragon,' he announced as they ate their meal one evening.

The Imperial Magician and the members of the Longevity Council applauded in approval. The government ministers didn't look quite so pleased.

Liu Che ordered all iron utensils and weapons to be replaced with bronze and had the iron sent away. When Ping told him of the other things that were harmful to dragons, the Emperor ordered the gardeners to chop down the two chinaberry trees in the garden. He also instructed servants to conduct a search for clothing and tapestries made of five-coloured thread and remove them from the lodge.

Kai now had three separate chambers – one for sleeping, one for eating and another one that didn't seem to have any particular purpose. They were now called the Dragon Quarters. Ping had a separate room, but it was very small compared to Kai's.

Kai was allowed to go anywhere he liked in the gardens and he trampled bushes, ate flowers and stirred up mud in the ponds. He followed the young Emperor wherever he went. He tried to climb on to his lap when he was sitting on the imperial throne receiving his ministers and making important decisions. When he wasn't with the Emperor, Kai was jumping out from behind trees to frighten the servants, leaving muddy footprints all over the halls and causing chaos in the kitchens.

For the first time in her life, Ping could relax. All she was required to do was translate dragon speech. Though she saw little of him during the day, Kai always came to sleep with her at night. Even though he had a large sleeping chamber of his own he always chose to curl up alongside Ping on her straw mattress. His vocabulary increased as he tried to tell Ping about his adventures each evening. His scales turned a lustrous purple, the colour of lilac blossoms.

Ping had stopped trying to think of a plan to escape. Kai was so happy and healthy, she decided that getting arrested was one of the best things that had happened to her. *Who knows why disasters turn out to bring good fortune?* Danzi had said to her more than once. Surely he would have approved of Kai living in this sort of captivity?

The servants put up with Kai's bad behaviour without complaint – even when he bit them. But though Hua was clean in his habits and didn't bite anyone, the few times they caught sight of the rat there was always a fuss and people talked of traps and cages.

'You must stay out of sight, Hua,' Ping said, when they were alone in the evening.

She stroked the rat's warm fur. It was a mystery to her

why people didn't like him. She brought him leftovers from her meals (she could never eat all the food that was served to her) and the rat got into the habit of sleeping during the day and going out at night.

Ping had been for a long walk right to the western edge of the garden where it ended on the banks of the Yellow River. She had spent most of the afternoon watching boats and water birds on the river. Then she walked back up to Ming Yang Lodge, wondering what would be for dinner that evening. Her thoughts were interrupted outside Late Spring Villa.

'Excuse me, madam.'

The Dragon Attendant was standing in front of Ping, trying to decide if he should bow to her or not. The man's name was Xiao Zheng, but Kai had taken to calling him Saggypants. This was because his trousers were too big for him and he was always hitching them up. His eyes were shiny with tears.

'I can't find the imperial dragon,' he said, wringing his hands.

'Were you trying to clean his ears again?'

The Dragon Attendant nodded miserably. He was a tall man about four-times-ten years old. He had a droopy face that looked sad most of the time. He also looked a little lop-sided. This was because one of his feet was bare.

'He took my shoe.'

Ping bit her lip to stop herself smiling.

'I'll help you find him,' she said.

The Dragon Attendant had already searched the places where Kai usually hid (in the pools, in the cellar where vegetables were stored, behind the piles of animal manure used to fertilize the gardens) but couldn't find him anywhere.

'I bet I know where he is,' Ping said.

Ping strode into the Chamber of Spreading Clouds. 'I know you're in here somewhere,' she said.

Instead of a hiding dragon, she found the Emperor and his Imperial Magician in the chamber. They were both poring over bamboo books. A silk hanging at the other end of the room settled back against the wall as if someone had just hurried past it. There was a brief silence. Dong Fang Suo was retying the ends of a book that had come undone. The Emperor looked annoyed by her interruption, but it was Dong Fang Suo who broke the silence.

'How dare you burst unannounced into the Emperor's presence!' he said.

He rolled up the book he was looking at and tucked something under his gown. Ping had never heard the Imperial Magician speak so angrily. She knelt down and bowed to the Emperor, glad to be able to hide her flushed face.

'Excuse me, Your Imperial Majesty,' she said. 'I didn't know you were here. I was looking for Kai. He sometimes hides in here.'

'His Imperial Majesty does not want to be disturbed,' Dong Fang Suo continued.

His outburst had made him break out into a sweat. He mopped his brow with his sleeve.

'It's all right, Dong,' Liu Che said. 'Ping wasn't to know I would be here.'

He rolled up the book he was reading and put it back in a chest that was overflowing with books. 'Kai isn't here. I haven't seen him today.'

Ping didn't ask about the books, but the Emperor explained their presence anyway.

'These bamboo books have arrived from the capital Chang'an,' the Emperor said. 'They are all the books in the imperial library concerning dragons. I sent messengers to fetch them.'

'They must have arrived very quickly,' Ping said, remembering how long it had taken her and Danzi to journey from Chang'an even though they had travelled much of the way on the rushing Yellow River. It was only a week since Kai's sudden appearance at Ming Yang Lodge.

'Messengers ran day and night and were there in less than four days. A swift boat carried the books from Chang'an.'

She looked at a book that lay open on the floor. It was made of thin strips of bamboo bound together side by side. Each strip had a column of characters written on it. To her, the characters were meaningless jumbles.

Ping sighed. 'I wish I could read them.'

The Emperor took the book and ran his finger down a column of characters.

'It says that Emperors have kept dragons for thousands of years,' he said, following the characters with his finger. 'They bring luck.'

'Danzi told me that if the imperial dragons are happy, it is a good omen for the Emperor,' Ping told him. 'If they are miserable, it is a sign that he isn't managing the empire well.'

At that moment Kai came running into the room. He had something in his mouth.

'What have you got there, Kai?'

'Nothing,' he said.

The little dragon stuck his head under a low table in an attempt to hide.

'I can still see you,' Ping said.

She pulled the dragon out from under the table by his tail.

Ping tried to take whatever it was from his mouth. He wouldn't let go. She pulled until it ripped in two. She held up her half. It was a piece of chewed leather, slimy with dragon saliva. It took her a while to work out what it was – or rather what it had been.

'Kai!' Ping exclaimed. 'You shouldn't be chewing Saggypants's shoe. That's very naughty!'

The Emperor laughed. 'Who is Saggypants?'

'That's what Kai calls the Dragon Attendant,' Ping replied.

Kai found his silk ball in a corner of the chamber. He put it into the Emperor's lap.

'Lu-lu play,' he said.

'What does he want, Ping?'

'He wants you to play ball with him, Your Imperial Majesty.'

The Emperor picked up the ball and examined it as if he had never seen such a thing before. He put it down at the dragon's feet. Kai's spines drooped. Liu Che looked uncomfortable. Ping got the feeling he'd never had much chance to play with a ball.

Ping threw the ball for Kai, who chased it across the room, skidding around on the polished wooden floor.

The Emperor smiled. 'I think we can safely say that the imperial dragon is happy,' he said, getting to his feet. 'Appoint scholars to read these books most carefully, Dong. I want to find out everything I can about dragons. Of all the creatures in the empire, they live the longest. We must discover what it is that gives them such longevity.'

'If I could learn to read, I could save you the trouble of appointing people to do the job,' Ping said.

'Unfortunately, at the moment there is no one with the time to give reading lessons,' Liu Che said.

'I can teach Ping to read,' said a quiet voice from the doorway.

It was Princess Yangxin. She had just entered. It was the first time Ping had heard her speak.

Ping thought she saw a flicker of annoyance pass over the Emperor's face.

'That won't be necessary,' Liu Che said. 'I'm sure some-one can be found for these duties.'

'I would like to take on this task,' the Princess persisted. 'It would help me pass the days.'

The Emperor's mouth softened. He took his sister's hand and smiled at her. 'Very well,' he said.

Ping thought she must have misread his expression. Liu Che would never be annoyed with his sister.

The next morning Princess Yangxin's lady-in-waiting came to take Ping to her first reading lesson. Ping had seen Lady An before. She was always near the Princess – sitting in the shadows, walking a few steps behind, watching in case her mistress needed anything. Lady An was a woman of about three-times-ten years old who moved with the same quiet grace as the Princess. She hardly said a word to Ping, but her gentle face was friendly and encouraging. She led Ping to the Rustling Bamboo Pavilion where Ping had seen the Princess crying.

Ping stopped at the bamboo canes that ringed the pavil-ion. Lady An showed her the secret to getting through the bamboo curtain. The canes were not planted in a circle at all, it was an illusion. They were actually planted in a spiral and a narrow path curled alongside the canes and eventually found its way to the pavilion. Ping waited for Lady An to follow her, but the older woman shook her head.

'Come in, Ping,' the Princess said.

Ping bowed to the Princess. 'It is very generous of you to spend your time teaching me, Your Imperial Majesty.'

It was the first time Ping had seen Princess Yangxin close up. Her hair was arranged in an elegant swirl, held in place with silver combs. A jade bird decoration was perched on top. It had delicate wings made of silver as thin as silk cloth that trembled whenever the Princess moved her head. She wore a pale blue gown with beads and tiny silver discs sewn on to it in flower patterns. The ornaments that hung from her ears were lotus flowers made of gold. The Princess's eyes still looked sad, but her mouth was upturned in a small smile. She was older than her brother. Ping guessed she was about twice-ten years old.

Ping felt plain and clumsy in the company of this beautiful young woman, whose every move was graceful. Even when she brushed away a fly, it seemed like a part of an elegant dance. Ping was wearing a new gown and had taken care to brush her hair and plait it neatly, but sitting next to the Princess, she still felt like a grubby slave.

When Danzi had taught Ping to count, ten numbers were all she had needed to learn. All the other thousands and thousands of numbers could be formed using just those ten numbers. She had expected that learning to read would be just as easy once she understood the system.

'Words are not as simple as numbers,' the Princess explained as she unrolled a bamboo book. 'There is a different character for each word. To learn to read you must learn thousands of individual characters.'

Ping's heart sank. She looked at the book that was laid open on the Princess's lap. Each character consisted of a combination of strokes – lines, curves and dots. It seemed impossible to differentiate one from another. The Princess pointed out that some characters had only three or four strokes, while others had as many as twice-ten.

Ping wanted to learn the character for *dragon* first, but it was far too complicated. She started instead with *Kai*, which had only four strokes. Her own name was harder, consisting of ten-and-one strokes, but she wanted to be able to write it. The Princess had brought ink, brushes and a length of undyed silk for Ping to practise her characters on.

'That seems like a terrible waste of silk,' Ping said, imagining the lengths of cloth she would use up before she got the characters right.

'We have plenty of silk,' the Princess replied. 'But if you would rather, you can use calfskin. The ink will wash off, so you can use the calfskin over and over again.'

Ping picked up the brush and dipped it in the ink. Her hand trembled as she tried to copy the four strokes that the Princess had made on the calfskin. The Princess's characters were light and flowing, just like her movements. Ping's were fat and splodgy.

'Perhaps you'd write better if you used your right hand,' the Princess said.

'No,' replied Ping. 'My writing would be much worse.' She tried again.

'It will take a lot of practice until I get them right,' she said. 'I can't bear the thought of wasting all that ink. Can't I write the characters in the dirt with a stick first, until I get the stroke order and length right? Then I can use ink.'

They went out into the garden and found a garden bed that had been dug over and would remain unplanted till spring. Ping found a straight stick and drew the two characters in the dirt. She preferred this method, which enabled her to quickly erase her ugly attempts at copying the Princess's beautiful characters.

Princess Yangxin tried to encourage her.

'You will need to recognize at least two thousand characters to be able to read a book,' she said airily, as if it was no more difficult than learning how to milk a goat or sweep out an ox stall. 'If you learn two characters each day you will soon be there.'

Ping wasn't much good with characters, but she had become quite skilled with numbers. She made a calculation in her head. At the rate of two characters a day it would take more than two years before she could read a book. She had only just got used to the fact that she had a future at all, now that Liu Che had decided not to execute her. She hadn't really given much thought to the years ahead, but it seemed that the Princess at least was expecting her to stay at the Garden of the Purple Dragon.

'But you'll be returning to Yan soon, won't you?' Ping asked.

The Princess's smile disappeared.

'No,' she replied quietly. 'I will not be returning to Yan.'

CHAPTER FOURTEEN

THE RAT AND THE PRINCESS

Kai no longer complained that he was hungry. He seemed to get bigger every day. In fact he was getting quite podgy. Every evening he and Ping ate with the Emperor, the Princess and the ministers in the Hall of Cool Fragrance. The meals were long and lavish, consisting of six courses. Kai wasn't the only one who was getting fatter.

Ping looked from her bowl, piled with pickled pork in jackal broth, baked crane stuffed with lentils and bitter herbs, to the Emperor's bowl, which contained one egg and some seeds.

'Aren't you hungry, Liu Che?' Ping asked.

Unlike Ping and Kai, the Emperor was looking thinner.

'The Longevity Council has devised a special diet for me. They say it will help prolong my life.' He picked up a sunflower seed with his chopsticks and ate it as if it was a tasty delicacy. 'I am to eat small meals consisting of cranes' eggs, leeks, sunflower seeds and peaches. Instead of wine, I must drink potions which contain ground pearls and gold dust.'

Ping remembered the huge meals Liu Che had eaten on her first visit to Ming Yang Lodge. Then he had thought a five-course banquet was a light meal.

Each day Ping went to the Rustling Bamboo Pavilion and Princess Yangxin patiently taught her two new characters. The lessons didn't take long. Afterwards, Ping walked in the Garden of the Purple Dragon, looking at the flowers and the autumn leaves – just for their beauty, not because they might contain caterpillars. If she saw dragonflies flit on the surface of pools, she taught herself to enjoy the scene and not jump up to catch them.

It seemed strange not to have to tend to Kai's needs, but whenever she saw him frolicking around the garden, she couldn't deny that he was happier and healthier than he had ever been. Now that others were caring for his daily needs, she could concentrate on learning to read, so that she could study the books and become as knowledgeable as the Dragonkeepers of old. It would take a long time. She imagined what the garden would look like at other times of the year, and looked forward to being there in spring.

Ping didn't have to worry about Kai now that he had the Emperor's protection. Kai was soon as familiar with Ming Yang Lodge and the Garden of the Purple Dragon as if he had lived there all his life. He chased pheasants, swam in the ornamental pools, and hid from the unfortunate Saggypants. He knew that it was the Dragon Attendant's job to take care of him, but Kai chose to make his life as difficult as possible.

Ping finally had the security and companionship that she had been wishing for. She was Liu Che's friend again, Hua came to visit her most nights, but she still wasn't at peace. She couldn't understand why, deep down, she felt uneasy. Something was troubling her, like an itch or a splinter in her foot. She didn't know what it was until one afternoon when she was sitting in a quiet chamber talking to Dong Fang Suo – or at least the Imperial Magician was questioning her.

'But if you have this second sight concerning dragons,' the Imperial Magician asked, 'why didn't you know that the dragon stone was an egg?'

It was a cold, drizzly afternoon and they were sitting in Late Spring Villa on the western slope of Ming Yang hill. Latticed windows in the shape of four-petalled flowers looked out on three sides. The windows were open despite the chilly weather. Dong Fang Suo had been quizzing Ping about her dragon-keeping skills. She was listening to the soft call of doves sheltering under the eaves and only half her attention was on the Imperial Magician's questions.

'I didn't say I was a good Dragonkeeper,' Ping replied. 'I still know very little about dragon rearing. Danzi kept the knowledge from me.' She felt a familiar ripple of frustration with the old dragon. 'He didn't think I was ready for it.'

Dong Fang Suo nodded wisely and stifled a yawn.

Ping watched the raindrops drip from the corner of the roof. A thought came to her that she hadn't considered since she had been living on Tai Shan.

'Dong Fang Suo, there's something I'd like to speak to you about,' Ping said.

The Imperial Magician stopped nodding and raised one caterpillar eyebrow.

'Even if I live to be extremely old, I will die while Kai is still a very young dragon,' Ping said. 'If he's to be properly cared for he'll need other Dragonkeepers after I die.'

Ping glanced over to where Kai had discovered his own image in a bronze mirror.

'I imagine you have a long life to look forward to,' Dong Fang Suo replied. 'We won't need to think about other Dragonkeepers for many years.'

Kai was standing stock-still, gaping at the other dragon who had appeared in front of him.

'Yes, but unexpected things can happen. What if I become ill? What if the necromancer still wants me dead?'

The mention of the necromancer seemed to jolt the Imperial Magician awake.

Kai was startled when the other dragon sat down and scratched its ear at exactly the same moment that he did. He hid behind a painted screen.

'You are under the protection of the Emperor now, Ping,' Dong Fang Suo continued. 'No one will harm you. Should you become ill you will have the best physicians in the empire taking care of you.'

The little dragon timidly crept up to the mirror again.

'I know we will be well cared for here,' Ping said, 'but . . .'

'If the Longevity Council can enable the Emperor to live for thousands of years as he wishes,' Dong Fang Suo interrupted, 'His Imperial Majesty will be the dragon's companion all his life.'

Ping had thought that Liu Che's pursuit of long life was just a whim, but it was becoming an obsession. He had changed a lot in the half year since she had seen him last. She wondered how different he would be in a thousand years.

Kai made a loud squawk to scare off the strange creature that was staring at him. Seeing the other dragon open its mouth wide alarmed him. He ran and buried his head under a cushion.

'He will still need a keeper,' Ping said.

The Imperial Magician yawned again. His afternoon nap was overdue.

'No one knows the importance of the dragon more than the Emperor.'

'I know the Emperor will care for Kai no matter what happens, but I'm the only one who can hear his voice. I'm the one who can understand what he says. Without me, he is no more than a dumb animal – a pet.'

Kai crouched down and then sprang at the mirror, banging his head on it. He yelped. The Dragon Attendant had been hovering around outside. He rushed in and fussed over him anxiously.

'He's just small and silly at the moment,' Ping continued, 'but as he grows he will become wise like Danzi. The Emperor might want to seek his advice. Without a Dragon-keeper he will have no way to communicate with Kai.'

'The Emperor looks forward to a long association with Kai, drawing on the dragon's knowledge and blessing.'

Kai's injured sounds stopped as soon as Saggypants offered him treats of crushed snails and chickens' feet.

Dong Fang Suo nodded as he thought about what Ping had said. He kept nodding. Ping waited for him to say something, but he didn't. His head came to rest on his chest. He had fallen asleep.

Ping left the Imperial Magician and went out into the garden. She looked out over the view. She could see the Tiger Forest, farmers' fields, a bend of the Yellow River. From that distance the walls surrounding the Garden of the Purple Dragon seemed small enough to jump over.

'It would be nice to go beyond the walls,' said a voice behind her.

Ping turned round. It was the Princess.

'But we are both confined by them.'

Ping looked back at the world beyond the walls. She had been enjoying life at Ming Yang Lodge so much, it hadn't occurred to her that she couldn't leave if she wanted to. But

Princess Yangxin was right. It seemed the Princess couldn't leave either. Ping looked back, but the Princess was gone.

Early one morning Ping was staring up at the Touching Heaven Tower. The golden Immortal stood as patient as ever, catching the star dew that made people live long. She had been lying awake since well before dawn thinking about what would happen to Kai after she died. It wouldn't be just a matter of finding a single Dragonkeeper to take her place. Even if she did find someone suitable, they would eventually die and another would have to be found. And another. Kai could live for twice a thousand years or more. Many good Dragonkeepers would have to be found. And she wouldn't be there to oversee their appointment. A thought had occurred to her in the dark hours of night. What if she could get some of the star dew to drink? Then she wouldn't have to worry about finding other Dragonkeepers. She could live as long as a dragon.

Ping's thoughts were disturbed by the sound of someone approaching. A shaman was walking up the hill towards the tower. She wanted to see how he climbed up the soaring tower to reach the star dew. She hid behind a tree and watched as he unlocked a door at the base of the tower. Touching Heaven Tower looked like it was solid stone from the outside, but it was actually hollow. Ping crept closer so that she could see what the shaman was doing.

She expected to see a ladder or stairs leading up inside

the tower, but there was neither. A bamboo tube disappeared up the wall. Below the tube there was a bronze jar. Ping smiled to herself. She had been very stupid to imagine that the shaman had to climb the tower every day and clamber up the statue on the top to empty the jade dish. The bamboo tube must lead all the way up to the top of the tower, through the middle of the statue and up to a hole in the bottom of the dish. The dew from the stars collected in the jade dish and then trickled down the bamboo tube into the jar below. All the shaman had to do was remove the jar each morning and replace it with an empty one. She watched the shaman walk carefully back down the hill carrying the precious dew. The builders of the tower were much cleverer than she was.

Ping had lingered so long in the Garden of Secluded Harmony that she was late for her daily lesson with Princess Yangxin. She hurried to the Rustling Bamboo Pavilion full of apologies.

The Princess greeted Ping with a smile. After Ping had practised the two new characters that the Princess had demonstrated, she ventured a question she had been thinking of for some days.

'Your Imperial Majesty, may I make a request?'

The Princess gracefully inclined her head.

'I want to be able to read as soon as possible,' Ping said. 'I'd like to learn more characters, perhaps six each day instead of two.'

Before the Princess could answer, Ping continued. 'I know this will mean that you have to spend more time teaching me each day, but the process won't take so long.'

'If you think you can learn six characters a day,' Princess Yangxin replied, 'I am happy to teach you. I am glad to have an occupation.'

It started to rain. Ping thought the Princess would end the lesson, but instead she sent Lady An to fetch a thick padded coat and an umbrella made of lacquered silk. The lesson continued. The rain stopped and after the lessons were over, Ping continued to sit with the Princess beneath the curve of a brilliant rainbow.

'The Emperor is looking thin,' Ping dared to say. 'I wish he was as concerned about himself as he is about you. It's not my place to question the Emperor, but I sometimes wonder if his preoccupation with achieving long life isn't . . .' Ping tried to think of the right word.

'Unhealthy?'

'Yes.'

'My brother's responsibilities are a heavy burden for a boy of sixteen years. He wants nothing more than to rule the empire well. Our father, as he grew old, became too concerned with his personal wealth and comfort. He left the running of the empire to his ministers. Some took advantage of this power. Liu Che thinks a long reign will be of great benefit to the empire.'

Lady An brought a tray with a teapot and cups on it.

'I didn't mean to criticize His Imperial Majesty,' Ping said, as Lady An poured tea into the cups.

The Princess smiled. 'I know you only have his best interests at heart, Ping. I am glad you are here. He enjoys your company.'

Ping blushed and waited until Lady An had left. 'Did he tell you that?'

The Princess sipped her tea.

'Even before I was married, he was being groomed to be Emperor. We didn't have many opportunities to be together. When I went to Yan, he was very lonely. He wrote to me about your friendship and I was pleased that he had found someone else he was comfortable with.'

'It must have been hard for you to live so far away.'

Princess Yangxin's beautiful smile withered like a flower in frost.

'I was just a child when I was married to the Duke of Yan – not much older than you are now, Ping. But I didn't have the experience of the world that you have. I was so lonely I thought I would die.'

Ping didn't know what to say. She wished she hadn't made the Princess remember such unhappy times.

'The Duke rejected me. He sent me back. It is a disgrace for the empire, but I don't care.' She smiled. 'It means I can be here with my brother.'

*

When the Emperor came into the Hall of Cool Fragrance that evening, he sat down and pushed his meagre meal aside.

'You must not sit out in the cold and the damp, Yangxin,' he said to his sister.

Ping glanced at the Princess. Nothing escaped the Emperor's attention.

'Ping's lessons must stop,' he said.

Ping's heart sank. Without her reading lessons how would she pass the long winter days?

'I don't think we need stop the lessons,' the Princess said. 'Couldn't we hold them in my chambers until spring?'

The Emperor didn't look pleased with this solution, but Princess Yangxin reached out and touched his hand. 'Please.'

'Very well, the lessons can continue . . . for now.'

Ping smiled her thanks at the Princess, but the Emperor remained out of sorts throughout the meal.

After everyone had left, Ping stayed to help Saggypants clean up Kai's mess.

'Have you served the Emperor long?' she asked him.

'All my life, madam,' the Dragon Attendant replied.

'How long has the Princess been here at Ming Yang Lodge?'

'Several months.'

'Did the Duke really send her back?' Ping couldn't believe that he would reject such a beautiful wife.

Saggypants looked around to make sure that no one was listening. 'The Princess was very lonely when she was in Yan, so the Duke allowed her mother, the Empress, to visit her twice a year. But on one of these visits, the Princess . . .' The Dragon Attendant lowered his voice even more. 'She formed an attachment to the Empress's senior imperial guard. When her husband found out, he was furious. He beheaded the man immediately. Then the Duke sent the Princess back . . . like . . . like a bolt of inferior silk cloth. She has come to live here at Ming Yang.'

Servants came to clear away the dishes from the banquet, and Saggypants hurried away as if he regretted saying so much.

The next day Ping entered the Princess's private chambers for the first time. They were on the north face of Ming Yang hill overlooking the serpentine Yellow River. Every wall was draped with silk paintings and embroideries. Every inch of the floor was covered with bamboo matting and woven rugs. There were large embroidered cushions scattered around the room. It was as if Liu Che thought his sister was so delicate she would be hurt if she so much as brushed her skin against a hard surface. It was also very hot. There was a bronze dish on legs piled with glowing coals in the centre of the room. All the window shutters were closed tight. Lamps burning orchid-scented oil gave off a soft light. The Princess was draped with a rug made of deep blue material studded with pearls. No one spoke louder than a whisper in the Princess's chamber. Ping had never experienced such comfort, but it was a little overwhelming, like a smothering embrace.

'My brother thinks I am as fragile as a camellia blossom,' the Princess said with a smile.

'His Imperial Majesty loves you,' Ping said. 'He's concerned for your health.'

The Princess's smile faded. 'He forgets that I lived for years in the shadow of the Great Wall, where even in summer the nights can be cold, and in winter it is impossible to go outside for three months because of the snow piled against the doors.'

She was silent for a few moments, then she wrote a character on a length of silk.

'*Cold*,' she said. 'Seven strokes.'

Now that they could no longer hold the lessons outdoors, Ping had to practise her characters on calfskin. Her writing had improved. She collected just the right amount of ink on her brush and balanced it lightly in her fingers. She wrote with a confident flick of her wrist. Her characters were like those drawn by a young child, but they were much improved. She wasn't as embarrassed by them as she had been at first. She had learned some of the more complicated characters such as *blue*, *chopsticks* and *write*. She had also learned the character for *dragon* and had no trouble remembering it, even though it consisted of ten-and-six strokes.

She had copied all the characters she had learned on to another piece of calfskin. Next to each character, she drew a small picture to help her remember its meaning. She planned to carry the calfskin with her, so that she could revise her characters whenever she wanted to.

The Princess invited Ping to stay for tea after her lesson.

'I would like to try to read a book,' Ping said to the Princess as they sipped tea and ate honey cakes.

'Thirty-eight characters are not nearly enough to read a book, Ping,' the Princess replied softly.

'I'd like to try.'

'You will be disappointed.'

Princess Yangxin sent Lady An to the library for a book. When she returned, the Princess undid the ties and spread it on a small table. Ping was hoping it would be one of the books about dragon-keeping. She looked at the characters in the first column. There was only one that she could read. It was the same with the other columns. There were no more than two characters in any column that Ping understood. The Princess read out the section. It was about the meaning of numbers. It had nothing to do with dragons.

'One is for the universe, whole and indivisible. Two is for the forces known as *yin* and *yang* – equal and opposite, they hold the universe together. Three is for the three sage emperors of old who ruled with perfect virtue and wisdom. Five is for the five elements – earth, water, fire, metal and wood. All the ten thousands of things under Heaven are made of these elements. Earth overcomes water, water overcomes fire, fire overcomes metal, metal overcomes wood, wood overcomes earth. In this way the universe is ever-changing.'

It was one thing to be able to read individual words. It was quite another thing to understand what they meant when they were strung together in sentences.

Ping was struggling to understand the meaning of this passage, when Hua appeared from among the folds of a floor rug. He scurried across the room. Ping smiled, wondering why he had come to see her now. But he wasn't hurrying to her. Ping realized he was making his way towards the Princess, holding a bamboo strip in his mouth. He sat at the Princess's feet and laid the strip on her satin slippers. The cushioned silence of the Princess's chamber was suddenly broken by the sound of screaming. All the servants were pointing at Hua and squealing with terror. Princess Yangxin jumped to her feet and leapt on to a table. Ping would never have guessed that the Princess could move so fast. One of the servants ran for a broom and tried to hit Hua with it.

'Stop!' shouted Ping. 'Leave him alone.'

She crawled over the cushions and picked up the rat. She felt the broom thwack on her back.

A vase was knocked over. The teapot was overturned as people ran back and forth.

'Your Imperial Majesty,' Ping said. 'Hua won't hurt anyone. He's a very well behaved rat.'

The Princess was staring at Hua with a look of disgust.

'Rats are filthy creatures,' one of the servants shouted.

It was the first time Ping had heard any of them speak above a whisper.

'No, he's clean, very clean. He doesn't have to rummage in rubbish for his food.'

Lady An was the only one who remained composed. She tried to calm the hysterical servants. Hua wriggled out of Ping's arms, causing a new wave of panic, and scurried out of the room. The Princess was still crouched on the table with her serving women gathered around her. Lady An coaxed Princess Yangxin down and led her trembling into her bedchamber.

Ping followed them to the doorway. 'Hua didn't mean to upset you,' she explained. 'He would never hurt anyone.'

Lady An came back to the doorway. 'The Princess has a particular fear of rats.'

'Why?'

Lady An pulled the curtain across the doorway without answering.

The Emperor was not in a talkative mood at the evening banquet. The Princess's place to his left was empty. Ping sat next to Kai, who had a special place on a cushion to the right of the Emperor. This made conversation with Liu Che difficult as Kai was continually bobbing about between them and making comments that no one but Ping could understand.

The Dragon Cook brought Kai a variety of roast and stewed birds.

'Birdies!' said Kai with delight.

He ate them all and then started on a selection of insects, and then six pheasant eggs. Kai's manners were terrible. He didn't pick up his food delicately in his talons as Danzi had, but wolfed everything down like a hungry dog. He put his foot in Ping's bowl of partridge stew. He spat out anything he didn't like the taste of. Ping scolded him over his bad manners, but the Dragon Attendant patiently mopped up the spilt food, picked up discarded bones, and wiped his paws. Kai took no notice of Ping.

Finally Kai had had enough to eat and he got up for some after-dinner amusement. This usually took the form of annoying the ministers and servants. One of his favourite games was to climb up on tables and plant stands and dive off on to a pile of cushions.

Now that there wasn't a noisy dragon between them, Ping asked Liu Che about the absent Princess.

'She is very distressed,' the Emperor replied. 'I will not tolerate the Princess being upset. My guards have captured your rat. It must be kept locked up.'

Ping had little appetite for the bear paw soup that had been served. Liu Che nibbled on a slice of peach.

'Why does Princess Yangxin hate rats so much?' Ping asked.

'That is none of your business!' the Emperor snapped.

They both pushed uneaten food around their bowls.

'I'm sorry, Your Imperial Majesty,' Ping said, looking at her hands in her lap.

The Emperor's stern mood softened.

'My sister has had an unhappy life. I suppose you have already heard the gossip,' he said. 'How she fell in love with a captain of the guards?'

Ping nodded. 'The Duke of Yan had him killed.'

'That wasn't the end of it,' Liu Che explained. 'As an added punishment, his body was strung up on the city wall. The Duke forced her to watch every day as rats gradually consumed the body.'

Ping's appetite disappeared completely. 'I didn't know.'

'I would much rather have had Hua put to death, however, the Longevity Council may wish to study him more. But if he escapes again I will order the servants to lay poison.'

Ping nodded quietly. 'As you wish, Your Imperial Majesty.'

Ping knew Hua was too clever to eat poison, but she wished he hadn't upset the Princess so.

A distressed cry from across the room broke the silence. Ping knew immediately who would be responsible. Kai was up to some sort of mischief. She went across the room to investigate.

The Dragon Attendant and several servants were gathered around a painted pottery vase that was almost as tall as Ping. Its curved sides bulged in the middle and then tapered at the neck. It was an elegant ornament decorated with patterns of clouds and strange animals. She could hear a muffled but familiar squawking. It was coming from inside the vase. Kai had tried to leap from a windowsill over the vase. He had dived into the vase instead. The servants were all talking at once, telling her that the vase was a hundred years old and had been painted by a famous artist using gold paint and the blood of a previous emperor. It was worth many thousands of *jin*.

'Stuck!' moaned Kai.

'Yes, I know you're stuck,' said Ping impatiently. 'You're a silly dragon.'

Ping ordered the servants to lay the vase gently on its side.

'Xiao Zheng, reach inside and pull the dragon out.'

The Dragon Attendant did as he was told.

Kai screeched in pain as if his talons were being pulled out.

'Ow!' he wailed. 'Saggypants hurt Kai's nose.'

The Dragon Attendant pulled as hard as he could, but though Kai's head emerged from the vase, his shoulders just became wedged.

'You got in there,' Ping said. 'You must be able to get out!'

She sent the Dragon Attendant to the kitchens for oil.

'Turn around, Kai,' Ping demanded. 'We might be able to pull you out backwards.'

'No pull tail,' said an unhappy voice inside the vase. Everyone else heard only a shrill piping, like someone blowing the highest note on a tin whistle.

'Well stay there then!' said Ping crossly.

After a moment's silence, Ping heard the dragon wriggle around inside the vase, moaning miserably.

The Dragon Attendant returned from the kitchens with a jar of oil.

'Pour it in the vase,' Ping said. 'It will make him slippery.'

'Stop, Saggypants!' said Kai as the Dragon Attendant poured in the oil.

Ping grabbed hold of Kai's tail and pulled as hard as she could, but the dragon remained stuck.

The servants suddenly dropped to the floor. The Emperor had come over to see what the fuss was.

'Break the vase,' he said.

'But Your Imperial Majesty . . .' Ping began.

Liu Che held up his hand to stop her.

'Do as I say,' he commanded.

One of the guards fetched an axe and hit the vase as hard as he could. It shattered to pieces, revealing an oily dragon with a shard of pottery balanced on his head.

'Broken,' said Kai.

The following day, when Ping went to the Princess's chamber for her reading lesson, the serving women wouldn't let her enter.

'The Princess is unwell,' they said.

She pleaded with Dong Fang Suo to convince the Emperor to let her continue her lessons. He was successful. Imperial ministers took over the job of teaching Ping to read and write. Without the Princess, it was not such an enjoyable experience. She'd been very patient, going over each character again and again, explaining the meaning of the components of each character and making up stories to help her remember them. But Ping and the Princess had talked about other things besides characters and books. Princess Yangxin spoke of her childhood and the bond she'd had with her brother ever since he was born. Ping had enjoyed hearing about the young Liu Che and his devotion to his sister. As they drank tea, Lady An had taught her how to tie up her hair in a neat knot. The lessons had lasted for entire afternoons.

Now a minister came each morning and wrote Ping's new characters on her calfskin. It was a different minister each day. He told her what each character meant. Ping recited the characters back to him and then he went away. Ping practised the characters by herself, in the garden if it wasn't raining or in her chamber if the weather was bad. In the afternoon, the minister returned to test her. If her characters weren't well formed, he made her write them again and again until she got them right.

Now that she understood the different components of the characters, it didn't take Ping long each day to learn six characters. Even when she persuaded the ministers to increase the daily number of new characters to ten-and-two, and she practised every character she knew, it still only took a few hours. She supervised Kai as he swam in the ponds. She tried to teach him not to trample the flowers. His attendants took care of most of his needs. Though the Emperor was always too busy with the Longevity Council to spend time with Ping, he still found time to be with Kai.

Ping missed the Princess's company. She walked every path in the garden until she knew each tree and rock. She watched ducks in their arrowhead formation fly away to warmer lands for the winter. She felt as lonely as she had at Huangling.

Ping went to visit Hua. She had managed to ensure that his cage only had a latch, so that Hua could use his dexterous claws to free himself every night. Ping felt bad that he had to spend so much time confined. He would have been better off if he'd stayed on the Isle of the Blest.

'It's not fair, Hua,' she told the rat. 'Kai can get away with all sorts of bad behaviour, and no one minds. Just breathing is enough to get you into trouble.'

Ping didn't like going back to the cages. She didn't want to be reminded of the time she'd been imprisoned. The monkeys and the black cat were no longer there. They had been freed to roam the Tiger Forest. She hoped that one day she would get a chance to wander in the wild forest.

CHAPTER FIFTEEN

HEAVEN'S ANGER

Ping couldn't sleep. Hailstones were battering the roofs. It sounded like the Immortals were pelting the lodge with rocks. An angry wind rattled shutters and lifted tiles off the roof above her chamber. Kai was curled up next to her. His bed consisted of a large feather mattress on a brick platform that was heated from beneath by hot coals. Most nights it was empty, while Ping and Kai were squashed together on Ping's straw mattress. She had suggested that she might sleep in the big bed where there would be more room, but Saggy-pants wouldn't hear of it. The bed was for the imperial dragon only. Ping would have brought the matter up with the Emperor but he was so busy she didn't want to bother him with such a trivial matter.

The sound of the wind whispering and whistling through the rafters frightened the little dragon. He had wriggled and whimpered for more than an hour. Ping had told him stories until he was finally asleep – curled up in a knot, taking up three-quarters of the bed and snoring softly. A flash of light lit up the room briefly. It was followed half a minute later by a deep rumble. Then the night was as black as a crow's wing again. She could hear a rustling sound. It was Hua rearranging some of the bedding straw to suit his own ratty purposes.

Storms had never kept Ping awake before. She was thinking about the books on dragons and their keepers.

'Those books are only to be read by members of the Longevity Council,' Dong Fang Suo had said when Ping had asked if she could look at them. Even though she still didn't know enough characters to be able to read them, his stubbornness annoyed her. If there were books on dragons and their care, why shouldn't the Imperial Dragonkeeper read them?

Ping lay on her side and then on her back, but she couldn't get comfortable. She got up and rearranged the blanket, which was all on Kai's side of the bed. She tried lying with her head at the bottom of the bed and her feet near Kai's nose. She had been in bed for hours, but still felt no closer to sleep. Her stomach rumbled. She hadn't felt hungry at the evening meal and had left her favourite dish (green goose with ginger sauce) untouched.

'I'm hungry now, though,' she whispered to Hua. 'Let's see if we can find something to eat in the kitchens.'

It was so dark, Ping had to feel her way to the door. She

checked that Kai was still snoring and then went out into the corridor. Small wicker baskets containing oil lamps were placed on the floor at intervals. It was at least two hours past midnight. Many of the lamps had burned up their supply of oil or had been blown out by gusts of wind. Only a few were still alight.

The corridors and halls were eerily empty. Through the shutters, she glimpsed one or two guards standing miserably under eaves with rain dripping off their caps, but no one was awake inside. Hua was enjoying this freedom. He darted around inspecting what was behind wall hangings and beneath holes in the floorboards. It reminded Ping of the times they had explored Huangling Palace together at night. The memory left her smiling, which was strange, since she had been a hungry, ill-treated slave back then.

Though she had intended to go to the kitchens, that wasn't where her feet were taking her. The lodge was not a neat symmetrical building like the palace at Huangling. It had been built to fit the contours of the hillside. It straggled crookedly across a slope and then abruptly turned uphill. The corridors changed direction unexpectedly and suddenly turned into stairs, sometimes leading up, sometimes down. Some chambers were completely separate, joined to the main building by enclosed passageways that zigzagged up and down the hillside.

Ping found herself in the walkway that led to the Hall of Peaceful Retreat where the Longevity Council worked on their potions and elixirs. She only ever saw the strange members of the council at the evening banquet. The rest of the day (and for all she knew the night as well), they studied and experimented. She had never been to the hall. Guards had barred her way whenever she tried to approach it.

During the day the walkway gave pleasant glimpses of hidden gardens and pools full of large goldfish. Now the shutters were all closed. Only two lamps were still burning in the passageway. Ping bent down to lift one from its wicker basket, shielding the flame with her hand as it flickered in a sudden gust of wind. A shutter blew open with a bang. Her heart pounded like a hammer beating metal. Through the open window she saw the wet garden lit up by a flash of lightning. It looked unnatural and frightening. Silvery shapes of twisted rocks loomed like ghosts. The branches of a weeping cherry tree were blown horizontal by the fierce wind. Then it was dark again.

Ping felt the floor slope down beneath her feet as she continued along the passageway. The wail of the wind died for a moment and she could hear the gentle pattering of Hua's feet on the polished floorboards. Then she heard another sound – heavy flat-footed steps. It sounded as if two or three guards were blundering clumsily down the passage behind her. There was a crash. Ping spun round. The first wicker basket had been knocked over, its oil spilled out. The flame from the wick licked greedily along the trail of oil. The wicker basket started to burn.

'Fire,' said a voice in Ping's head.

By the light of the flames Ping could see that the culprit wasn't a band of clumsy guards, just one small dragon.

Ping rushed back and stamped out the fire.

'Kai, you could have burned down the whole lodge,' Ping snapped. 'What are you doing here? You should be asleep.'

'Lonely,' said Kai. 'Frightened.'

The dragon's green eyes blinked in the lamplight. At any other time of the day, she might have been pleased with the improvement in his speech, which for the last week had consisted of nothing but bad words he'd learned from the imperial guards.

'Well, if you're coming with me, you have to be very, very quiet. Do you understand?'

Kai nodded. 'Quiet.'

There was no guard outside the Hall of Peaceful Retreat. Ping pushed the door open a chink, half expecting the strange Longevity Council members to be still at their work, but no light leaked out. She went into the hall. Her lamp spread only a small circle of light. She could see jars and bowls, a mortar and pestle on a bench. There was an unpleasant smell, sharp and sour, like vinegar and urine mixed together. It was a familiar smell, but Ping couldn't place it. The rumble in her stomach had become an ache.

Hua jumped up on to the bench and sniffed the contents of the bowls.

Kai made a high-pitched noise.

'Sssh, Kai. Remember what I said?'

'Quiet.'

Ping held up her lamp. Bamboo books were stacked on a shelf above the bench. They were neatly rolled, tied with thin ribbon and each had a tag hanging from it. One was spread open on a bench. Ping held the lamp close. She recognized the characters for *long* and *life*. She examined the tags on the other books. She found two that had the character for *dragon* written on them. She opened out one of these books. There were many characters that she could understand – *heart*, *eye*, *blood*. She couldn't make out the meaning of the sentences, but she had an unpleasant feeling that it was a list of uses for dragon parts. She pulled the other dragon book from the shelf. The neat stack of books collapsed with a thud.

'Sssh,' said Kai sternly. 'Quiet.'

Ping ran her finger down the columns of characters. The *dragon* character was repeated many times. She sighed with frustration. Though she knew many of the characters, she still couldn't make sense of it.

A noise startled Ping. She held up her lamp. A curtained doorway led off the hall to an inner chamber. The wind had died, the hail had stopped and there was just the patter of rain. She heard the noise again. Someone was on the other side of the curtain. The ache in Ping's stomach had turned to a sharp pain. But it wasn't hunger that had made her stomach hurt. It was the sense of dread that she felt when enemies were near.

Ping pinched the lamp wick between her finger and thumb. The room was black as an ink block. She crouched in a corner, holding Kai close to her, with her hand clamped around his mouth in case he made a noise. She heard the swish of the curtain as it was pulled back, and the slap of slippers across the floor. There was the smell of sweat and stale wine, the sound of fingernails scratching dry skin. Fingers fumbled with a catch. A shutter opened. A flash of lightning lit the room for a second. In the brief silver light, Ping saw the back of a man's head as he stood at the window. Thunder cracked the silence, booming and rumbling. There was another flash. The man spat out of the window and then turned towards Ping. She gasped, but the sound was drowned by another peel of thunder. She only saw his face for a moment, but the image burned in her mind. The man had a dark mark on one side of his face and a patch over his right eye. She would have known that face anywhere. It was the necromancer.

Ping covered her mouth with her hand to stop herself from crying out. The thunder died away and the high-pitched shriek of a tin whistle took its place. She had let go of the dragon's jaws.

'Bad man!' Kai screeched.

Ping felt the necromancer turn towards her in the darkness. The feeling of dread forced her to her knees. The foreboding had been diluted before, like watery soup. It hadn't reached its full strength until the necromancer was almost breathing in her face.

Lightning lit the room again. Ping tried to move, but couldn't.

'You thought you'd seen the last of me, didn't you?' He smiled. 'I believed you'd drowned, but then I heard villagers talking about a sorceress who'd been arrested. There were rumours about a devilish rat. I knew it was you.' His hands reached out towards Kai. 'That dragon whelp is mine.' The tips of his long black fingernails scraped the little dragon's scales.

Hua leapt at him. Then the room was black again. The necromancer cried out in pain. Ping's legs finally obeyed her. She was out of the door, Kai clutched to her, before the necromancer had time to draw another breath. She ran up the passageway. There were no lamps but it didn't matter. Her feet retraced her steps as surely as if the corridor was lit by ten-and-two torches.

'Guards!' Ping yelled.

Ping burst out of the door at the end of the passageway and into the dark and wet. There were no guards at the door. As she opened her mouth to shout for help, the sky lit up as if it were daylight. A heartbeat later there was a clap of thunder.

'Guards!' she yelled. 'Quick, there's an intruder.'

No guards came. Kai was strangely silent in her arms. He was terrified. Ping stood in the pouring rain, wondering what she should do. She had to get Kai to safety, but the lodge no longer seemed secure. Kai suddenly came to life. He thrust out with his strong paws. Ping couldn't hold him. He jumped down and ran off into the darkness. The lightning was now so frequent that the garden was more often lit than in darkness. The thunder was a constant rumble. The Hall of Peaceful Retreat loomed black behind her, crouched on the hillside like an animal ready to attack. The garden seemed safer. This time her second sight didn't fail her. Even though she couldn't see him, Ping knew that Kai was running up the hill towards the Garden of Secluded Harmony. She ran after him.

Ping could hear the sound of the bells on the Touching Heaven Tower jangling frantically in the strong wind. Kai finally came to a halt at the foot of the tower. A bolt of brilliant light zigzagged across the sky and hit the finger of one of the gold statue's upstretched hands with a shower of sparks. At the exact same time there was a deafening crack as if Heaven itself had been split in half. The upper part of the tower burst into flames. The statue of the Immortal glowed in the light of the fire and then tilted to one side. It fell end over end. Ping was halfway across the bridge that led to the tower. She felt it shake beneath her as the statue hit the bridge. Then one of the cornerstones splashed into the surrounding lake.

'Kai!' she called out, her heart gripped with fear. 'Where are you?'

Lightning pulsed across the sky again and again. The thunder was a continual roar. Rain poured from the sky like a waterfall. A stone block fell from the tower, then another, crushing the bridge in front of her. Ping was frozen in indecision. She couldn't turn and save herself until she had found Kai. She tried to focus her second sight to find the invisible thread that led to the little dragon. She felt the rush of air as another stone fell just in front of her. Sharp claws dug into her skin as the dragon leapt into her arms. Ping held him close then turned and ran.

The wind carried the sound of anxious, frightened voices. Guttering torches were making their way up the hill. The light of the flames revealed spears, shields and red leather tunics. The lightning strike had roused the guards at last. Captains shouted orders. Their words were sharp and harsh, but with tremors of fear and confusion.

Liu Che appeared on the edge of the lake, his hair hanging in wet strings, a padded coat thrown roughly over his shoulders. He was still in his nightshirt. Servants tried to shelter him from the rain with a silk umbrella, but the wind tore the fragile fabric to tatters. Ping tried to go to him but the guards pushed her back. Dong Fang Suo came puffing up behind the Emperor. It was the first time Ping had seen him without his ministerial cap. He had a round bald patch on the top of his head.

The stones had stopped falling. The lightning was becoming less frequent. The thunderclaps lagged behind. Finally the lightning stopped and the angry roar of the thunder faded to an irritable rumble.

The Touching Heaven Tower no longer reached up to Heaven. Where the lofty tower had stood, there was nothing but a pile of stones and smouldering rafters. The golden statue of the Immortal lay face down in the rubble. The jade dish was smashed to pieces.

A pale light beneath the heavy clouds faintly outlined the eastern horizon. It was almost dawn. There would be no star dew for the Emperor to drink that morning.

CHAPTER SIXTEEN

THE BAMBOO BOOKS

Ping waited outside the door of the Chamber of Spreading Clouds. At last she had been summoned by the Emperor and could tell him about the necromancer. Guards stood stiff and stern-faced on either side of the door. Inside the chamber, the Emperor was meeting with his shaman and seers. They had been shut in there for hours. As far as Ping could see, Liu Che didn't need seers to explain the fall of the tower. There was only one way to account for it. Heaven was not happy with the Emperor. He had built a tower to reach up to the dwelling place of the Immortals and they had used their heavenly power to smash it down. How could it be anything but a bad omen?

To make matters worse, Kai was unwell. Ping thought this was the result of eating ten-and-four roast swallows at the banquet the night before, but she didn't trust her second sight any more. It had let her down. Perhaps the storm had weakened it, but she couldn't be sure. The fact remained that for the first time Kai hadn't eaten his breakfast and he had refused to get out of bed. A sick dragon was another bad omen for the Emperor.

Eventually the shaman and seers filed out of the chamber with grim faces. The guards led Ping in. Liu Che sat with his arms folded across his chest and a scowl on his face. His hair was now arranged in a neat knot and he was wearing a yellow gown with a pattern of black spirals embroidered around the hem and cuffs. He didn't smile when Ping knelt before him.

'How is Kai?' he asked.

'He has an upset stomach.' Ping tried to sound confident. 'I'm sure there's nothing to be worried about.'

Her reassurances didn't remove the creases from the Emperor's brow.

'I will send for the imperial physician at Chang'an,' he said. 'He may have suggestions for how to treat Kai.'

'I don't think that will be necessary,' Ping said. 'I'm more concerned about his safety than his health.'

'What do you mean? Kai is safe here at Ming Yang Lodge.'

'That's what I believed.' She paused before she continued. 'Last night I saw the necromancer.'

The Emperor looked surprised. Ping wasn't sure he understood who she was talking about.

'The man who tried to kill me on Tai Shan. He tried to take Kai.'

'You saw him?' the Emperor stammered. 'Where?'

Ping didn't answer immediately. No one had seen her creeping around the night before. She could easily have lied and said she'd seen him in a different part of the lodge. But she didn't think it wise to risk offending Heaven any further by lying.

'He was in the Hall of Peaceful Retreat.'

Liu Che glared at her.

'When was this?'

Ping couldn't look him in the eye.

'Perhaps three hours past midnight.'

The Emperor drew his mouth into a thin line.

'You have exceptional freedom here at Ming Yang Lodge, Ping. But it seems you are determined to try my patience by sneaking into the few places you are forbidden to enter.'

'I'm sorry.' Ping bowed her head to the floor. 'I didn't mean to disobey Your Imperial Majesty.'

'So you accidentally stumbled into the Hall of Peaceful Retreat in the middle of the night?'

'No, but I didn't set out to go there. That's where my feet led me. I didn't realize it then, but my second sight was drawing me there.'

The Emperor stood up. Ping could feel him towering over her.

'I know I deserve punishment, but the necromancer was here in the lodge. He tried to take Kai. He must have been spying on us. It would be easy for him, he's a shape-changer.'

She expected the Emperor to call for the captain of the guards immediately. But he didn't.

'Why were you at the tower last night, Ping?' he asked in a calm, cold voice.

'I . . . I don't know. I wanted to get as far away from the necromancer as possible. Kai ran up to the Garden of Secluded Harmony. I followed him.' The Emperor didn't seem to understand the urgency of the situation. 'The necromancer thinks Kai belongs to him,' Ping persisted. 'He must be captured.'

Ping could see Liu Che's thoughts were going in a different direction.

'You were there when the tower fell?'

'Yes. I saw the lightning strike the tower as surely as if it was aimed straight at it.'

The Emperor was silent.

'It's unfortunate about the tower,' Ping said. 'But you must think about Kai. He has to be protected. The necromancer could still be in the gardens.'

The Emperor nodded slowly. Ping didn't see him make a sign, but the captain stepped forward none the less.

Ping was expecting Liu Che to order the captain to set guards outside the Dragon Quarters or to conduct a search of the grounds. He didn't do either.

'Bring me the guard who was supposed to be on duty outside the Hall of Peaceful Retreat last night,' he said.

The captain hurried out.

'What did you do in the Longevity Council's chambers, Ping?'

'I looked at the dragon-keeping books,' Ping said, fiddling nervously with her purple ribbon of office.

'I suppose your hands just happened to rest on them.'

'I want to know all there is to know about dragon-keeping,' Ping replied. 'So that I can properly fulfil the role Your Imperial Majesty has given me.'

'Books are to be read by scholars, not just anyone.'

Ping sat back on her heels and looked the Emperor in the eye. 'I am not just anyone. I am the Imperial Dragonkeeper.'

Ping saw anger flash in his eyes, but his mouth remained clamped tight.

'I am not trying to keep the contents of the books from you, Ping.' His tone changed. He was trying to sound friendly, but his anger was still there, like soup simmering in a lidded pot. 'You haven't learned enough characters to be able to read a book yet.'

'I thought I might be able to gain a little knowledge from them.'

'A little knowledge is dangerous,' the Emperor said. 'I planned to give them to you when you were able to read them. I thought that Princess Yangxin would go through the books with you. But you offended my sister.'

'I didn't mean to upset the Princess.'

'You don't mean to do a lot of things, Ping, but somehow you end up doing them.'

'I'm truly sorry I've added to your worries, but I was concerned about Kai. I wanted to learn more about raising a young dragon.'

The young Emperor was silent for a while. Then he nodded. 'I will send the books to the Dragon Quarters, Ping, and I will ask Dong Fang Suo if there is someone we can spare to help you read them.'

'You are most kind, Your Imperial Majesty.'

'I have more urgent concerns than a disobedient Dragon-keeper,' he said. 'I'm sure I don't have to tell you how the seers interpreted the collapse of the tower. The harmony of the universe has been disrupted. I have to meet with my ministers to work out what has offended Heaven so.' Kai was asleep when Ping returned to their chambers.

He still wasn't well. His scales were dull, his spines were drooping. Three servants were hovering about the bed.

'You can go,' she said. 'I'll take care of him.'

They left willingly. No one wanted to be associated with a sick dragon. If his condition worsened, they would be to blame. Kai looked small and helpless in the big bed. She hoped she was right and he had nothing more than a case of overeating.

He woke around midday, but though the Dragon Cook had brought an enticing platter of roasted cicadas, stewed worms and sparrow soup, the dragon ate little. He lay on his back with his feet in the air so that Ping could rub his stomach.

There was a knock at the door and a servant let in one of the junior imperial ministers who had been taking turns to teach Ping her characters. He was carrying the box of bamboo books.

'The ministers have finished with them,' he said. 'They say you are permitted to read them.'

The junior minister began reading the dragon books to Ping. She tried to follow the characters, but his finger flew down the columns and she couldn't keep up.

The first book was a list of all the Dragonkeepers for three-times-a-hundred years. There were twice-ten-and-three names. The minister read them all out to Ping. They were all males. Ping's name wasn't on the list. Neither was Master Lan's. The last name was Lao Lan, who was Master Lan's father.

'Some of the Dragonkeepers had very short terms of office,' Ping said. 'What happened to them?'

'Some were old when they took up the position,' the minister explained. 'One died when he fell from the back of a flying dragon. One was executed for allowing a dragon to bite a prince. One died in some sort of accident.'

Ping couldn't help thinking that dragon-keeping was a very precarious profession.

'There were twelve dragons then,' the minister said.

Being a dragon was far more dangerous. So many dragons had died. It brought tears to Ping's eyes.

Ping didn't see Liu Che the next day. He ate in his chambers and was busy with his ministers behind closed doors. In the afternoon the junior minister came and continued to read from the bamboo books. He read out events that were recorded during each Emperor's reign.

'When Emperor Shen Jing died, the red dragon dropped a pearl from its mouth. Rays of sunlight shone on him and green clouds floated in the sky.'

Ping didn't understand the significance of green clouds. Neither did the junior minister.

'After Emperor Nan had reigned for nineteen years, there were floods. Wild dragons were seen outside the city.'

Ping wanted to know what happened to the pearl and the wild dragons, but there was no more detail. Each entry was very short.

'In the first year of the reign of Emperor Gao, the dragons flourished and were happy.

'In the spring of Emperor Zhen Ding's fifth year, the dragons fought in the pool of Wei.'

The entries stopped when Liu Che's grandfather took the throne. The junior minister fingered the frayed ends of the string binding the strips together.

'The last strip is missing. It must have fallen off over the years.'

'Does it say anything about how Dragonkeepers were chosen?' Ping asked.

The minister scanned through another book.

'It says that Dragonkeepers are always drawn from the same families – the Huan or the Yu.'

'I wonder how Master Lan's father came to be Dragon-keeper?'

The minister read further. 'According to this, his was just a temporary position as feeder of the dragons until a new Dragonkeeper was appointed.'

'Was there a new appointment?'

'No. That's the last entry.'

'Does it say where the dragon-keeping families lived?'

'The Dragonkeeper before Lao Lan was Yu Cheng Gong. It says he came from the village of Lu-lin, near the city of Mang. The Huans have not been Dragonkeepers for many generations. The last Huan keeper lived east of the mountains and west of the River Hong in the village of Xiu-xin.'

The minister looked up from the book.

'Your name should be added to the list. What is your family name?'

'I don't know,' said Ping.

'It must be either Yu or Huan.'

Danzi had told her that Dragonkeepers had only ever come from the same two families, but it had never occurred to her that she must belong to one of them. Was the last Yu on the list one of her ancestors? The thought echoed in her mind. It was some time before she could concentrate on what the minister was saying again.

Ping didn't learn much from the bamboo books. She had hoped they would fill in all the gaps in her dragon knowledge. Instead they had only left her with more questions. There were no remedies for sick dragons. In the end she remembered that Danzi had found a drink of arsenic very beneficial to his health. She went to the imperial herbalist and asked if he had any. He gave her three small steel-grey crystals. She dissolved them in water, taking great care not to get any of the mixture on her hands. Arsenic was poisonous to humans, but Kai slurped up the draft with pleasure.

As she sat in the last of the afternoon sun that streamed through the latticed windows of the Dragon Quarters, Ping thought that she probably had all the knowledge she needed to keep Kai happy and healthy. Perhaps her head actually contained more information about dragons than any book in the empire.

Reading the bamboo books had left her with only two questions that she wanted to know the answer to. Was her name Yu or Huan? And where was her family now?

CHAPTER SEVENTEEN

PLANS AND DECEPTIONS

A week after the fall of the tower, Ping found herself standing in the largest and most lavishly decorated chamber she had ever seen. The Emperor had sent for her, but the imperial guard didn't take her to the Chamber of Spreading Clouds. Instead, he lead her to the Emperor's quarters. It was the first time she had been in Liu Che's private chambers. One wall was entirely made up of latticework shutters. The sunlight from outside shone through them, making a bright pattern of lotus flowers on the bamboo matting. Through an open door, Ping could see out on to a wide balcony where Liu Che was reclining on a couch. Dong Fang Suo was speaking to him, twisting his ribbons of office anxiously.

'But I think it is unwise to send another boat to search for the Isle of the Blest,' the Imperial Magician said. 'The wreckage of the first boat was washed ashore last week. Good men died.'

'Build a bigger boat,' the Emperor said. 'I have also heard about the fungus of everlasting life that can be found in the mountains beyond the western border of the empire. Arrange an expedition, Dong.'

The Imperial Magician looked unhappy, but raised no objections. 'Whatever Your Imperial Majesty commands.'

The Emperor noticed Ping standing in the doorway.

'How is Kai?' he called out cheerfully. 'I haven't seen him out in the gardens.'

Ping bowed to the Emperor.

'He is fully recovered, Your Imperial Majesty,' she replied. 'I just wanted to keep an eye on him indoors for a day or two. He can go out again tomorrow.'

'I'm very pleased to hear that,' Liu Che said. 'Come out on to the balcony so that I don't have to shout.'

The balcony was as wide and long as three houses put together. It jutted out from the building and seemed to hang in the air high above the gardens. Ping didn't want to go out on to the balcony. It wasn't the height that bothered her. She had spent much of her life on top of mountains. It was the flimsy structure that concerned her. She was worried it would collapse and send her plunging down the hillside. Liu Che laughed at her reluctance.

'It's perfectly safe,' he said getting up and walking over to the scarlet-painted balustrade, which to Ping's eyes appeared to be made of nothing more than thin sticks arranged in a geometric pattern.

'The balcony is held up by strong beams resting on posts made of tree trunks that I couldn't reach around, Ping,' the Emperor said. 'It would support a team of oxen.'

Ping felt a sudden pain in her stomach but it wasn't because of her fear of the balcony.

'The necromancer,' she whispered. 'I can feel him. He's somewhere near.'

'I know,' the Emperor said with a smile.

Ping stared at the Emperor.

'The imperial guards have captured him,' he said.

Ping didn't speak.

'That's why I summoned you,' Liu Che said. 'I thought you'd be overjoyed.'

'I am pleased, very pleased,' Ping stammered. 'I'm just surprised he was caught so easily.'

'Why? You don't have a very high opinion of my guards if you think they can't capture one man who pretends to have magical powers.'

Ping's experience with the necromancer had convinced her that his powers were very real.

'Where is he? Can I see him?'

'Yes,' Liu Che said. 'But only if you're quick. He is about to be transported to Chang'an.'

The Emperor laughed at her confusion and pointed down over the balustrade. Ping stepped on to the balcony as if it were made of eggshell. She grabbed hold of the scarlet rail and looked down. A waterfall tinkled cheerfully beside the balcony on its way to a pool far below. But Ping wasn't admiring the view. In the courtyard next to the pool, a man wearing a cloak was being led from the stables in chains. As the guards pushed him roughly into a wagon (the same one that had brought her to Ming Yang Lodge), he turned and looked up. Ping saw the necromancer's tattooed face. She clutched her stomach. The guards tied the leather cover over him. The captain shouted an order and the driver flicked the ox with his whip. The wagon rattled off, escorted by ten imperial guards. The sight didn't give Ping as much pleasure as she thought it would.

When Ping entered the Hall of Cool Fragrance for the midday meal, the Emperor was looking very pleased.

'The seers have decided what I must do to appease Heaven,' he said excitedly, as she bowed and took her place. 'I am to hold a special festival. Shamans will build a mound made of earth of five colours. Five fires of thornwood branches and fern stalks will be erected on top. Water buffalo, goats and pigs will be sacrificed. I will kneel before Heaven on a mat made from holy plants. White pheasants will be released. Afterwards there will be a feast with music and songs of praise. I will invite the land owners and imperial administrators from nearby. All the villages within a day's march will receive meat and wine so that my subjects can take part in the festivities and show Heaven that they are happy with my reign. Isn't that right, Dong?'

He turned to the Imperial Magician, who was sitting on his other side.

'That is correct, Your Imperial Majesty,' Dong Fang Suo replied. 'Incense will carry our prayers to Heaven. Kai must take part too, so that Heaven can see how happy the dragon is.'

Liu Che nodded enthusiastically. 'My dragon is well, the necromancer is captured, and after the festival all will be put to rights!'

'I'm sure that Heaven will realize that you are a good and wise ruler,' Ping replied.

The servants brought out the meal. Usually after she had experienced a foreboding, Ping had no appetite. The Emperor's happy mood was infectious, though, and the pleasant smells of boiled quail and fried fish with sour sauce made her mouth water. She allowed the serving maid to fill her bowl. Since he was in a good mood, Ping felt bold enough to tell Liu Che about a plan of her own.

'We have been reading about the old dragon-keeping families,' she told him.

The Emperor's servant brought him a single crane's egg. He turned it over with his chopsticks.

'I would like to find out if they still exist,' Ping continued. 'If something happens to me, you will need to know where to find another Dragonkeeper.'

'I am sure Heaven will grant you a long life,' the Emperor replied.

'Even if that's the case, you will still need to find a new Dragonkeeper one day. Kai will need many Dragonkeepers throughout his long life. I think we should search for the old dragon-keeping families and find out if they have died out. If I could just go to the villages of Lu-lin and Xiu-xin . . .'

The Emperor didn't seem at all interested in the subject. His egg lay untouched in his bowl.

'Ping, you shouldn't bother His Imperial Majesty while he is eating,' Dong Fang Suo said.

The servants brought out the next course. Ripe persimmons and tea scented with the flowers of the sweet olive tree were placed in front of Ping. They gave the Emperor three slices of peach and a cup of cloudy water.

'It is important that you digest your food carefully, Your Imperial Majesty,' Dong Fang Suo continued. 'Only then will you get the full benefit of the diet the Longevity Council has devised for you.'

Liu Che ate one peach slice. Ping could see that his good mood had evaporated. The Longevity Council's diet was so meagre, it was no wonder the Emperor was irritable. She would have to be patient and wait until the Emperor was in a more receptive mood.

A minister approached the Emperor. He was thin, straight and had a serious little mouth. His gown fell in neat folds as if each one had been carefully arranged. Even though it was late in the day, not a wisp of hair had escaped from under his ministerial cap. He knelt down in one graceful movement and bowed before the Emperor.

'I have received another letter from the Grand Counsellor, Your Imperial Majesty,' the minister said. 'He urgently requests that you return to Chang'an immediately to attend to the government of the empire.'

The Emperor waved the minister away irritably. 'The empire can wait until after my festival.'

The minister didn't move. Liu Che turned towards Ping. There was a sly glint in his eye.

'Perhaps you are right, Ping,' he said in a voice loud enough for the minister to hear. 'It is wise to prepare for all possibilities. Eventually, the day will come when I will need a new Dragonkeeper.'

Ping was delighted.

He looked at the minister, who was still kneeling in front of him. 'Minister Ji, you can conduct the search. Ping wants to find out if the old dragon-keeping families still exist. Where did you say they are to be found?'

Ping's smile faded. 'Lu-lin and Xiu-xin, Your Imperial Majesty.'

'But I don't need to go myself to achieve that, Your Imperial Majesty,' Minister Ji said. 'I can write to the subprefect. A messenger can deliver a letter in less time than it will take for me to travel there in a carriage.'

'I think a personal visit would be more appropriate, Minister Ji.'

Liu Che smiled like someone who had outwitted his opponent in a game of draughts.

Ping tried to look pleased.

After the meal, Ping went for a walk. It was her favourite time for walking in the gardens. Everyone else rested after the midday meal, so she had the gardens to herself. Kai didn't feel like an afternoon nap either. He scampered back and forth along the path. For once he wasn't misbehaving. It was good to see him back in full health. The Dragon Attendant yawned as he trailed after Kai. He wouldn't rest unless Kai did.

Ping felt guilty. It wasn't right to be deceitful, not to anybody. Especially not to the Emperor. She hadn't entirely told him the truth. She did think it would be a good idea to know where to find another Dragonkeeper, but like the Emperor she didn't expect they would need one for many years. There was another reason why she had wanted to search for the dragon-keeping families – she had hoped to find her own family. Somewhere in the empire were her parents who had sold her as a slave. She might have brothers and sisters. She wanted to meet them. Would they want to meet her?

She watched Kai enjoying himself. He was chasing something. It was only an insect, but he stalked it as if it were a tiger. He crouched low, ready to pounce. Then he raised his head and bared his teeth. That didn't seem to be the right position for pouncing. He raised his behind and lowered his head instead. Ping laughed.

A movement in a nearby bush caught her eye. She thought it might be a rabbit or a lizard, but it wasn't. It was a rat.

'Hua!' Ping exclaimed. She glanced at Saggypants, who was now dozing on a stone bench. 'You should be in your cage. If anyone sees you there'll be trouble.'

She picked him up and nestled him in the crook of her arm. She stroked his warm fur, which looked beautiful in the autumn sun. The rat wriggled out of her grasp and went back into the bush. When he re-emerged, he had something in his mouth. It was a bamboo strip. The same one he'd had when he frightened the Princess. He laid the strip in Ping's lap. She picked it up and studied the characters. Even though she had now learned almost twice-a-hundred characters, she still could only read five of the characters on the bamboo strip, not enough to make any sense of it.

'I don't know what it says, Hua,' Ping said, a little annoyed with him for giving her the bamboo strip, which only proved how little she'd learned.

Kai wriggled his behind. He was about to pounce. Hua suddenly lost interest in the bamboo strip. He ran over to Kai and snatched up the insect that the little dragon had been chasing. Kai made disappointed sounds.

'Hua!' Ping said sharply. 'Kai was playing with that.'

It was only then that she saw what Hua had trapped

between his teeth. It was a centipede. She jumped to her feet and scooped the dragon into her arms. Hua crunched the centipede and swallowed it.

Ping held the dragon tightly, even though his spines stuck into her. She turned angrily to the Dragon Attendant.

'Saggypants – I mean Xiao Zheng – you're supposed to be watching Kai.'

The Dragon Attendant woke with a start.

'I'm sorry, madam,' he stammered.

'I told you to keep an eye out for centipedes!' Ping said.

'You mentioned iron, five-coloured thread and the leaves of the chinaberry tree, but you said nothing about centipedes.' The Dragon Attendant's bottom lip started to tremble. 'I thought the little fellow ate all creepy-crawly things.'

'No! Centipedes are very dangerous. If they crawl inside the dragon's ear, they'll eat his brain.'

As soon as she had said it, Ping thought it sounded rather ridiculous. But Danzi had been terrified of centipedes, so she wasn't prepared to take the chance.

Ping looked around for Hua, sorry that she had snapped at him. She could ask the junior minister to read the strip for her. But the rat was nowhere to be seen. He had disappeared and taken the bamboo strip with him.

CHAPTER EIGHTEEN

FIRST FROST

The first frost had left the ground white and crunchy. Autumn had been in no hurry to leave, but winter had finally arrived. Kai had refused to get out of bed to go for a walk before breakfast. The colder weather didn't keep Ping indoors. She liked the quiet stillness of the garden in the early morning.

She saw Liu Che alone in a small pavilion in a secluded part of the garden. He was wearing a padded coat over his gown, but he looked thin and cold. He was scratching his arms inside his sleeves. When she got up close, she could see that his face was greyish and he smelt as if he had vomited.

'What's wrong, Liu Che,' Ping said. 'Shall I fetch a physician?'

'I'm not ill,' he said. His breathing was laboured. 'I have just eaten my daily portion of wolfsbane.'

Ping knew of the plant. 'But that's poisonous!'

'I have been advised to eat small amounts,' Liu Che replied. 'It is known to prolong life. There are just a few side effects – a little nausea, an itchy rash.'

He scratched his neck and then his lower leg.

'You weren't at the evening banquet last night, Your Imperial Majesty,' Ping said.

'I wasn't hungry.'

'It's too cold for you to be sitting outside, if you're unwell,' Ping said.

'Out here as the day dawns is the only time I get a few minutes alone.'

'You seem troubled.'

Liu Che sighed. 'I have a lot of things on my mind at the moment, Ping. Every detail of the festival must be correct so that Heaven isn't further offended.'

'But your ministers and shaman should take care of that.'

'They seem unable to make the smallest decision without consulting me. I have to tell them how many white pheasants are required, how high the sacrificial mound should be, what sort of grasses the holy mats should be made of. It takes me away from my longevity regime, which is much more important.'

'I wish I could help.'

'There are some things that only I can do. '

He shivered. Ping thought about running to get a rug for him. 'The seers are anxious that I discover exactly what has offended Heaven. I can't think what it is. I have reduced taxes, enlarged the school my father set up, I have defended the empire's borders. I have done nothing wrong.'

'You're a good Emperor, Liu Che.'

Two servants came hurrying up the path.

The Emperor sighed. 'My hiding place has been discovered.'

The servants sank to their knees and bowed.

'Your Imperial Majesty,' one said. 'The Longevity Council wishes to report on their experimentation with frogs.'

'And Minister Ji wishes to see you,' said the other.

'Has Minister Ji returned already?' asked Ping. It was only two weeks since she had proposed a search for the dragon-keeping families.

Before the Emperor could answer, Minister Ji came striding towards the pavilion. Liu Che closed his eyes as if he wished he were somewhere else.

'I arrived back at Ming Yang Lodge after midnight,' the minister said, 'and I have been up all night writing my report.'

The minister's gown was as neat and clean as always. His ribbons of office were uncreased. He didn't look like someone who had been up all night after a long journey.

'Tell Ping your findings, Minister Ji. I have more urgent matters to consider.'

The minister reluctantly held out the scroll to Ping. Her face flushed despite the cold air.

'Ping can't read,' the Emperor said.

Liu Che looked off into the distance again as if the contents of Minister Ji's report didn't interest him in the slightest. The minister unrolled the silk scroll and started to read. Ping held her breath.

'On the first day of the third week of the second-last month of the first year of the reign of the Emperor Wu, we departed from Ming Yang Lodge. We spent the first night at the Su-chang garrison. On the second day—'

'I don't need to know the details,' Ping said impatiently.

Minister Ji glared at her and rolled up his scroll again.

'I called on the sub-prefect for the district of Nanyang,' he said. 'Both Xiu-xin and Lu-lin are in this district. It seems likely that the Yu and Huan families are related in some way. Perhaps they are both descended from an original ancient dragon-keeping family who—'

'Did you find the dragon-keeping families?'

Minister Ji looked at the Emperor as if he thought it was below his dignity to be talking to Ping. The Emperor didn't notice.

'The sub-prefect informed me that Xiu-xin was destroyed by floods some years ago. He is not aware of a Huan family under his administration,' the minister continued in a voice that could have frozen a pond. 'Fortunately, the third assistant sub-prefect was in the room at the time. He was born in Xiu–xin and he remembered a family of Huans from his childhood.'

Ping's heartbeat suddenly increased, as if she'd just run two *li* without stopping.

'But he said that Mr Huan died before the floods and Mrs Huan left the village with her two children. No one heard from her again. She was very poor and there was a rumour that they died from disease.'

Ping's heart sank. 'What about the Yu family?' she asked.

'The sub-prefect informed me that there is a family by the name of Yu living in Lu-lin,' the minister replied.

Ping's heart started racing again.

'Mr Yu is currently in the business of raising silkworms.'

'Does he have children?' Ping asked.

'The sub-prefect mentioned many daughters.'

'I wasn't expecting to find another female Dragon-keeper,' Ping said, smiling at the minister.

The minister didn't smile back. 'No, I understand we are looking for a proper Dragonkeeper this time,' he said sharply. 'A male one.'

The Emperor turned towards Minister Ji.

'Were there any sons?' the Emperor asked. He had been listening after all.

'I believe the sub-prefect referred to one son.'

'Was he left-handed?' Ping asked. 'Did he seem like a possible Dragonkeeper?'

'I had no orders to question the sub-prefect or speak to any of the family members,' the minister replied curtly.

Ping turned to the Emperor. 'We must find out more about this family.'

'After the festival, Ping.'

'But I could go and interview the Yu family. If I can't help with the festival preparations, I can do this.'

The minister opened his mouth to object.

'Kai would enjoy the journey.'

The Emperor frowned. 'Kai cannot leave the lodge. He has to rehearse his part in the festival.'

'It would be good for him to see some of the empire,' Ping insisted. 'There is herb lore he has to learn. He can practise his shape-changing.'

'He must get used to the drums and gongs, so that he isn't startled by them at the festival.'

'If there is a boy in the Yu family, as Minister Ji says, Kai's reaction to him will be important.'

'Is that so?'

'Yes.' Ping sensed that the Emperor's resolve was wavering. 'It's in the books.' The lie tumbled easily out of her mouth. 'A young dragon recognizes a potential Dragon-keeper.'

Dong Fang Suo came panting up the path, blasts of white vapour issuing from his mouth like a steaming kettle. He made an attempt at a bow, which involved no more than a brief bend at the knees. An administrator was behind the Imperial Magician with a pile of goat-skin scrolls.

'The seers are awaiting your response, Your Imperial

Majesty. They must have an answer today. And your new robes need to be fitted.'

'And what do you want?' the Emperor snapped at the administrator.

'These documents need your approval and your seal before they can be sent to Chang'an, Your Imperial Majesty. And the emissary from Yan has been waiting for an audience for three days. He is getting very angry.'

'It is impossible to get a moment's peace! There is always someone making demands on me!'

Dong Fang Suo made another feeble attempt at a bow. 'Remember what the Longevity Council said about taking calm, shallow breaths.'

'Silence!' The Emperor's voice rang out over the garden. He stood up and everyone fell to their knees.

'Dong, *you* go to Lu-lin to interview the Yu family.'

'But the festival is only three weeks away,' the Imperial Magician complained.

'If Dong Fang Suo is too busy, I should go,' Ping interrupted.

'You can both go! Take Kai! Just make sure he returns in time for the festival. Maybe now I'll get some peace!'

'Whatever Your Imperial Majesty commands,' Dong Fang Suo said.

The Emperor strode off down the path, knocking the scrolls from the kneeling administrator's hands on to a garden bed.

Ping knew she should have been sorry that she had contributed to the Emperor's frustration. She should have felt guilty for lying to the Emperor as well. But she couldn't stop a smile from creeping across her face.

That afternoon, Lady An came looking for Ping in the gardens.

'Princess Yangxin has heard that you are going on a journey,' she said. 'She has asked me to help you choose some warmer clothes.'

'But this gown is warm enough.'

Ping looked down at the new gown she was wearing.

'Your gown is suitable only for the lodge,' Lady An said. 'You will need a thicker gown for travelling. Follow me.'

It was the first time Ping had spoken to Lady An since the incident with Hua in the Princess's chambers.

'How is Princess Yangxin?' Ping asked.

'The Princess is well enough,' Lady An replied. Her voice was full of concern and Ping had the feeling that by 'well enough' she meant 'unhappy'.

She took Ping to a dressing room that was small by the standards of the lodge, but still big enough to house a family of ten-and-two. Around the walls there were many chests and baskets. On one wall was a large bronze mirror with a border of painted spotted leopards. At the other end of the room there was a black lacquered screen decorated with swirling red patterns, supported on delicate gold feet shaped like dragons. Lady An laid out a choice of gowns. The rich colours and embroidery glowed in the afternoon sun filtering through the lattice windows.

'I don't want to wear anything fancy,' Ping said.

'This is the plainest,' said Lady An.

She held up a gown and Ping fingered the cloth.

'But this gown is thinner than the one I'm wearing.'

'The thread is finer and tightly woven,' Lady An said. 'It will be much warmer.'

The cloth was dark red and had a diamond pattern woven through it in green. Around the neck and cuffs the gown was trimmed with silk the same shade of green as the pattern. Ping took off her own gown. Lady An was shocked to see all the scratches and scars on her arms.

'Has someone been beating you?' she asked.

Ping laughed. 'No. These are just Kai's scratches.'

She turned away so that Lady An couldn't see the larger scar where she had bled herself to feed the dragon.

Lady An went to one of the baskets and returned with a jar of balm.

'This will soothe and heal them,' she said.

'They don't hurt that much,' Ping assured her, but Lady An insisted that she rub the balm into her scratched skin.

'You will need something else to wear underneath the gown in the cold weather,' she said.

'I've lived through many cold winters with only a thread-bare jacket and trousers,' Ping said.

Lady An handed her a thick padded undergarment, which was made of silk floss sewn between two layers of cloth.

Ping tried on the gown and the undergarment. They both fitted well.

She looked into the dim corners of the room. She couldn't shake the feeling that she was being watched.

Lady An also gave her an embroidered silk pouch, a pair of silk mittens and a coat to wear over the gown when it got very cold. Finally she gave her a new length of purple ribbon.

'This is for your imperial seal,' she said.

Ping tied her Imperial Dragonkeeper's seal to her belt with the ribbon and looked at her image in the mirror. Only the ministers, the Imperial Magician and the seers wore seals of imperial office. Though she was the highest ranking imperial servant in the lodge, Lady An didn't have one. Ping ran her hands over her new warm gown. As far as she knew, she was the only female in the entire empire who wore an imperial seal.

Lady An opened one of the smaller boxes that was full of hair ornaments and took out a silver comb. From a basket of cosmetics, she took a jar of sweet-smelling oil. She combed the oil through Ping's hair, showed her how to hold her hair in place with the silver comb and gave her the jar of oil. Ping looked at her reflection in the bronze mirror again. She hardly recognized herself.

'Would you like some jewellery?' asked Lady An, opening a casket of bracelets and necklaces.

Ping shook her head.

'I already look very grand,' she said. 'Shouldn't I look more . . . simple if I'm visiting peasant villages?'

'You are the Emperor's representative. You must dress in the correct way. And you have picked the plainest garment in the whole of Ming Yang Lodge, Ping,' Lady An replied with a smile.

Ping regarded her reflection, hoping that she could keep the gown clean and uncreased and her hair tidy. She didn't hear a sound, but she became aware that someone else was in the room. She turned to find Princess Yangxin standing next to the screen.

'You are going beyond the walls of Ming Yang Lodge,' the Princess said. 'I envy you.'

Ping bowed.

'Perhaps the Emperor will permit you to come with me.'

'He won't. I am an embarrassment to my family. I have to stay confined here at Ming Yang.'

Ping looked up at the Princess.

'Take care, Ping.'

The Princess turned and left the room with a rustle of silk.

CHAPTER NINETEEN

BEYOND THE WALLS

Now that the necromancer was imprisoned, Ping was looking forward to travelling beyond the walls of the Garden of the Purple Dragon again. She would have preferred to go alone with Kai so they could walk along quiet country paths and she could teach him the names of birds and the uses of plants, but the Emperor wouldn't hear of his dragon, the last imperial dragon, walking unprotected around the countryside. Besides, the weather had turned bitterly cold.

The journey didn't take long to arrange. Two days later, Ping, Kai and Dong Fang Suo were ready to leave. Since they would be staying at inns, Ping had no need to take her cooking utensils. She put her mirror, comb and jar of oil in her new silk pouch along with one gold coin and a few copper cash in case she wanted to buy anything along the way. She tucked Danzi's scale and a piece of dragon–stone shard in an inner pocket of the pouch, not wishing to be separated from these keepsakes.

A carriage was waiting for them in the courtyard at dawn. It wasn't a rough wagon like the one she had arrived in, but a fine imperial-yellow carriage with the Emperor's symbols of a blue crane and a red bat painted on the sides, a canopy to keep off the rain, and shutters that could be closed if it was windy. Inside were cushioned benches and rugs.

Kai had been excited about the trip until he saw the carriage and the large tan horse that was to pull it. Then he ran and hid in the stables. It didn't take Ping long to find him. She could see his tail sticking out from under a pile of straw.

'It won't be like when we were in the wagon, Kai,' Ping explained, as she tried to lift him into the carriage.

He wrapped his front legs around one of the wheel spokes.

'Don't like wagon.'

'We won't be locked in. You'll be able to get out and run around,' Ping said. 'And Saggypants has packed a special box of food just for you.'

'Saggypants coming?' Kai asked.

Though the Dragon Attendant spent all his time running around tending to the dragon's smallest need, he wasn't very good at playing games. Kai didn't like him much.

'No,' replied Ping, 'Just you, me and Fatso.'

'OK,' said Kai, letting go of the wheel. 'Kai go.'

*

The driver flicked the reins and the carriage set off. Four imperial guards rode behind them on fine black horses. The Emperor had wanted to send a whole section of guards to protect Kai, but Ping had persuaded him to send just four. Ping smiled to herself as they passed under the southern gateway. She was proud of the high regard Liu Che had for her opinion. She looked up at the three characters that were written on the gateway in gold. She could understand them now. They read *Long Live the Emperor*.

Pulled by the galloping horse, the carriage rattled through the Tiger Forest at a fast pace. Ping had hoped that they might catch a glimpse of tigers, but, if they were there, the thunder of the horses' hooves would give them plenty of warning of their approach. The only animals she saw were deer and foxes and they were far away.

Once Kai realized how fast the carriage was travelling and that the side shutters could be left open, he was enthusiastic about the trip. He wanted to stick his head out of the carriage so that he could feel the wind in his ears. He climbed over Ping and the Imperial Magician, so that he could look first out of one side of the carriage then the other.

Dong Fang Suo wasn't as pleased about the journey as Ping. His smile looked a little forced.

'Is something wrong?' Ping asked.

He didn't answer straightaway. 'The Emperor is not

entirely happy with the efforts of the Longevity Council,' he said. 'He can't understand my reluctance to risk the lives of his subjects by sending them off into unknown lands and over the Ocean. He thinks we should have come up with more schemes to lengthen his life.'

'You're doing your best, Dong Fang Suo,' Ping replied.

'It is not enough.'

Ping felt sorry for the Imperial Magician, but she soon forgot about his concerns. Her excitement was growing. Though she was pleased to have a change of scenery, and keen to find where the next Dragonkeeper would come from, it felt as if dragonflies were flitting around in her stomach. She was going in search of her family.

When they passed through the gate in the wall that surrounded the Tiger Forest and started to travel through fields and villages, Ping pulled the little dragon back inside. He sat on the seat with one ear inside out making low, sad noises.

'Ping not nice,' he said.

'It's Lu-lu's idea. He doesn't want anyone to see you,' she told him.

Ping was happy to go along with Liu Che's wishes. She could imagine the fuss Kai would cause in every village they passed through.

Ping picked up Kai's latest ball. His satin ball hadn't lasted long. He had shredded it to pieces. One of his attendants had made him a ball made of wound hemp string. That one had proved to be a nuisance, as servants were forever tripping over lengths of unravelled string. Finally someone had come up with the idea of a sturdy ball made of goatskin stuffed with nutshells. So far this one had survived. She threw it to the little dragon and he caught it expertly in his jaws. Then with a twist of his head, he threw it back again. There wasn't much room in the carriage, but it kept him occupied for an hour.

It had taken a lot of persuasion for Dong Fang Suo to allow her to bring the rat along. Hua was happy to sleep among the comfortable rugs and cushions. Ping was glad that he didn't have to spend all his time in a cage; glad he was with her again.

Telling stories was another thing that kept Kai amused. Ping spoke the words aloud. His understanding of spoken words was much better now, and she only had to stop to explain a few unfamiliar words in her head. Ping told him the stories that Lao Ma had told her when they had worked together at Huangling Palace. Kai liked the tale of the dragon who re-drew the riverbeds with its tail after Emperor Yu had dried up the Great Flood. He also liked the story of the naughty princess who was turned into a frog and imprisoned in the moon. He had heard them many times before, but he still enjoyed them. She asked Dong Fang Suo if he had any stories to tell. He told a long-winded tale about an imperial guard who lost all his money gambling.

'Ping's stories good,' Kai said. 'Fatso's stories bad.'

There were times when Ping was glad that she was the only one who could understand the dragon.

The village of Lu-lin, where the Yu family lived, was more than five-times-a-hundred *li* away. It sounded like such a long way, Ping couldn't believe they would be able to go there and back in a few weeks. Because they were on imperial business, they were permitted to travel on the middle section of the imperial road, which was made from flat stone slabs. It was a swift and smooth journey.

After the third day, Ping was beginning to wish she hadn't talked Liu Che into allowing her to bring Kai along. He was bored and restless. Hua did his best to help entertain the little dragon. They played a game called *Where is the Rat?* that Ping had invented. Hua was very ingenious at finding places to hide in the confined space of the carriage. He hid behind cushions, under the hem of Ping's gown and on top of the sleeping Imperial Magician's hat.

Whenever they stopped to eat or to stay the night at an inn, Kai had to shape-change. He could never quite decide what shape he wanted to take. He would start off as a bowl or a bucket, then he would catch sight of something new and change into that instead. Fortunately it was usually dark by the time they stopped for the night and the weary innkeepers didn't notice that Ping arrived with a pot and left with a pumpkin.

They spent the seventh night at an inn in the city of Mang.

Ping didn't sleep well. The closer they had got to the village of Lu-lin, the more anxious she had become. The next day she might be reunited with her family. She tried not to, but she couldn't stop herself imagining what it would be like to meet her parents. As they had travelled, she had managed to keep these thoughts at the back of her mind, but now her stomach was churning like water boiling on a blazing fire. Her feelings about her family swapped and changed. One moment she understood how desperate they must have been to sell her. The next she was angry with them for caring so little about her. She wondered if her mother still thought about her. Did she have brothers and sisters? Did they know about the sacrifice she'd made for them? Or had no one told them that she even existed?

Lu-lin was a neglected little village surrounded by mulberry orchards. Dong Fang Suo explained to Ping that mulberry trees were grown not only for their sweet fruit, but also for their leaves, which were the only thing that silkworms ate. She nodded, but she already knew. The trees' summer foliage was long gone. The branches were bare and brown and blown by a bitter wind. Ping was glad of the coat Lady An had given her.

As they approached Lu-lin, a pack of skinny dogs surrounded the carriage, barking furiously. The houses were in need of repair. The few pigs were as thin as the dogs, so were the chickens.

'I thought that raising silkworms was a profitable business,' Ping said.

'That is usually the case,' said Dong Fang Suo, climbing down from the carriage with the help of a guard.

'Birdies!' said Kai. His long red tongue licked his lips.

'Leave the chickens alone, Kai! They belong to these poor people. We'll have dinner later.'

Ping looked at the children working in vegetable fields and tending water buffalo. They all had runny noses and hunger in their eyes. Would that have been her life if she hadn't been sold to Master Lan?

'You have to shape-change now, Kai,' she said.

Kai thought for a moment. Ping looked away and when she turned back there was a chicken sitting alongside her. It was much plumper than the ones that were scratching around in the dirt. She was afraid the hungry inhabitants would try to steal it.

'No, Kai,' she scolded. 'Nothing that people can eat!'

The air shimmered and the chicken turned into a jar.

The arrival of an imperial carriage accompanied by four guards caused quite a commotion, as it had everywhere they had stopped. The village elder welcomed them, bowing and thanking them for honouring his village with a visit. Children left their chores and came to stare at the visitors. Women came out of their houses to see what all the fuss was about, shielding their eyes from the slanting rays of sunlight.

The elder sat them in his courtyard and brought wine for

the weary travellers. No doubt they sat outdoors because he was ashamed of his humble home. Ping had told Kai to stay in the wagon in his jar shape. She hoped Dong Fang Suo would be quick. She knew the dragon would soon grow tired of sitting still. The Imperial Magician shivered, pulled his coat around him and accepted the wine offered to him. He made polite enquiries about the silk crop.

'Heaven has not blessed us,' the elder said. 'Our crop has been poor for three years in a row. Our trees have been struck by disease. The leaves turn yellow, and brown spots appear on them. The silkworms won't eat them.'

'I am sorry to hear of your misfortune,' Dong Fang Suo replied.

Ping impatiently fiddled with the cuff of her coat while the elder told the Imperial Magician all the remedies they had tried. It was more than an hour before Dong was able to ask after the Yu family.

'Yes, they live here,' the elder said, 'as they have done for many generations.'

Ping could hear nothing but the hammering of her heart. This was the moment she had waiting for ever since they had left the Garden of the Purple Dragon.

The elder led them to a particularly dilapidated house. Before Dong Fang Suo had a chance to knock, the door was flung open. A man and a woman stood at the door. They were thin and, judging from their worn clothes, very poor, but both were smiling.

'Welcome, welcome!' They spoke as if they were greeting old friends, but they stood in the doorway, so that it was impossible to get into the house. 'We have waited for this moment for so long.'

They were taking no notice of Ping. Their smiles were all for Dong Fang Suo. She couldn't understand their excitement.

Mr Yu was a small man, who once might have been as fat as Dong. The fat had disappeared, though, and the skin on his face hung like bags that had been full of grain, but were now empty. Mrs Yu was taller, but had a stooped back which brought her down to her husband's size. Three small children, all girls, hid behind their mother's gown. Ping stared at Mr and Mrs Yu, searching for a resemblance – in their eyes, in their smiles, in the way that they moved.

From somewhere inside the folds of his gown, Dong Fang Suo produced three jujubes. The little girls' eyes lit up, but they wouldn't take the fruit.

'Will you permit your daughters to accept this small gift?' Dong Fang Suo asked.

Mrs Yu pushed the little girls forward. They took the fruit, ate them hungrily, and then were sent off to feed the chickens. Dong Fang Suo tried to move inside the house.

'My home is too humble for such honoured guests,' said Mr Yu, standing bowing and smiling in the doorway.

'A humble home is a palace in the eyes of Heaven,' said

Dong Fang Suo, pushing past him. The Imperial Magician was determined to get out of the wind.

Four older girls were working inside the house. They were bent over a large bowl of steaming water. In the dim light, Ping couldn't make out what they were doing. They stood up, bowed and started to leave.

'Please don't let us interrupt you,' Dong Fang Suo said.

The girls glanced at their parents and went back to their work. Ping stared at them. Were these girls her elder sisters?

Mrs Yu didn't say a word. She just smiled and smiled. Ping couldn't understand how such poor people could be so happy.

The house was indeed very humble. It consisted of a single room with a floor of trampled earth, and no furniture, just one ancient mattress and an unlit stove. The wind found its way through holes in the walls. The grey sky showed through the roof. The blankets looked old and worn. Ping had grown used to the comforts and luxuries of the imperial lodge. Even the shepherd's hut on Tai Shan seemed luxurious compared to the Yu family's house. Mr Yu invited them to sit on a worn and smelly water-buffalo skin on the floor. They were offered more wine. The Yus' wine was rather sour millet wine that hadn't been strained properly.

'You have fine daughters,' Dong Fang Suo said.

'Yes,' said Mr Yu, dismissing his seven daughters with a wave of his hand. 'That is my misfortune.'

'They must be a great help to their mother,' the Imperial Magician said politely.

'They are hard-working, I suppose, but unfortunately only one of them is betrothed.'

Now that her eyes were used to the dim light, Ping could see what the girls were doing. Each one had a pile of white balls in her lap. Silkworm cocoons. A small charcoal fire beneath the large bowl kept the water hot. In fact, it looked close to boiling. The girls soaked the balls in the hot water and then turned them over and over until they found the end of the silk thread. Then they unravelled the thread and wound it on to reels. Ping watched in amazement. Each silkworm cocoon unravelled in one long, unbroken thread. Each thread must have been more than a *li* long. The girls' fingers were white and wrinkled from being in the hot water.

Ping wondered if the Yus had another daughter – a daughter they had been forced to sell because of the burden of so many girls.

'Heaven has blessed us though,' said Mr Yu proudly. 'We have one son.'

A young boy stepped out of the shadows. Ping thought he looked about two years younger than her. He was very skinny.

'Here he is!' said Mr Yu, indicating the boy as if he were a prize ox or a rare jewel.

Actually he was a most unremarkable boy. Ping thought

that if he'd stood among twice-ten boys of the same age, she wouldn't have been able to pick him out. Except for one thing. His hair was very short, too short to plait or tie in a knot. It hung about his ears and in a fringe over his forehead. He stood with his head bowed and fiddled with the belt tied around his frayed jacket.

Mrs Yu beamed at the boy and held out her hand for him to take. Her fingers were stiff and bony, like birds' claws. They were wrinkled like her daughters', but in places the skin was peeling off to reveal red raw patches beneath – no doubt the result of spending years immersed in hot water. Mrs Yu couldn't keep silent any longer.

'We have guessed the reason for your visit,' she said happily. 'You have come for Jun!'

She smiled proudly at her son, while Mr Yu poured more wine, spilling some on Dong Fang Suo's gown in his excitement. He poured a cup for the boy and handed it to him. The boy took the cup with his left hand. Mrs Yu glanced at the Imperial Magician to make sure that he had noticed. It was strange to see parents so pleased to have a left-handed child. Master Lan had told Ping what a curse it was to be left-handed and how she brought him nothing but bad luck because of it.

'You are aware that members of your family have held imperial office?' Dong Fang Suo asked.

'Yes, of course,' Mr Yu replied. 'My grandfather held the position about thirty years ago. He was one of a long line of

Yu men who had the job. He died unexpectedly while in office. I was only a small boy, but I remember the imperial minister coming to tell us that he'd had an accident. He tested my father and me to see if we had the right characteristics. Neither of us did. We have lived in poverty ever since.'

'Jun has the characteristics though,' Mrs Yu continued. 'He uses his left hand – and he can predict things that are going to happen.'

Dong Fang Suo sat up straight. 'He has second sight?'

Ping studied the boy's face. She had thought she would know if she met a fellow Dragonkeeper. She had expected her second sight would leave her in no doubt, but she felt no connection to the boy at all.

'Yes,' said Mrs Yu proudly. 'He knows when storms are coming. And he can tell whether an unborn baby will be a boy or a girl.'

Dong Fang Suo looked at the boy with interest.

'I've never heard of a Dragonkeeper having second sight before they come into contact with a dragon. Have you, Ping?'

Ping didn't get a chance to answer.

'That's how we knew you were coming to offer him the position of Imperial Dragonkeeper!' exclaimed Mr Yu.

'We have not come to offer him a position, I'm afraid,' the Imperial Magician said. 'The position is already filled.'

Mr and Mrs Yu's happiness melted like ice in hot water.

'Ping is the Imperial Dragonkeeper,' Dong Fang Suo said. The couple looked at Ping for the first time.

'A girl?' Mr Yu sneered. 'How can the Imperial Dragon-keeper be a girl?'

'Who can explain the ways of Heaven?' said Dong Fang Suo.

'But we were depending on it,' Mrs Yu said. 'We paid the village elder a lot of money to teach Jun how to read and write. It kept him from his work in the orchard.'

'We were looking forward to him earning an imperial salary,' Mr Yu said. 'My grandfather earned six sacks of grain and five rolls of cash every year.'

Mr Yu spoke as if this were a fortune, but it wasn't a large sum. The gold coin in Ping's pocket was worth more than that.

'Can't you reconsider? Surely the Emperor would prefer a male Dragonkeeper,' pleaded Mrs Yu.

'Just a few years of this salary would save us,' Mr Yu continued. 'It wouldn't matter that we have no dowries for our other daughters. It wouldn't matter if the mulberry leaves withered and died.'

Ping had been waiting for the right time to ask the question that was burning in her mind. She couldn't wait any longer. Dong Fang Suo opened his mouth to say something else, but Ping spoke first.

'Have you seen this before?' she said and she pulled out the bamboo square that was hanging around her neck. Mr Yu held the character upside down as he stared at it. Ping knew it meant nothing to him.

He shook his head. 'I have never seen it.'

It was no surprise to Ping. The first moment she had seen Mr and Mrs Yu, she had known deep down that they weren't her parents. She also had a vague feeling that there was something Mr and Mrs Yu weren't telling them. But this sensation was overwhelmed by her sadness. She hadn't found her family.

'We would still like Jun to be trained,' Dong Fang Suo said, with a quick sideways look at Ping, 'in case the position becomes vacant. You will be compensated for your son's absence.'

The Imperial Magician pulled a gold coin from his pouch and gave it to Mr Yu. The couple brightened.

'Jun will come with us to Ming Yang Lodge . . .'

A scream from outside the house interrupted the Imperial Magician. Ping knew that the little dragon would be the cause of all the fuss. Kai had been alone in the carriage for too long.

Ping followed the noise. It was coming from a tumble-down shed at the back of the Yu house. As she expected, Kai was there. And he was no longer in the shape of a jar. The three younger Yu girls were staring at the purple dragon. The littlest was screaming at the top of her voice. Kai had knocked some small terracotta jars from a shelf.

'Caterpillars,' he said, though the others only heard a

sound like a cheerful melody played on a flute. 'Kai smell caterpillars.'

'It's all right,' Ping reassured them. 'He won't hurt you.' She patted the screaming girl on the back, trying to console her.

'I'm sorry he has broken these jars.'

She picked up several pieces of pottery. Kai was snuffling through the scattered contents – hundreds of tiny black balls.

'Kai, don't!' Ping said.

She picked him up. Some of the tiny balls were stuck to his wet pink nose.

'I'm afraid he's ruined your poppy seeds,' she said, brushing the balls off his nose.

'I don't think they are poppy seeds, Ping,' said Dong Fang Suo. 'I suspect they are silkworm eggs, saved for next season's crop.'

'Oh,' said Ping, trying to gather up the tiny eggs. Each egg would grow into a silkworm that would spin a long length of silk to form its cocoon. They were precious. 'I'm so sorry.'

The little girl finally stopped screaming and settled into a sniffly cry.

Dong Fang Suo gave Mr Yu another gold coin.

Kai was wriggling in Ping's arms. He stuck his talons in Ping's arm. She let go of him with a shout of pain. Jun had just entered. Kai scurried over to him, making high and happy flute sounds. The boy stared at Kai, but he wasn't afraid of him. He reached out and touched the little dragon's head.

Mr and Mrs Yu beamed with pleasure. Ping tried to smile too.

'It looks like we have found another Dragonkeeper candidate, Ping,' Dong Fang Suo said. 'Our journey has been successful.'

'Kai like Boy,' said the little dragon.

Ping's half-smile shrivelled like an autumn leaf. She felt a sensation she had never felt before. It took a while for her to put a name to it. It was jealousy.

CHAPTER TWENTY

TWISTING SNAKE RAVINE

The horse was harnessed to the carriage before dawn. Dong Fang Suo had been anxious to return to Ming Yang Lodge as soon as possible. There were many things he had to attend to before the festival. He had spent an uncomfortable night, even though the village elder had insisted on giving up his own bed to such an important guest. Two of the guards had been despatched the night before with a message for the Emperor telling him of their success. If the Imperial Magician was aware of Ping's low spirits, he showed no sign.

Despite the early hour, every inhabitant of Lu-lin was at the village gate jostling for a good view. Frightened children clung to their parents' gowns or cried to be lifted up. They all wanted to catch a glimpse of the amazing creature that had suddenly materialized in their village.

Kai was aware of all the attention on him and growled and blew out clouds of mist.

Jun kissed his mother and sisters goodbye and climbed into the carriage. Mr Yu handed his son a worn silk scroll.

'You must continue your studies,' he said. 'We will pray to Heaven that you are successful.' He gave Ping an unfriendly glance. 'It's your birthright.'

The boy nodded.

He waved to his family as they drove off. He leaned out of the carriage, watching them grow smaller and smaller until the miserable village of Lu-lin disappeared from view.

The carriage wasn't built to carry three people and a fidgety dragon. Dong Fang Suo took up more space than Ping and the boy together. Kai soon grew bored. Unless they were travelling through heavily populated areas, Ping had given up trying to stop him from hanging out of the carriage. He clambered over them, treading on the boy's scroll and the Imperial Magician's stomach.

The sky was overcast and Dong Fang Suo predicted snow.

'I expect you have many questions,' he said to the boy, smiling broadly, 'about dragons and their ways.'

Jun shook his head and tried to hide behind his fringe.

'About the Emperor and the imperial palace?' the Imperial Magician asked, his smile shrinking.

The boy shook his head again and concentrated on his scroll. Every few minutes he sighed deeply. It seemed he wasn't as pleased as his parents about the change in his fortunes. Ping saw him wipe his eyes with his sleeve. He missed his family, even though they were poor. He's lucky to have a family to miss, Ping thought bitterly to herself.

Half an hour later, the Imperial Magician tried again to engage the boy in conversation, but Jun's head was bowed and he was silent.

Kai was hanging out of the carriage, trying to catch leaves that were falling from trees. Ping held on to his tail, just in case he leaned out too far.

As she watched the wet, empty fields roll past the carriage, Ping had plenty of time to think. She knew now that Mr and Mrs Yu were not her parents. If she was a true Dragonkeeper, it could only mean that the Huans were her family. But Minister Ji had said they were all dead. She would never find her family.

Kai was trying to get Jun to play with him. The dragon hadn't left the boy's side since the moment he'd first seen him. He had insisted on sleeping at the foot of Jun's bed — even though it was just a pile of straw in the shed.

The boy let out a cry of surprise. Ping looked round, thinking Kai might have bitten him. But it was Hua who had caused his alarm. The rat had crawled out from under a cushion.

Dong Fang Suo chuckled. 'That is Ping's rat,' he said. '*You* don't have any unpleasant pets, do you? No snakes or spiders under your jacket?'

Ping stroked Hua. She hadn't realized that the Imperial Magician didn't like him.

She looked over at the scroll Jun was studying. It was covered with characters — hundreds of them. Ping recognized only a few. He was obviously a much better reader than she was.

Dong Fang Suo was signalling to her, raising one caterpillar eyebrow and jerking his head in Jun's direction. He wanted her to talk to the boy. Ping didn't feel like making polite conversation. She didn't want to put him at his ease. She wished she'd never met him. She had imagined finding an assistant, someone to take her place if she was unwell, someone who would produce a future Dragonkeeper from among his children. She hadn't expected to find a rival.

Dong Fang Suo was insistent. He kicked her in the shin. Ping couldn't think of anything to talk about. She looked out of the window for inspiration. They were driving past a village surrounded by fields. Farmers were at their work. She noticed other children, boys and girls, with short hair like Jun's. A few were completely bald.

'Is there some reason why you have your hair cut short?' she asked the boy. 'Is it a local custom?'

The boy blushed.

Dong Fang Suo cleared his throat. 'I think you'll find, Ping,' he said with a nervous giggle, 'that the children have had their hair shaved off to remove an infestation of head lice. Those with short hair are still waiting for their hair to grow back.'

'Oh,' said Ping. 'When I was at Huangling I had lice, but

Master Lan made me rub a foul-smelling ointment in my hair.'

Dong Fang Suo glared at Ping. 'That would be beyond the means of most peasants.'

Ping had hated the stinging ointment. She hadn't realized it was a luxury.

Ping didn't make any other attempts at conversation. She watched the boy's fingers run quickly down the columns of characters on his scroll. She was glad she had forgotten to bring the calfskin on which she had written the few characters that she had learned. Even though she'd had plenty of free time to study, Ping had found learning to read difficult. This boy had learned to read between his chores in the mulberry orchards.

Kai was excited that Jun was travelling with them.

'Boy, play ball,' he said, dropping his goatskin ball on Jun's scroll and nudging his arm with his nose.

Jun tried to ignore him, but eventually gave in to Kai's persistence. He threw the ball to the dragon, again and again. Kai tossed it back enthusiastically. The boy had much more patience than Ping for playing games, but even he grew tired of it eventually.

'That's enough for now, Kai,' the Imperial Magician said. 'Give Jun a rest.'

The little dragon's spines drooped. He made low, unhappy sounds.

'Later?'

Jun patted the dragon on the head. 'I'll play with you again later.'

Ping stared at the boy. 'Could you understand what Kai said?'

Jun nodded and buried his head in his scroll again.

Ping was shocked. She had been caring for Kai for six months before she could understand his sounds. Jun had been in his presence for less than a day. Her dislike for the boy was growing.

'The Emperor will be very pleased we've found you,' Dong Fang Suo said. 'If you pass the tests, you will require some training.'

Ping wondered what tests and training he had in mind. She had never undergone any tests and the only training she'd had was from Danzi.

'I'll play with you, Kai,' Ping said, holding out her hand for the ball.

Kai snatched up the ball and dropped it in Jun's lap.

'No,' he said firmly. 'Kai play with boy . . . later.'

Ping's jealousy festered like an unclean cut.

The next day Jun still had his head bent over his scroll.

'What is written on your scroll?' Dong Fang Suo asked.

He held it up for the Imperial Magician to see.

'It's all the characters I've learned,' the boy replied. 'Arranged in small poems and stories to help me remember them.' It was the first time he'd said more than five words together.

'You have done well to learn so many characters.'

'Our village elder was a government official when he was younger. He taught me to read and write.'

'Ping has been learning to read, but she doesn't know half so many characters.'

Ping stared out through the shutters. She didn't need to be reminded of her ignorance.

Towards the end of the second day, Jun finally ventured a question of his own.

'Are there other dragons in the world, sir?' he asked Dong Fang Suo.

The Imperial Magician seemed very pleased with this question.

'There are occasional reports of dragon sightings on the edges of the empire far from human settlement,' he replied enthusiastically. 'They could be merely tales told by travellers to impress their listeners, but I think there are other dragons . . . somewhere.'

'Wild dragons?'

'I believe so, living in the wilderness, I don't know where.' Dong Fang Suo smiled at the boy. 'I can see you are already thinking like a Dragonkeeper.'

Ping seethed.

They stayed that night at an inn. Ping was glad to have a room to herself. The previous night they had stopped at a military garrison. Dong Fang Suo had been given a room in the officers' quarters, but Ping had had to sleep in the stable with Kai, the horse . . . and Jun. She was looking forward to a good night's sleep on a comfortable mattress.

Very late at night, or perhaps very early in the morning, she was wide awake immediately, as if woken by a loud noise. But the only sound was someone talking in a low voice in the courtyard below. She couldn't hear what was being said.

Kai had wriggled around so that his tail and his back feet were against her face. She got up to turn him around again. Then she went to the window. Dong Fang Suo was in the courtyard. He was whispering urgently to a messenger who was standing next to a steaming horse. The messenger mounted his horse and rode off. Dong Fang Suo stayed in the courtyard, staring down at his lumpy feet.

'Whatever His Imperial Majesty commands,' Ping heard him say to himself.

She went back to bed, but she couldn't get back to sleep.

There was something odd about the Imperial Magician the next day that Ping couldn't put her finger on. He was unusually quiet and made no mention of the messenger in the night. He didn't try to get Jun to talk again either. Ping didn't mind the silence. She had quite enough conversation with the dragon's endless questions.

'Nearly home?' he asked about ten-and-seven times each hour.

'Dinner time?' was his next favourite question.

'What's that?' he asked every time he saw something he didn't know the name of.

Ping had to explain everything from piglets to pawlonia trees, from winnowing to weaving looms.

Eventually Kai tired of asking questions and curled up between Ping and the boy – his nose on Jun's lap – and went to sleep. Dong Fang Suo usually dozed as well, but it seemed he was not sleepy. He stared out of the carriage, absently winding his ribbons of office around his fingers.

For the first day since they had left the Garden of the Purple Dragon, the sky was clear. They had left the snow clouds in the south. The air was still cold but there was no wind. The faint aroma of cinnamon bark filled the carriage as the road left villages behind and wound its way through a cassia wood. Ping breathed in the fragrant air.

She was startled when Jun suddenly spoke to her.

'Have you lived at the imperial palace all your life?' he asked shyly, looking at her through his fringe.

Ping shook her head. She didn't want to tell him anything about herself.

'Did you always know that you were a Dragonkeeper?'

She wanted the boy to think that she had been trained to be a Dragonkeeper since birth.

Kai woke from his nap.

'Story,' he said.

The tale of how Ping had become a Dragonkeeper was one of Kai's favourite stories. He loved to hear about her adventures with his father. She relented. She would tell Kai the story aloud. He still needed to improve his understanding of speech. And Jun would hear it. Then he would know that her life had been harder than his. He would realize that she was the true Dragonkeeper – the one who had travelled with a wise old dragon, the one who had carried the dragon stone across the empire, the one who had witnessed Kai's birth.

She told him about Danzi and her years on Huangling Mountain. She explained how Hua had been her only friend. She showed the boy Danzi's scale and the purple shard, but wouldn't let him hold them.

'You have had a very exciting life,' Jun said enviously.

Dong Fang Suo, who had hardly said anything all morning, suddenly spoke.

'According to the old spell books, the shell of a dragon egg has many interesting properties,' he said, leaning forward and peering at the shard.

Ping felt a sudden possessiveness. She took it back from Jun, slipped it into her silk pouch with the dragon scale and continued her story.

She had got to the part where Danzi gave her the Dragonkeeper mirror.

'Each of Danzi's true Dragonkeepers has carried this

mirror,' she said proudly. 'It is hundreds of years old.' She polished the mirror and held it out to Jun. 'You can hold it if you're very careful.'

She was telling the boy about how she'd defeated Diao and outwitted the necromancer when the carriage stopped. Ping had been so engrossed in telling her story that she hadn't noticed the change in the countryside. They were returning to Ming Yang Lodge by a different route. The cassia wood had disappeared and the road was winding through a narrow valley. Steep cliffs of rock the colour of unpolished iron rose up on either side. The valley was just wide enough for a single carriage to pass through. Dong Fang Suo put his head out of the window to see what was happening.

The Imperial Magician seemed nervous – as if he couldn't bear any delay. Ping didn't see that there was any need to hurry. They had plenty of time to get back to Ming Yang before the Emperor's festival. One of the guards came and explained that there was a rock in their path.

'We are harnessing the horses to it, so that it can be hauled out of the way,' the guard explained. 'There will be time for you to get out and stretch your legs.'

He opened the carriage door.

'Where are we?' Ping asked.

'This is Twisting Snake Ravine,' Dong Fang Suo said.

The Imperial Magician stood up, changed his mind and sat down again.

Ping peered ahead at the rock that had stopped their progress. It didn't look so big.

Kai suddenly said. 'Pee.'

'Can't you wait half an hour until we get out of this ravine?' Ping asked.

'No,' said the little dragon.

Ping knew it was not a good idea to argue with Kai on the subject. The last thing she wanted was the smell of dragon urine in the carriage.

The Imperial Magician suddenly grabbed hold of her sleeve.

'No, don't get out, Ping.'

He looked like he had more to say, but the words appeared to get stuck in his throat.

'Pee now,' said Kai more urgently and hopped down from the carriage.

Ping shook Dong Fang Suo's hand from her arm. 'I have to keep an eye on Kai, so he doesn't wander off.'

There was barely room between the rock face and the carriage for her to climb down.

Dark rock towered above them on both sides, so smooth and steep it looked as if it had been cut with a knife. A band of blue was all that could be seen of the sky. Ping had the uncomfortable feeling that she was being watched.

Kai sniffed around behind the carriage. It always took the dragon some time to find the right place to pee. He preferred a tree, but there were none. Several tufts of grass had forced their way between rocks. One spindly bush had managed to find a patch of earth to grow in. A few frail, pale flowers were struggling to stay alive. Kai sniffed at one rock after another.

'Hurry up, Kai,' said Ping impatiently.

Ping's stomach ached. She remembered the last time her stomach hurt. She scanned the rock surfaces, but there was no ledge wide enough for anyone to conceal themselves on the cliffs. There wasn't a breath of wind and the narrow space was eerily silent.

Jun jumped down from the carriage. He kicked a stone around.

Finally the little dragon decided that the bush met his requirements. He lifted his leg. A pool of dark green liquid spread over the dry earth. Ping stood at a distance to avoid the smell, thinking that the bush would be dead before nightfall. She waited. It always amazed her just how much urine one little dragon could hold. He finished at last, but then he started sniffing around the rocks.

'Kai, come here right now,' Ping scolded.

She went over to pick him up. As soon as she got near him, he scurried away with the tinkling sound of dragon laughter.

'I'm not playing games, Kai,' she said urgently.

She looked up and down the cliffs again. She saw a flash of light out of the corner of her eye. She turned to the carriage in time to see Jun with the little dragon under his arm jump up into the carriage. The boy had her mirror in his hand.

Ping was about to run towards the carriage, when something high on the opposite cliff caught her eye. It was a snake, black with orange bands. It must have been huge if she could see it from that distance. One of the snake's eyes was looking straight at her. A glint of sunlight reflected in it. Ping couldn't tear her eyes away from it. She tried to move but couldn't. It was as if her feet had taken root in the earth. She heard the sound of the horse and carriage thundering away, but the snake's eye wouldn't release her gaze. She heard the two guards leap on to their horses and gallop after the carriage.

Then she heard a rumbling. At first she thought it was thunder. No rain was falling, but pebbles were showering on her. Larger rocks cascaded down. One struck her on the side of the head. The snake finally looked away and slithered across the rock high above. A shadow fell on her. She looked up. There was another rock falling. This one was as big as an ox. It was heading straight for her. Her feet agreed to move at last. But the rock was moving faster than she was. The band of blue sky disappeared.

CHAPTER TWENTY-ONE

ONE GRAIN OF SAND

Even though her eyes were open, Ping could see nothing. She hadn't expected to see anything ever again – she had expected to be dead. Perhaps I'm a ghost, she thought. Perhaps ghosts can't see. Or had the crashing boulder left her blind?

After a while she realized that the darkness had shades and in fact she could just see a sliver of light out of the corner of her left eye. She couldn't move her head to look at it though. She was aware of various parts of her body – her head, her arms, her chest. They all hurt.

The boulder had crashed its way to the bottom of the ravine and come to rest up against the rock face. There was a small triangular space formed by the fallen rock, the cliff and the ground. It was no more than a few inches deep. Ping's body lay in this narrow cavity, not crushed, but trapped. Her head was twisted to one side. The rock pressed against her cheek. Blood was running slowly down her neck. The boulder was squashing her chest, so she could only take small, shallow breaths. She couldn't move at all.

As soon as she had seen the boulder hurtling towards her, she had known she was powerless to avoid its crushing weight. It was as if the rock had been poised for thousands of years on that hill, waiting for the moment when she stood beneath it, to fall, to crush her. As if a blast of *qi* power had dislodged it and aimed it straight for her. She should have been able to leap clear, but the snake had distracted her and then her feet had refused to move.

The ravine was as silent as it had been before the rock fall. No birds were singing. There was no wind. Neither were there any anxious voices, no sounds of digging, nor anyone calling her name. There was no voice in her head either. She couldn't feel Kai. She was alone. Completely alone.

She tried to think of reasons why she should be alone. Her mind wasn't working well. Perhaps Dong Fang Suo had gone for help. She waited. It was hard to tell how much time passed. No one came. The slender thread that had linked her to Kai had broken. He'd moved too far away. Dong Fang Suo hadn't gone for help. He must have thought she was dead. Left her to rot in Twisting Snake Ravine. But she wasn't dead. Not yet. Her death would be slow.

She heard a scratchy, scrabbling sound. Something furry brushed against her face. She smelt a certain ratty smell.

'Hua,' she said, though the sound came out like a frog's croak. 'I should have known you wouldn't leave me.'

She felt something cool in her mouth. It was moist and sweet. Some sort of flower that contained nectar. Hua had been away looking for something to revive her.

There was only one way that she could survive. The rock would have to be moved. And there was only one way that the rock would move. She had to shift it herself.

There was no anger in her. Her anger over Jun had been squeezed out of her by the rock. She would have to find some other way to focus her *qi* power. She would need more than she had ever generated before.

She worked through all the mind exercises that Danzi had taught her. She pictured a garden full of peonies and counted each flower. She counted backwards from five hundreds.

She knew that she couldn't summon enough *qi* power to lift the entire boulder. She imagined the angle of the rock against the cliff. Less power would be required to tip it sideways. She didn't breathe, she didn't move a muscle, all the *qi* within her was concentrated on shifting the boulder.

It didn't move. Not even a hair's breadth.

If Danzi had been there she could have done it. She would have been able to draw strength from him. He was far away though. Far, far away. She thought of her mirror. If she could feel the cool bronze, that might help. But she didn't have the mirror. She had carried it with her ever since she had left Black Dragon Pool, but Jun had it now.

If the rock were no bigger than a melon, she still wouldn't have had the strength to move it.

'I can't do it.' Her voice was just a whisper.

But she had to. She had to find Kai.

She heard Hua scratching around in the sandy soil.

'You won't be able to dig me out, Hua,' she said, but the rat kept scratching until he had made his way to her left hand.

Then she felt the rat place something in her palm. It was cold and smooth but had a sharp edge. She knew exactly what it was. It was the shard of dragon stone.

'Hua, you always know what I want even before I do.'

She touched the shard with her fingertips, feeling its smoothness and its sharpness. She felt her mind focus. She concentrated again, imagining her body covered all over with tiny ink dots, each one no bigger than a needle prick. She drew *qi* power from every single dot. She could feel the grainy surface of the rock pressing against her right cheek. This time she focused on just one small point on the boulder, a single grain of sand. The rest of the boulder didn't exist. The ravine didn't exist. There was nothing in the world but that one grain of sand. Sweat dripped from her brow. She felt the power within her form into the narrowest of beams. She focused it on the grain of sand. The boulder shifted. It tipped sideways, crashing over with a rush of air and a thud that shook the earth beneath her.

A cloud of dust slowly settled. The strip of blue sky above

the ravine was the most beautiful thing Ping had ever seen. She didn't move. She could feel Hua's whiskers against her cheek. She tried to turn towards him, but couldn't. There wasn't a *shu* of strength left in her body. The rat ran off again.

Ping was sore and bruised, but she knew that she hadn't broken any bones. It was her head that hurt most, where the smaller rock had hit her. It ached and burned and made it hard for her to think. She had to think, she knew that, but she didn't want to. There were images from before the rock fall. Not moving memories, just three still pictures as if someone had painted those moments so she wouldn't forget them. She wished she could forget them. She wanted to go back to before the rock fall and make things happen a different way.

She looked at the three pictures. The first was of Dong Fang Suo. He was sitting silently in the carriage. There had been something different about the Imperial Magician that had been troubling her all that morning and she finally realised what it was. He had stopped smiling.

The second picture was of a snake, a black and orange snake that wouldn't release her gaze. She'd seen another snake like that before, back on Tai Shan, the day the necromancer had killed her goat. The snake was the shape-changed necromancer, she was sure of it. He had sent the boulder down to kill her.

The final picture was of Kai. He had his ball clenched in

his teeth. He was half-turned away from her, half-turned towards Jun. His eyes were hard, like small brown pebbles.

She was sure that Dong Fang Suo was in league with the necromancer. Together they had conspired to kill her. She had told Liu Che that Kai could identify any potential Dragonkeepers. It was just an excuse so that the Emperor would let her bring him along, but Kai had done his job well – too well. He had convinced Dong Fang Suo that Jun wasn't just a potential Dragonkeeper – but the only one.

The bamboo books had said clearly that Dragonkeepers were always the sons of either the Yu or the Huan family. Jun was left-handed, he had second sight and he could hear Kai's words in his head. He had all the attributes of a Dragon-keeper. She had handed him the Dragonkeeper's mirror herself. And Kai had liked him from the beginning. Had Kai accepted Jun as his keeper? It was the only reason she could think of for the misery she felt.

The loss of Kai was more painful than all her wounds and bruises. Just saying his name aloud hurt. It was as if she'd lost part of herself, some piece of her body that was as essential for life as her heart or lungs. She couldn't feel his presence, couldn't feel the thread joining her to him. But she was sure he wasn't dead. She would have known if he was. Tears streamed down her face

How could she have believed that she was such an impor-tant person as an Imperial Dragonkeeper? What had come over her? Her life ever since she left Huangling seemed like a dream that she'd just woken from. The sort of dream where the more you think about it the harder it is to remember. One by one the details of this previous dream life faded, until all memory of it vanished completely.

CHAPTER TWENTY-TWO

A FIELD OF CABBAGES

Hua returned with another nectar-filled flower. Ping felt the few drops of sweet liquid moisten her tongue and run down her throat. A tiny amount of strength returned to a spot somewhere near her left elbow. She used it to roll, slowly, painfully, on to her side. Then she could see Hua. His eyes were the colour of the sky. He was such a handsome rat, even with the chunk missing from his ear. She would have told him so, but she didn't want to waste her energy in speaking. She had a big challenge ahead of her. She had to stand up.

Getting to her feet would take more energy than she had. Walking was unimaginable. She didn't like the dark cliffs. She hated the way they loomed over her, threatening to come crashing down on her at any moment. She looked up at the strip of blue. She liked the blue. If she could get away from the rock there would be more blue. Hua sat beside her. Every so often he squeaked as if encouraging her to get up.

She moved one muscle. Then another. It took so much concentration to move an arm, to turn her head. She knew that once she'd been able to run to get away from bad people. She knew she had done many complicated things like chopping vegetables, washing gowns. How clever her body had been once upon a time. She got to her knees. Then she had to rest for several minutes. It might have been longer. But she was determined. She would stand.

Her body felt as if it were made from rags. It seemed impossible that it could stand upright and support her weight without sagging and falling over. But Ping had already achieved the impossible once that day. She had to do it again. It took her a long time, but at last her weak, aching limbs agreed to take her weight, first on her knees, then on her feet.

The dark rock walls rose up on either side of her. They were falling. She covered her head with her arms, but no rocks came crashing down. She looked up again, then closed her eyes to stop the dark rock spinning around her head. It was just dizziness.

With a great effort, Ping lifted one foot and moved it forward. She stopped to rest. She didn't know where she was going. She looked forward and then back. The twists in the ravine meant that she couldn't see the road ahead or the road behind her. Which way would she go? It didn't seem to matter. All she had to do was get away from the oppressive cliff walls. She lifted her other foot. She kept moving forward. It saved her the effort of having to turn around.

Eventually, her legs became used to supporting her again. Her feet remembered how to walk without her having to remind them to take every step. Hua ran alongside her, as she stumbled along, occasionally squeaking encouragement.

The steep cliffs on either side of the road slowly shrank to softer hills and then levelled out to rocky uneven ground. Grass and bushes found places to grow. She was out of the ravine at last, but there was no blue. The sky had turned grey. Ping stopped to rest. She was afraid that if she sat down, she wouldn't be able to get up again.

She kept walking. It was cold, very cold. Her fingers and toes were numb. It grew dark. Water started to drip from the grey sky. She tilted her head back and opened her mouth to drink. What was that called? Rain. It drenched her, but she kept walking. She couldn't remember where she was going. She was sure there was something important she should be doing.

Every now and again, Ping stopped dead in her tracks, overcome by a feeling that she had lost something, but she couldn't remember what it was.

She touched the side of her aching head. It was sticky. She looked at her fingers but it was too dark to see what the sticky stuff was. If she didn't know where she was going, what was the point of continuing? She stopped walking and sat down. Hua brought her some berries. She didn't have the strength to eat them. Her eyelids were heavy, so she closed them.

When Ping opened her eyes, it was daylight. She didn't know where she was. She was wet and cold, but her face was burning, her head throbbing. It wasn't raining but she could hear the sound of running water. There was a stream, fast-flowing and deep. She crawled to it and drank deeply. She splashed cold water on her face. The stream was slurping and gurgling around rocks in a hurry to get somewhere. Since she had nowhere to go, she would follow the stream.

Ping trudged along the muddy bank, not looking ahead, placing one muddy foot in front of the other. Perhaps the stream was going to Ocean. She had been going to Ocean once, though she couldn't think why. Perhaps she never got there. Perhaps that was where she was supposed to be going now.

Then she lost the stream. It sneaked away when she wasn't looking. She kept going anyway. She walked straight ahead, through woods, over fields. The sun wasn't shining but she was hot, very hot. She was shivering, but sweat dripped off her.

Now she was in the middle of a field of cabbages. Some-one was shouting at her, waving a hoe. People were gathering around her like flies around ox dung. It seemed like such a long time since she'd seen a face. They all looked so funny with their different shaped noses sticking out of the middle. She laughed. Some of them wore short aprons around their waists. Some held spades. They all had dirty hands. They were talking, but she couldn't make any sense of their babbling.

Ping's stomach suddenly began turning somersaults. The crowd parted and one woman stepped forward. The babble of voices died. The woman spoke and her words made sense.

'What happened to you?'

The woman's voice echoed in her ears. It reverberated inside her head. Ping felt dizzy.

The voice spoke again. 'Where are you from?'

Ping looked at the woman who was speaking. A word exploded inside her head. She tried to say the word, but her mouth had gone dry. Silver dust specks filled her eyes. The world was spinning again.

Ping woke inside a house that smelt of beeswax. She was lying on a couch, covered with a blanket made of undyed silk. Someone was leaning over her, splashing her face with cool water that smelt of jasmine flowers. It wasn't the woman in the cabbage field; it was a girl.

The girl called out to someone outside the room. 'She's awake.'

She sounded annoyed, as if she had better things to do than watch over a swooning stranger. The girl would have been pretty if she wasn't scowling. Her hair was in a neat knot held in place with three combs, even though she couldn't have been more than nine years old – far too young to be wearing combs in her hair.

The couch was in a well-furnished room. There was a polished table with legs carved into the shape of bears. The polished table top, which balanced on the bears' heads, was the source of the beeswax smell. A silk painting hung on one wall. It was a picture of a scholar standing under a bough laden with cherry blossom. A woman entered the room. It was the woman from the cabbage field. She was carrying a small boy.

'Are you feeling better?' the woman asked, putting the child down.

Ping felt the whirling sensation. She didn't dare look at the woman in case she fainted again. The emotions swirling inside her made her tremble. There was fear, joy and anger, mixed with a desperate longing. Ping opened her mouth, but couldn't speak.

'What's wrong with her?' said the girl impatiently. 'Is she dumb?'

Ping looked at the woman's face. Her cheeks were plump, her lips soft. Her hair was neatly coiled but there were grey strands among the black. Her eyes were lined with black to accentuate their lovely shape. They were full of concern for the stranger lying on her couch.

'Your fever has broken,' she said.

The woman's gown was made of finely spun hemp, dyed

dark blue. It had bands around the neck and cuffs in matching blue satin embroidered with small yellow flowers.

Ping pulled the length of red silk thread from under her gown. Her hand shook as she held out the bamboo square. The character on it was now almost too faint to read, but the woman's face changed as soon as she saw it. The colour in her cheeks faded. The concern in her eyes changed to shock.

The girl peered at the character. 'It says *Ping*.'

The woman nodded as she continued to stare at Ping. Now it was she who was speechless. Ping finally allowed herself to speak the word that had exploded in her mind back in the cabbage field.

'Mother.'

CHAPTER TWENTY-THREE

REUNION

Ping wanted to throw her arms around her mother. She wanted to touch her, to hold her hands in her own. But her mother didn't move. She didn't speak. She just stared at Ping. The expression in her eyes wasn't one of unexpected joy. It seemed to Ping more like hurt.

A man came into the room. He was tall and well dressed.

'This is Ping,' Ping's mother said in a whisper.

His brow furrowed. He looked at his wife.

'My eldest child,' Ping's mother explained. 'Ping, this is your stepfather Master Chang.'

The man looked at Ping in surprise. 'Well,' was all he could manage to say.

He had the dark skin of a man who worked out in the sun, a thick moustache and a tuft of hair growing beneath his bottom lip. His serious face broke into a smile and he called for a servant to bring some broth.

'We were wondering who this stranger was who stumbled into our fields two days ago. We never imagined . . .' He shook his head in wonder. 'What happened to you? Were you on your way to visit your mother after all these years? Did you have an accident?'

What had happened to her? Ping couldn't remember.

'I've cleaned the wound on your head,' Ping's mother said. 'It should start to heal now. It was a nasty blow. It must have caused you some memory loss.'

The servant handed her a lacquered cup. Ping raised it to her lips with shaking hands and sipped the broth.

'Take your time,' Master Chang said. 'It will all come back.'

Ping's mother was now bathing a cut on her hand. 'You were holding a broken piece of stone; it was an unusual purple colour,' she said. 'You held it so tight, it cut your hand.'

Ping was wearing a thin shift. She knew it wasn't hers. She looked around. There was a gown on the end of the bed. It was dark red with a diamond pattern woven through it in green. The collar and cuffs were made of green silk. On top of the gown was a piece of purple stone.

'Your things are safe,' the girl said sulkily, 'if that's what you're looking for.'

The girl handed her a white jade seal on a purple ribbon and a silk pouch. Ping held the jade in her hand. There was a dragon carved on one end. One corner was chipped. With trembling fingers she reached for the purple shard. Then she looked inside the pouch. There was a dull, rough thing about the size of a beech leaf. At first she didn't know what it was. Then she remembered. It was a dragon's scale.

Memories dripped back into her mind like raindrops from the corner of a roof. She remembered Huangling Mountain and a big green dragon. She remembered a dark, scary night and the sharp smell of pickle cooking. Her mind seemed to know that she couldn't cope with remembering everything all at once. She remembered a beautiful purple stone with creamy swirls, and flying high above the world. She remembered meeting the Emperor. She saw him smile at her. There was a garden. With each drip the pain grew. She remembered the journey to interview the Yu family. She remembered a carriage racing away and leaving her behind, a boulder crashing from the cliff top. The final drops of memory trickled into Ping's mind. She remembered Kai and how he'd been taken from her. She lay back on the couch and longed for forgetfulness to return.

'I think she's going to faint again,' said the girl, without a hint of concern.

'Don't crowd round her,' Master Chang said. 'Open the shutters, Mei.'

'Would you tell me about my childhood,' Ping whispered. 'I have no memory of it.'

Her mother sat in silence for a moment. From her face,

Ping could tell it wasn't going to be a happy tale. She sipped the broth to give her strength to hear it.

'Your father worked in the cinnabar mines. I never saw him from one year to the next. Then the work made him sick and he came home,' her mother said. 'Just after your first brother was born.'

She didn't look at Ping as she spoke, but stared into her lap. 'I made a little money weaving bamboo baskets and hats to sell in the market, but I never earned enough to keep hunger very far away. It was a blessing from Heaven when Master Lan knocked on the door.'

The dizziness returned. Ping put the bowl down before she dropped it.

'A blessing?' she said in a small voice.

'He came to see your first brother. He said that the Huan family had a right to an imperial position. Apparently one of your father's ancestors had held the position and it should have been passed on from father to son, but for some reason only left-handed boys could take up the position. Neither your father nor grandfather was left-handed. Master Lan pulled a plum from his bag and handed it to your first brother. He reached for it with his right hand. When he'd finished eating it, Master Lan asked him to toss the plum stone outside. Your first brother threw the stone with his right hand too. We begged Master Lan to accept him for the position even though he wasn't left-handed. "What difference does it make which hand he uses?" I said. "He will work hard like his father. His father worked himself almost to death." But he wouldn't take him.'

Ping's mother stole a glance at Ping, as if she couldn't bear to look at her for too long.

'Then Master Lan noticed you winding thread on to a reel for me. "She uses the left hand," he said. We couldn't understand why he was suddenly interested in you. Only men can take up imperial positions. "Does she ever seem to know in advance anything that's going to happen?" he asked. I thought it was a very strange thing to enquire about. But as it happened you did say something odd just before a neighbour died. I thought she just had an upset stomach, but you said, "Auntie will be gone by morning." She died the next day. Master Lan was very interested when I told him this.'

It seemed that, like Jun, Ping had also had the beginnings of second sight before she had ever laid eyes on a dragon.

'Your first brother was sick,' Ping's mother was saying. 'And he wasn't getting better because he didn't have enough to eat. I knew I couldn't keep two children alive, so when he offered to take you to train as a lady's maid, I agreed. If one child could live well and not be hungry, that was a good thing.'

Tears started to roll down Ping's mother's face. 'Your father didn't last the year out. Your first brother died two months later.'

Master Chang put his hand on her shoulder to comfort her.

'I expected to hear from you, once you were settled in the palace,' Ping's mother continued. 'Master Lan said that, after a year or two of training, you would receive a generous allowance, and since all your needs would be provided for, you'd be able to send most of it to me.'

Ping could hardly believe her ears. Had Master Lan known that she was a Dragonkeeper all along, and told no one? Had he made her his slave, so that he could keep the position himself? She opened her mouth to speak. But no words came out.

'I sent a letter to Chang'an to tell Master Lan that I had moved to another town,' Ping's mother continued, 'but I never received any money.'

The sulky girl was standing with her arms folded. 'I suppose she was too busy to send any.'

'Sssh, Mei,' said Master Chang. 'Let your stepmother finish.'

'Heaven chose to smile on me, though,' Ping's mother continued, wiping her eyes and patting her husband's hand. 'Master Chang had just lost his first wife. He had a young child and no one to care for her. He saved me from poverty and despair.'

Ping still didn't speak, but thoughts were crowding her mind. How could she have let her young daughter go? How could she have not seen through Lan's lies?

Master Chang smiled at his second wife. 'It took years of hard work, but we are comfortable now.'

'Not as comfortable as she's been at the imperial palace,' said Mei.

Though Ping's gown was splattered with mud, it was made of fine cloth and her undergarment was padded with silk floss. They looked like they belonged to a rich woman. She had gold in her pouch, a silver comb in her hair and a jade seal of office hanging from her waist. Ping couldn't deny that she was well-off.

'I wish I could live in a palace and not in this ordinary house,' Mei said.

Master Chang frowned at his daughter.

'Mei, go and tell Yi Min that there will be a guest eating with us tonight.'

The girl glared at Ping and stomped off to the kitchen.

'It's amazing,' said Master Chang as if he'd just heard a storyteller's tale. 'Chance brought you here. And on the very day that your mother was in the fields to help with the final harvest before the snow.'

Ping knew it wasn't chance that had brought her. She hadn't been wandering aimlessly at all. Even though her mind was dazed with fever, her second sight had chosen her path for her.

Ping wanted to tell them that the imperial position Master Lan had given her was as his slave, that she'd had to sleep in the ox shed and clean pigsties. But there had been too much misery, too many years of loneliness and hunger to express in words.

'I was taken to Huangling Palace, not Chang'an,' she said instead.

'Where's that?' asked Master Chang. 'I've not heard of it.'

'It's on the edge of the empire far to the west. Your letter never reached me.'

Even if it had, Ping knew that Master Lan would have destroyed it. Her mother believed that she had been living in imperial comfort. Ping wanted to pour it all out, every minute of unhappiness, every blow, every cruel word. She wanted to shake Mei and tell her how lucky she was. She wanted to explain how it felt to be so cold you couldn't sleep, so hungry you'd eat scraps from the pig trough, so lonely you had no one in the world to turn to but a rat. Mei had something that was worth more than gold, more than fine clothes – she had a family.

Her mother had the plump, fragrant skin of a wealthy woman, but Ping could read her history in the lines on her face and the sorrow behind her eyes. The unexpected arrival of her daughter had ripped open a place inside her that she'd kept closed for years. If Ping told her the truth, it would only make her unhappy. Ping didn't want that.

Master Chang took hold of the little boy's hand and pulled him out from the protection of his mother's gown.

'This is your second brother, Liang,' he said.

'Hello,' Ping said.

The little boy was too shy to speak. He peeked at Ping and then looked down at the floor.

Ping's mother and stepfather asked her many questions about her life. She described the palace at Huangling (even though she'd only seen it in the dark, on the occasions she'd sneaked in at night to explore). She spoke about the old Emperor (though she'd only met him once and had been under arrest at the time). She told them about the lovely Garden of the Purple Dragon. She proudly told them of her friendship with the young Emperor.

'What exactly are your duties, Ping?' her stepfather asked.

'I was the Imperial Dragonkeeper,' she answered. Even though she'd lost the position, she couldn't stop a little bit of pride creeping into her voice.

Mei giggled. 'Dragonkeeper? There's no such thing as dragons. Everyone knows that.'

In that comfortable house, there was no hunger or hardship, and a busy town bustled outside the doors. Dragons didn't seem to have a place there. Ping had no desire to change their minds. It was better this way. She wouldn't have to tell them the whole heartbreaking story.

'Dragonkeeper is the title the position has had since ancient times,' Ping said. 'I was in charge of the care of some of the imperial animals.' That wasn't too far from the truth. 'I supervised their feeding and training.'

She told them about the Emperor's plan to turn the Tiger Forest into a reserve for wild animals from all over the empire.

The colour had returned to Ping's mother's face. After hearing about the palace and her daughter's comfortable life at Ming Yang Lodge, her smile returned.

'That's not at all what I expected you to be doing,' said her mother. 'I thought you'd be a lady's companion or an embroiderer.'

'But you talk about it as if it's in the past,' Master Chang said.

'Yes,' Ping replied. 'I no longer have the position.'

Now that she had found them, Ping wanted to stay with her family. Her previous life had evaporated like water in summer sun. She hoped she could have a new life with them. Even if they didn't want the burden of another daughter, she could stay as a servant. She could work in the fields. Anything as long as she could be with them. In this house, she could be happy. She could forget about her failure as a Dragonkeeper.

The little boy, Liang, came over to the couch. He had seen something move next to Ping. He lifted the blanket that was covering her, and Hua's head popped out.

Mei screamed. The rat's bright blue eyes blinked as he suddenly found himself in the light.

'He won't hurt you,' Ping assured the little boy. 'He's very tame and well behaved,' she added for the benefit of her mother, who was staring at the rat with distaste.

'I've never heard of anyone keeping a rat as a pet,' her mother said.

Master Chang shook his head again. 'They certainly breed rats big in imperial palaces,' he said as he went out to tend to his oxen.

Ping's mother and stepsister went to help prepare the evening meal. Ping looked from the doorway at the rest of her family's home. She was on the second storey of a large house. Stairs led down to a neat courtyard that had buildings on all sides. Ping could see three fat pigs in a pigsty and a coop full of chickens. Delicious smells were coming from the kitchen on one side of the courtyard. It was everything a home should be.

Liang reached out to pat Hua. His small fingers nestled in the rat's bluish fur.

'He's very soft.' It was the first time Ping had heard the boy speak. He had a sweet voice.

Liang stroked Hua and tickled him behind his ears. He had no fear of the rat. Ping felt a rush of love for her little half-brother.

'Would you like to hold him?' Ping asked.

He nodded. Ping placed Hua in the boy's lap.

'Have you really seen a dragon?' Liang said.

Ping glanced over her shoulder to make sure no one else could hear. She smiled down at the boy.

'Yes. I had two dragons in my care,' she whispered. 'One was a big dragon. He was very wise and brave, but he was also very old. He flew away to the Isle of the Blest. The other was a baby dragon. When he was happy, he made sounds like someone playing a pretty tune on a flute. Sometimes he was very naughty. His name was Kai.'

That was the best way to think about the little dragon, she decided. He was in the past. He didn't exist in her new life.

'I don't have any dragons any more though,' she said sadly.

'Were the dragons blue like the ones painted on our best bowls?' the boy asked.

'There might be blue dragons somewhere in the empire, but not my dragons. Kai was purple. The old dragon was green.'

Ping fished in her silk pouch and pulled out the dragon's scale.

'This is one of the old dragon's scales.' She ran her fingers over the rough scale.

'And this,' she found the dragon-stone shard, 'is part of the egg that the baby dragon hatched from.'

'Can I touch it?' Liang asked.

Ping put the shard of dragon stone in the boy's outstretched hands. He smiled. He had a tooth missing.

The evening meal was served in the room where Ping had woken up. It was the best room, the one where the family received guests, not where they normally ate. The table was set with white bowls covered in blue dragon designs. The maid served three dishes, each made from grain and vegetables grown in Master Chang's fields.

Ping listened to the stories of their day – Mei had torn her favourite gown, little Liang had found a lizard in the courtyard, Master Chang had given a sack of grain to a family whose father was ill.

'I had an interesting day,' said Ping's mother. 'I found my long-lost daughter.'

Everyone smiled – even Mei.

After the meal, Ping's mother bathed the wound on Ping's head with a soothing lotion.

'It's healing well,' she said.

'You must stay as long as you like, Ping,' said Master Chang. 'If you don't mind sharing a mattress with your step-sister.'

'I'm not having a rat in my room!' Mei said, folding her arms crossly.

'Perhaps you can put your rat in the barn,' suggested Master Chang.

When the two girls were alone Ping tried to talk to Mei, but she wasn't in the mood for conversation. The only time she spoke was to point out that her hair combs were only made of ebony, not silver. Then she lay down and turned to face the wall.

Ping was sleeping under the same roof as her family for the first time since she was a small child. She felt safe and warm. All her burdens had been lifted from her shoulders. She would stay at her mother's side. She would win over her stepsister and be her friend. She would tell little Liang stories and he would grow to love her. All these things would come to pass, she was sure of it.

She took the dragon scale out of her pouch again and felt its rough texture. She lifted it to her nose to catch its distinctive smell. She held it up in the moonlight and its dull green colour became brighter. It was a souvenir of her past life. Nothing more.

CHAPTER TWENTY-FOUR

THE TIGER FOREST

Ping could see the moon through the trees. The full moon. Dark tree branches criss-crossed its face, so that it looked as if it had been sliced into irregular pieces. One of the pieces broke off. That's a shame, Ping thought. The moon is broken. It will never be whole again. The slice of moon was falling from the sky. It was getting larger. Ping ran through the trees towards it. She wanted to know where it landed. She wanted to look at a piece of the moon up close. She wanted to see it more than anything.

She ran until she came out of the trees into a clearing. The bright light was just above her. It wasn't a slice of the moon at all. It was a dragon. Her dragon.

'Danzi, I haven't seen you for such a long time.'

The anxious lose their guiding thread. The pure and tranquil see harm and are not frightened.

The dragon swooped low and Ping grabbed one of his

258

paws as he soared up into the dark sky again. Her feet left the ground. The dragon flapped up into the dark night sky. She looked at the shining dragon shape above her. Every scale was glowing like green jade in lamplight. Danzi flapped higher and higher. The darkened world shrank beneath her with amazing speed. She could see mountain slopes below, outlined faintly in the moonlight. It looked like a ghost world.

A snaking stream was the only thing that wasn't sleeping. Its serpentine windings were lit by tiny flakes of moonlight as it hurried along its way. Ping had felt like that stream. Always rushing, always striving, never being able to rest, but somehow always staying in the same place.

'I can only really rest when I'm up here with you, Danzi,' Ping said. 'Up here I don't have to walk, I don't have to think, but I fly because of you.'

Those who do not leave their beds are not always safe. Do not fear the dangers of the path.

Ping's heart soared. But only for a moment. Her fingers stiffened with cold. She felt her grip on the dragon's paw loosen. The moon went behind a cloud. The dragon shape disappeared, as if someone had blown out a candle. A rush of icy air told her she was falling, falling, falling.

Ping woke from the dream with a start. The dragon scale was still in her hand. Danzi's dream words had never made any sense before. They were just as puzzling as they had been when he was there in the flesh, but this time his meaning was clear. She'd chosen safety instead of the path that was her destiny. Like a coward she'd wanted to hide in the comfort of her family's home.

She couldn't stay with her family. Jun wasn't the Dragonkeeper – she was. Danzi had said so. Of all the people in the empire and beyond, the old dragon had chosen her to take care of his only heir. She wasn't ready to give up that role yet. Her desire to be with her family was strong, but not as strong as her need to care for Kai.

She had almost made the same mistake as her mother – the one thing that Ping had blamed her for all the time she'd lived at Huangling. Her mother had listened to someone else's advice instead of listening to her heart. She had given over her only daughter to the care of a stranger. Ping had almost done the same thing. Dong Fang Suo had decided that she was no longer the Dragonkeeper, and she had let him take Kai away from her. The Imperial Magician was wrong. She would have to tell Liu Che. Convince him that she was the true Dragonkeeper.

Ping ate breakfast with her family. She imagined eating with them every morning – enjoying her mother's steaming buns, hearing her stepfather's plans and Mei's complaints, helping Liang put on his socks. This comfortable family life wasn't her destiny though. Heaven had chosen a different path for her.

'I'll be leaving after breakfast,' she said.

'You're not going already?' said her mother.

'Stay longer,' said Master Chang. 'It's not the season for travelling.'

She reached out and touched her mother's hand. 'It's been my greatest wish to find you. I would love to stay, but I have to return to my duties.'

'I thought you said you'd lost the position,' Mei said.

'The bump on my head made my memory play tricks on me,' Ping said. 'I was just having a holiday. I have to return to Ming Yang Lodge.'

Ping didn't tie her hair up in a knot like Lady An had taught her. Instead she tied it back in a plait.

'It's more suitable for travelling,' she explained and gave the silver hair comb to Mei. 'It used to belong to Princess Yangxin. I'd like you to have it.'

She gave the jar of hair oil to her mother and her one gold coin to Master Chang. He didn't want to take it. She knew that the family didn't need more money, but she had nothing else to offer them.

'It won't make up for all that I would have sent you, if I'd known where you were,' she said. 'But it's all I have with me.'

She stood outside her family's house with her bag over her shoulder. Her mother looked puzzled by her daughter's sudden decision to leave.

'We thought you'd stay for a few days at least,' said Master Chang.

'I wish I could stay forever,' Ping said.

She wanted to say more, but she was afraid she wouldn't be able to keep back the tears that were threatening to spill down her face.

Her mother took her hand.

'Mothers know their daughters will leave from the day they are born.' Her eyes were filled with tears as well. 'You just left a little earlier than most. I'm proud of you, Ping. You bring honour to your father's family.'

Ping hugged her mother tightly. Master Chang told her she was welcome in his house any time. Mei allowed Ping to hug her. Ping bent down and kissed Liang on the cheek.

'Kai would like you,' she whispered.

Master Chang gave Ping a bag of dried fruit and nuts for her journey. He told her she only had to walk to the next garrison along the imperial road. From there she would be able to get a carriage back to Ming Yang Lodge.

Ping collected Hua from the barn and then waved as she walked away from her family.

'I'll come back and visit you when I can,' she called back to them, but she had a feeling she never would.

She felt Hua's warmth inside the folds of her gown. She was glad she wasn't travelling entirely alone.

The next carriage wasn't due to leave for another four days. Ping couldn't wait. She would have to walk back to Ming Yang Lodge. Though every step took her further away from her family, it also took her closer to Kai. She searched for the thread that connected her to Kai, but it eluded her.

As she walked, Ping thought about what her mother had said. She was only a girl. Of course her mother would put the welfare of a son before hers. And she was right. Even if she had stayed with them, in a year or two Master Chang would have found her a husband and she would have been sent off to live among strangers. It was better this way. Her mother believed that Ping was happier than she would have been if she had stayed with her.

Even so, Ping had lost something. Through all her hardship at Huangling, she had always had a tiny hope in her heart. She had dreamed that one day she would find her mother and be able to stay in the warmth and comfort of a family. That small hope had disappeared. Whatever her future held, that wasn't it. But that hope had been replaced by certain knowledge of where her path lay.

It hadn't been the family reunion she was expecting, but Ping didn't feel sad. She knew her mother was safe and well. She had a half-brother. A stepsister. She didn't have to worry about them. Master Chang would take care of them.

It felt strange to have no one to look after but herself. Ping could think about things without dragon words interrupting her train of thought. There had been so many times since Kai had hatched that she had longed to have a break from dragon rearing. To have a few days without the baby dragon's nonsense in her head, without being jumped on and scratched. Now she had that freedom, she felt like an arm or a leg was missing. She missed Kai's voice in her head, his happy sounds as he ran around the garden discovering new things, his spines sticking in her side as she slept. She was looking forward to being with him once more.

Ping was back on the imperial road by the end of the first day. She was sorry she'd left her coat in the carriage. Dark clouds hung low and heavy. An icy wind promised snow.

There were a few people on the imperial road, but they all bowed their heads against the wind. That suited Ping. She didn't want to waste time in conversation. Whenever she could, she begged a ride from farmers driving carts.

Two days after she had left her family, Ping arrived in a town they'd passed through on the journey to Lu-lin. The smell of roasting meat diverted her from her straight path to a market stall. It was where Dong Fang Suo had bought a midday meal on their journey to Lu-lin. Kai had been delighted because the man sold roasted swallow. Ping bought a baked quail with her few copper coins.

'I didn't expect to see you again,' the meat seller said.

Ping was surprised that he even remembered her.

'The gentleman stopped at my stall again on his return journey,' the man said. 'I asked after you. He said that you'd stayed in Lu-lin with your family. That was the purpose of the journey, so he said.'

'How long ago?'

'Must have been three or four days ago. He was in a great hurry,' the meat seller said. 'It was almost dark when they arrived. They bought food to take with them. There was music coming from the carriage. It sounded like someone playing a flute. The saddest tune I've ever heard.'

Ping left the town immediately, eating as she walked. She had to get back to the Garden of the Purple Dragon as soon as possible.

Dong Fang Suo had lied to the meat seller. The last time she'd seen the Imperial Magician she hadn't even met her family. She felt a stab of hatred for the old man. He had betrayed her. He was a feeble old man and, even though he called himself a magician, he had no magical powers.

'He wanted me dead, and he got the necromancer to do the job for him.'

She spoke the words aloud to see how they sounded. They didn't sound as absurd as she thought they would. Dong Fang Suo wanted Jun to take Ping's place. Liu Che wouldn't have agreed. He would want Ping to be Dragonkeeper. If she were dead, though, there would be no debate.

Each day, Ping walked from before dawn till well after dark. She no longer accepted rides on wagons. She was stronger now and could walk faster than an ox. The closer she got to the Garden of the Purple Dragon, the more anxious she became. She still couldn't feel Kai. She slept less and less until finally she didn't stop to sleep at all, but walked through the night. Hua kept pace with her. At night he ran beside her. During the day he scurried through the fields or the bushes, where no one could see him. When he grew weary, he climbed up to rest in the folds of her gown.

Ping came to a crossroad. She turned off the main imperial road and on to the smaller, quieter road that led to the Garden of the Purple Dragon. It had been six days since the rock fall. She'd planned to announce that she was the Imperial Dragonkeeper and demand an escort through the Tiger Forest, but when she reached the wall surrounding the forest, the gate was open and unguarded. Perhaps the Emperor had decided that the forest with its dangerous inhabitants was deterrent enough to his enemies. She would have to walk through unprotected.

Through the trees the clouds were turning orange. It would soon be dark. In the distance she could hear the high call of monkeys and the roar of other animals she couldn't identify. Bears perhaps? She wanted to get back to Ming Yang Lodge as soon as she could, but she couldn't risk the forest at night. Ping climbed the steps up into the empty gate tower. She found food and a mattress. She stroked Hua's warm fur for comfort. She didn't realize how exhausted she was until she lay down. She slept like a squirrel in winter.

Before dawn, Ping was walking again. The forest track was peaceful after the bustle of the imperial road. There were no shouted greetings as travellers passed by. No clop of galloping horses or creak of wheels. No panting of imperial messengers. The only sounds were the calls of birds and animals as the dawn roused them.

Most of the trees in the forest were ancient junipers. Their foliage had a bluish tinge and their bark hung in peeling strips. Ping chewed on juniper berries. They had a bitter taste, but they kept her alert. Apart from the birds and the unseen animals that rustled through the undergrowth, the silent trees were the only witnesses to her journey.

Late in the afternoon, Ping heard the sound of rushing water. She left the path to look for the stream. Three deer were drinking on the opposite bank. They didn't notice Ping at first. Then suddenly they all looked up together. Ping thought she must have made a noise to disturb them, but the startled creatures weren't looking in her direction. They were looking behind them. The trees were dense, their branches criss-crossed each other like latticework. Some of the dark branches moved. The deer darted away. Ping peered into the forest. Something was moving.

An animal stepped out of the trees. It padded toward the edge of the stream on large paws. It stopped to sniff the air. It was huge. Its fur wasn't yellow, as she had been told, but honey-brown, striped with black bands. It crouched down and lapped at the water with a large, pink tongue. The markings on the animal's lowered head were beautiful. They looked as if an artist had painted them on with a brush dipped in black ink. The tiger looked up. Though she hadn't moved, hadn't so much as taken a breath, Ping knew that it had heard her. It looked straight into her eyes. Its lips curled back, wrinkling the fur around its nose, making its white whiskers stand on end, baring its huge teeth. The tiger's deep roar reverberated through the trees.

The birds stopped singing. No small creatures rustled through the bushes. Everything was silent out of respect for the tiger's terrible strength. She imagined its claws raking deep into her skin, those huge teeth tearing her flesh. The creature was designed to kill. The tiger took a step towards her. Ping looked into its eyes and felt her own power, her own strength. It wasn't her destiny to be killed by a tiger. The creature roared again, then turned and stalked back into the forest.

Ping drank from the stream. She should have felt the thread joining her to Kai by now. She hurried back to the path. The sun was low. She had to get to Ming Yang Lodge before dark. Ping had started her journey counting the days until she would be with Kai again, then she had counted the hours. At last she was able to estimate the time in minutes. She started to run.

She was looking for the lights of Ming Yang Lodge, but there were none. She had expected the gates to be closed, guards to call out their customary challenge 'Who presumes to disturb the peace of the Son of Heaven?' But the gates were wide open, and the watchtowers empty.

Ping walked through the gates.

CHAPTER TWENTY-FIVE

BLOOD AND FIRE

Ping entered the darkened Garden of the Purple Dragon. Even in the half-light, it looked like a different place to the one she had left a little more than two weeks ago. Where there had been garden beds of winter lilies and irises just beginning to open, now there was a huge, dark mound of earth. On top of the mound were the smouldering ashes of five fires and a large bronze cauldron lying on its side. The surrounding earth was trampled as if a crowd of people had been stamping and dancing on it, but there was no one around. Animal bones and fruit peel littered the ground. Cups and wine jars lay abandoned under shrubs. The smell of cold animal fat and ashes didn't quite overwhelm the pungent traces of incense. Plants had been flattened, tree branches broken. A single duck quacking miserably beside a rubbish-filled pond was the only sign of life.

Ping had wondered what sort of reception she would

receive when she returned to Ming Yang Lodge, but she hadn't expected this. She couldn't understand it. The Emperor's festival to appease Heaven wasn't due to start till the following day. Had she lost track of the days? Or had the Emperor been too impatient to wait for the auspicious day that the seers had set?

Ping's heart was pounding, panic rising in her throat. She still couldn't feel the thread joining her to Kai.

She went inside Ming Yang Lodge. It was dark and eerily quiet. She found a lamp and Hua lit it with one of his spit-balls. She ran to the Dragon Quarters. Kai's bed had been stripped of its blankets. His goatskin ball was lying on the floor.

She ran to the dining hall. Hua scurried after her. It was empty. So were the kitchens. There were no servants. The pots and kettles were all packed away. The Chamber of Spreading Clouds was just as empty. The furniture was draped with cloths. There were no imperial guards any-where. She went to the Princess's chambers. They were completely bare. The chests and baskets of gowns, the boxes of jewellery and cosmetics were all gone. The wall hangings had been taken down, the mats and cushions removed. She ran along corridors, not knowing where she was going.

She became aware of a faint sound. It was like the high-est notes of a flute played on a far mountain. Each note was so full of sadness and pain it made her heart ache. It was Kai. He was calling to her. Something or someone was hurting him. Ping tried to work out where the flute notes were coming from, but the more she listened, the fainter they seemed.

She felt a sense of foreboding spread over her like a cold sweat. Something bad was going to happen. She reached into her pouch to touch Danzi's scale to calm herself. Instead her hand closed around the dragon-stone shard. Her mind suddenly focused. It homed in on the faint sound like a well-aimed arrow seeking its target. She could feel the thread at last, tugging her, leading her towards Kai. She put down the lamp and strode forward, eyes closed. What she saw was just a distraction. She didn't stop until a door barred her way.

Ping opened her eyes. She knew exactly where she was. Behind the door was the Hall of Peaceful Retreat, where the Longevity Council did their mysterious work — where she had seen the necromancer. She could hear the dragon's voice in her mind, but there were no words, just low miserable moans.

Ping pushed the door open. The room was lit by several lamps. She could see details that had been hidden in the dark on her previous visit. Symbols were painted on the walls — strangely shaped mushrooms, a woman carrying a tray of seven enormous peaches, the characters for *never* and *decay*. Ping recognized the sharp, sour smell from her previous visit. She remembered why it was familiar — she had smelt it in Wucheng.

Bowls and jars were spread out on a bench. There was a

mortar and pestle where someone had left off grinding tortoise shell to a powder, an open bamboo book and some dried plants. The unpleasant smell was coming from bowls containing dark, sinister mixtures. One bowl held a thick dark liquid, in which Ping recognized birds' feet, pine needles and pieces of dog flesh with fur still attached. Maggots squirmed in it. In another there was a rancid mixture of pig lard, teasel and black beetles. Alongside the bowl was a needle threaded with brown silk. This familiar tool seemed out of place. Hua sniffed a third bowl. It contained just one thing – a large, bloody liver. This wasn't rotting. It was bathed in fresh blood. A piece had been hacked from it.

Ping thought they must have been the elixirs and spells that the Longevity Council was experimenting with. Ping had always been uneasy about Liu Che's obsession with longevity, she had worried about his health – now she was concerned more about his soul. But she didn't have time to worry about the Emperor. Kai was all that mattered. The invisible thread pulled her towards the curtained doorway where the necromancer had been hidden on the night that the tower fell. Ping drew the curtain aside.

The necromancer wasn't there – but Kai was. There was just enough light from the other room to see him. He was strapped down on a bench. He slowly turned his head towards her. She ran to him. His green eyes were as dull as stagnant water. His lips were the colour of old meat. Blood was oozing from a gash in the little dragon's tail. Ping gasped. The edges of the wound had been pinned back to stop it from healing. Drops of purple blood dripped into a flask beneath the bench.

'Ping.' The dragon's voice was faint.

Ping pulled the pins out of his tail and ripped the hem from her gown to bandage the wound. She picked Kai up, cradling him in her arms. He was barely conscious.

'Who did this to you?' Tears were running down her face. She couldn't speak without sobbing, so she said the words in her mind.

'Bad man,' Kai replied.

She knew who he meant.

There would always be those who sought Kai, whether it was for the properties of his body parts or his value in gold. Her job was to protect him from such greedy people. She had failed. She had believed she and Kai were safe. It hadn't occurred to her until it was too late that there might be enemies within the walls of Ming Yang Lodge.

A feeling of dread struck Ping. She found it hard to breathe. She felt a prickling sensation on the back of her neck. Someone had come into the room. Someone who meant to harm Kai. She swung around, scanning the dim corners. She couldn't see anyone. Hua made a sound, a squeal of warning. His fur was standing on end. He reared on his hind legs and launched a spitball. It missed its target, but in the brief flare of fire Ping saw what the rat had seen.

A snake with black and orange markings was slithering

across the floor. Kai whimpered. Ping could feel his fear as if it was a solid presence in the room. The snake was more than six feet long and as thick as a man's arm. It raised its head. It only had one eye. There was a scar where its other eye should have been. The snake's one yellow eye glinted in the lamplight, staring at Hua. The rat froze, his paws were stuck to the floor, and he seemed unable to drag his eyes away from the yellow eye. Ping had seen a similar yellow glint high on the cliff at Twisting Snake Ravine. It had had that same effect on her. The snake turned away from Hua and towards Ping, its forked tongue darting in and out.

The snake started to twist and shimmer. Ping felt her stomach heave as the snake transformed into a cloaked figure with a ginger beard, a tattooed face and a patch over one eye. He was holding a knife in one hand – a kitchen knife like the ones the imperial cooks used to cut up meat. In his other hand was the hacked-off piece of liver, still dripping blood. Ping had seen the necromancer taken away from Ming Yang Lodge in chains. Somehow he had got free and he and the Imperial Magician had banded together.

Without thinking Ping focused her *qi* on a large jar and sent it flying across the room. It hit the necromancer on the head and smashed to pieces. He sagged to his knees with a groan. Ping's heart leapt. It was the first time she'd felt pleasure at hurting anything. His cloak slipped from his shoulders and she could see that he was wearing a strange vest. It was made up of flat squares of green jade. There were holes in the corners of each square and they were linked with what looked like gold wire. Liu Che had told her about the properties of jade. Important people were buried in suits of jade so that their bodies didn't decay after they died. The jade shielded the corpses from forces trying to attack them. The jade vest had formed a shield which kept the necromancer hidden from her second sight until she was standing an arm's length from him.

Claw-like black fingernails reached out for Kai, just as they had grasped for the dragon stone in Wucheng. She held the dragon tighter and summoned her *qi* power again. Anger burned within her like a pool of molten metal. She had never been so furious in her life. Still on his knees, the necromancer raised the knife, ready to throw it. Ping released a burst of *qi* power. The knife, leapt from his hand and clanged against the wall behind him. The tattoo on his face looked more like a tame cat than a fierce wild creature. There was fear in his one eye, instead of the hypnotic glint. Ping felt triumph swell within her.

She moved towards him, rejoicing in the fact that he was on his knees before her. She got ready to strike again. Her foot collided with something. She looked down. It was an arm. In the dim light, she hadn't seen a body lying on the matting. In the moments that she was distracted, the necromancer picked up a bronze pot and swung it at her, knocking her sideways.

Ping hit the floor. It took a moment or two for her eyes

to focus. She recognized the body on the floor. It was Saggy-pants. His face was white, his eyes wide and staring, but his skin was still warm. The Dragon Attendant's jacket was pulled open and his saggy trousers slashed to lay bare his belly. His hands were bound above his head and tied to the bench leg. There was a large hole in the right-hand side of his stomach. Dark blood had formed congealed pools on the bamboo matting around him. Ping remembered the liver in the bowl. From the expression on his face, Ping was sure that the Dragon Attendant had still been alive when his liver had been cut out of him.

She retched, but her stomach was empty. Nothing came out but a trickle of yellow bile. Kai was making a high-pitched keening sound. It was a sound of pain, terror and desolation. Ping tried to get up. Barbed metal discs spun through the air towards her. The barbs just missed her flesh, but pinned her sleeves to the floor so that she couldn't get up. Her anger changed to fear; her own power had been smothered like a cupped flame.

The necromancer had the threaded needle in his hand. He turned away from her, so she couldn't see what he was doing. She heard him groan with pain and hoped she'd hurt him. She had to refocus her *qi* while he was distracted, gather together every *shu* of strength and power within her. She wrenched her left arm up from the floor, ripping her sleeve. Then she pulled out the barbed discs that pinned her to the floor. She got to her feet. Ping had never felt such anger. She sent out a bolt of *qi* and it was strong, much stronger than anything she'd been able to summon before. The necromancer staggered when it hit him, but when he turned towards her, a sound like a crackling bark came out of his mouth. It was laughter. Bolt after bolt shot from Ping's arm. They were useless. Just a few minutes ago, the necromancer had resorted to hitting her with a bronze pot and using barbed discs to disable her. Something had changed. Now power radiated from him like heat from a blazing fire.

She raised her hand again.

'Keep trying,' the necromancer laughed as he moved towards her, the knife still in his hand. 'You won't be able to bend back my little finger.'

Ping tried anyway. He sucked her strength from her before she was able to focus it. She couldn't summon a single bolt of *qi*. His one eye stared at her. She looked away. She had to avoid his stare. She had to escape or she would end up like the unfortunate Dragon Attendant. She couldn't help Kai if she were dead. What little strength she had left, she used to run to the door and didn't look back. She ran down corridors, up stairs, turning this way and that in the vain hope that she would lose the necromancer.

She found herself outside the Emperor's private quarters. It was forbidden to enter without being invited in by the Emperor, but the chambers were almost at the top of Ming Yang hill. There was nowhere else to go. She entered with the smallest hope that Liu Che might be there and would help her.

The lattice doorways leading to the balcony were all closed. The sky was overcast. The lotus patterns of light on the matting were only faint grey. No lamps were lit. The furniture was draped with cloths.

The feeling of dread hit her so hard, it knocked her off her feet. All hope drained from her. She turned around. The necromancer was standing in the doorway, his mouth twisted into a smile that had nothing to do with joy or happiness. Ping shuddered. His one eye glinted at her. It bored into her like a drill. She couldn't tear her gaze away. She could see deep into his evil soul – and what she saw made her very afraid.

His eye released her, but she still couldn't get up. All she could see were the wooden floorboards squashed up against her face. The necromancer was still laughing, relishing his victory over her. He held the knife in front of him.

As she stared at the dark floorboards, something appeared through one of the knotholes. It was so close that she couldn't get it into focus. Then she saw that it was a trembling pink nose. A set of whiskers followed, then two bright blue eyes and two ears, one with a chunk missing. Hua had recovered and found her. He somehow managed to squeeze his body through the hole. The sight of the rat helped her find a little strength – just a trace, like a drop of water in an empty bucket.

The necromancer walked unhurriedly across the room. He knelt down beside Ping and held the knife blade against her belly. An unlit lamp was the only thing in reach that she could use as a weapon. She grabbed it and struck him on the head. Oil ran into his eyes and on to his cloak. He swung the knife blindly at Ping. She rolled aside, but felt a searing pain as the blade slashed her right arm. There was a flash, followed a moment later by another. Hua was launching his spitballs. The necromancer's cloak suddenly burst into flame. He let out a howl of pain and fear as the flames flicked up his face. He fought to undo the cloak's clasp. His cries sounded like music to Ping.

The necromancer flung his burning cloak from him. Flames spread to a cushion and then to a rug. The fire raced across the bamboo matting faster than a galloping horse. It flared up between Ping and the necromancer. Ping felt a wave of relief. He couldn't get to her – but the fire also cut off any chance of escape. Through smoke and flames, Ping saw the necromancer turn and stride out of the room.

As she ran out on to the balcony, she could feel the heat on the back of her neck. Tongues of fire were already licking through the latticework of the doors. She looked around frantically. There was no escape. Behind her was the roaring fire. In front was a drop of four *chang* to the courtyard below. Hua clawed his way up the back of her gown. He knew what she had to do. She leapt over the scarlet balustrade. There was no other choice.

Ping fell headfirst. She could hear a tinkling sound over the rush of air. It was the waterfall that tumbled down the hillside into a pool far below. She felt a surge of joy. The pool would break her fall. She looked down. Her relief changed to panic. The pool wasn't directly below her. She would hit the ground and break her neck. She closed her eyes. Something smacked into her; it wasn't as hard as earth, but intense pain shot through her chest. She'd fallen into the branches of a willow tree. They didn't break, but bent beneath her weight.

She reached out and wrapped her arms around as many of the tree's drooping branches as she could. They slipped through her embrace, but they had slowed her fall. She grasped hold of one strong willow bough. It didn't snap; it bent and flexed like a length of rope and took her weight. She used the momentum of her fall to swing out over the pool. Then she let go of the branch.

The slap of the water was painful, but she was more concerned about drowning. She thrashed about in the water trying to keep her head above the surface. She sank down until she bumped against the slippery, algae-covered bottom of the pool. She didn't allow herself to panic. She remembered how she had floated up through the green waters of the well with Kai. She pushed herself off the bottom and kicked her legs. As she resurfaced, she clutched a strangely shaped rock that jutted out of the water. Hua swam up to her. She caught her breath and then splashed her way to the edge of the pool.

Ping dragged herself out of the water. Spots of blood were dripping into the pool. Ping ripped a strip from her sleeve and bandaged her arm as best she could with one hand. She had to ignore the pain. She picked up Hua and put him in her gown. Far above her the fire lit up the night sky. Orange flames were engulfing the balustrades of the Emperor's balcony. She had escaped from the necromancer, but Kai was still inside the blazing lodge.

CHAPTER TWENTY-SIX

MUDDY WATERS

The pain in Ping's chest made it difficult to run. She knew a little about the arrangement of bones in a body from butchering goats for Master Lan. One of her ribs had broken in the fall. As she stumbled towards the lower buildings of Ming Yang Lodge, her feet seemed to move in slow motion. Sparks showered down from the fire above. Other buildings had started to burn. If the servants and the imperial guards had been there, they might have been able to control the fire. But the flames were spreading unchecked – to the kitchens, to the Princess's chambers. Whichever way Ping turned, the fire kept driving her back. She couldn't get near the Hall of Peaceful Retreat. The entire lodge, every building, every pavilion, every piece of furniture was made of wood. Like a ravenous monster, the fire devoured everything in its path. Nothing was going to stop it.

Ping's mind was a chaos of nightmare images – of the

dead Dragon Attendant; of the necromancer's grinning face; of burning buildings; of Kai limp and bleeding.

She couldn't find the end of the fragile thread that joined her to the dragon. Her second sight searched blindly, but found nothing. Ping felt in her pouch for the shard of dragon stone. It wasn't there. Her silk pouch had been ripped, probably by the willow branches, and the shard had fallen out. She had only just come to understand its power to focus her mind — and now she'd lost it. She should have kept the sturdy leather pouch that she'd had since Huangling instead of accepting the flimsy silk one. It was just another mistake to add to the long list of mistakes she'd made. Despair enveloped her like a black shroud.

She had no power over the five elements. She couldn't fight fire. All she could do was watch the lodge burn. The smoke made her eyes sting; tears streamed down her face. The dawn light revealed a desolate landscape. The imperial chambers were reduced to blackened ruins. Flames still licked and curled around the lower buildings. The trees were bare of all but a few scorched leaves. The lotus leaves on the ponds had withered. The smoke from the burning buildings had shrivelled the flowers. Not long ago, Ping had wanted the necromancer to die a horrible death, now she was praying he had escaped the fire. It was the only way Kai could have survived.

Ping crawled through the thick, black smoke that threatened to choke her as it had everything that had grown in the garden. She made her way down Ming Yang hill, past Late Spring Villa, until she found herself on the banks of the Yellow River. The river rushed by, eager to get to Ocean, unaware of the devastated lodge or her misery. Its muddy waters were as impenetrable as ever, stretching as far as she could see and giving no clue as to what lay beneath the surface. Ping drank some of the yellowish water and tried to wash the smoke from her eyes.

Crouched on the river bank, she tried to shut out the horrors of the night. She couldn't. Saggypants was dead. The imperial lodge was destroyed. The necromancer had overpowered her. Then there was the most important thing. The one she was trying to keep out of her mind because it was unbearable.

'I can't feel the thread,' she said to Hua.

Her second sight was unreliable, it came and went like a flame flickering in a breeze. She didn't know how to control it. She felt sensations, but didn't know their meaning. It was like trying to peer through the muddy waters of the river. The only thing she wanted to feel was the connection between her and Kai, but it wasn't there. Hua crawled inside the folds of her gown. She curled up, trying to shut out the ugly, blackened world and her failure.

'I've found her,' a voice said.

Ping opened her eyes. A breeze had thinned the smoke. She didn't know how long she'd been there. An imperial guard was looking down at her. There were footsteps and other guards came along the path. Minister Ji was among them.

'I've been searching for you for over an hour,' he said crossly.

'How did you know I was back at Ming Yang Lodge?'

The minister didn't answer. He turned and walked away. 'Follow me,' he said.

His calmness infuriated Ping. She wanted to stand up and shake him, but she didn't have the strength. She grabbed hold of the hem of his gown.

'I've lost Kai,' she sobbed. This time the tears weren't because of the smoke.

Minister Ji brushed her hands from his gown as if they were a pair of spiders.

'Your distress is entirely unnecessary,' the minister said. 'The imperial dragon is with the Emperor. I have been instructed to take you to him.'

Ping couldn't believe her ears.

'But I saw him.' Ping tried to think how long ago it had been. It seemed like days, but it couldn't have been more than a few hours. 'He was weak and bleeding. The necromancer had him.'

'The Emperor did not instruct me to stand and argue the point with you.' He turned round and strode off along the path.

Ping followed. Minister Ji seemed unconcerned about the ruined lodge.

'Ming Yang Lodge is burning,' she said. She needed to confirm that she wasn't going mad, that she hadn't imagined the fire.

'Most unfortunate,' Minister Ji agreed. 'Rebuilding it will be an expense the empire could do without.'

The minister walked calmly and without hurry away from Ming Yang hill. Ping tried to rearrange the facts in her head so that they made sense. How had Minister Ji known that she was back at Ming Yang Lodge? Who had rescued Kai? It was like trying to fit together the pieces of two broken jars that were jumbled together. Nothing fitted. Nothing made sense.

They came to a small inlet cut into the river bank, where a boat was tied up away from the rush of the river.

'Where are you taking me?' Ping said.

The minister didn't answer. He walked up the gangplank. Ping followed him.

The boat was smaller than the one that had carried her and Danzi down the Yellow River. But this one had a team of ten rowers, each wearing nothing put a pair of short trousers. The skin of their muscled arms was taut and shiny. With so many rowers, Ping thought that they must have been going back up the river against the current. Minister Ji sat down in the middle of the boat and arranged his gown. Ping collapsed next to him. Hua wriggled inside the folds of her gown.

A boatman untied the boat and pushed it out into the rushing current. At his command the rowers dipped their oars into the water and started rowing for all they were worth. They weren't rowing upstream against the current. Nor were they allowing the river to carry the boat downstream. They were rowing across the river. Their muscles flexed as they plunged their oars into the yellow water again and again. They chanted a song to help keep their oar strokes in time. The boat made its way slowly across the great river, but Ping could feel the current pulling them downstream at the same time.

The river must have been at least four *li* wide. As they got closer to the opposite bank, she could see a bamboo thicket. The bamboo canes grew right to the water's edge. They reached up to the grey sky and the newly grown tips bent back and forth in the wind as if they couldn't decide which way to go. Ping could see no buildings among the bamboo, no dock that the boat was heading for. Meanwhile the current tugged them further and further downstream. If they were rowing across to a dock on the opposite bank, they would miss it. Neither Minister Ji nor the rowers seemed concerned. The rhythm of the oars dipping into the water never varied.

The opposite bank was now only a few *chang* away. Something large and black loomed into view. It was the imperial barge. Ping was suddenly aware of Kai. It was faint, but she could feel his presence again. Hope swelled within her. He was nearby. The rowers dipped their oars into the water with the exact same rhythm. Another ten-and-five strokes brought them to the dock where the imperial barge was moored. The two mooring sites on either side of the river had been built to take into account the pull of the current and the strength of the rowers.

The barge hadn't been repainted in the new imperial yellow; it was still black. Bearers were busy unloading chests and baskets from the barge and stacking them on the dock where a wide road led off to the north. Some of the chests looked familiar. Ping followed Minister Ji up the gangplank, her legs shaky with fatigue and anticipation.

The deck was crowded with ministers, guards and servants. Liu Che was sitting on a throne on the deck. He was so thin that his gown hung off him. He was sitting with the heel of one gold embroidered shoe resting on the opposite knee as if nothing unusual had happened. Kai was on a satin cushion at the Emperor's side. He lifted his head as if it took a great effort.

'Ping,' said the dragon.

Ping was so relieved to see him again, she didn't care what she had been through. Minister Ji bowed to the Emperor and took his place with the other imperial ministers. Ping tried to go to the dragon, but guards barred her way.

'Are you all right, Kai?' She spoke to the dragon with her mind.

'Kai OK.'

His flute sounds were faint.

Dong Fang Suo was on his knees before the Emperor. 'You are stripped of your position as Imperial Magician,' the Emperor announced.

Ping felt her heart lift. She didn't have to tell Liu Che about Dong Fang Suo's treachery. He already knew. The old magician crouched in front of the Emperor like a beaten dog. His face looked as crumpled as his gown. Ping glared at him triumphantly. At last she could rest. The Emperor would take care of things. She bowed before him.

'Dong Fang Suo left me to die, Your Imperial Majesty,' Ping said. 'I was crushed by a falling boulder. It wasn't an accident. He's in league with the necromancer.'

'Be silent!' Minister Ji snapped. 'The Emperor did not give you permission to speak.'

Guards pushed her to her knees and forced her head to the deck. Ping waited for Liu Che to tell the minister she could speak, but the Emperor said nothing. She turned her head so that she could see him. His eyes were as cold as polished stones, his mouth a thin, straight line. His hollow cheeks made him look older and sinister.

'I'm not very happy with Dong Fang Suo either,' the Emperor said. 'I told him to make sure you were dead.'

Ping thought she couldn't have heard him properly.

'I have appointed a new Imperial Magician.' The Emperor waved his hand.

Dread extinguished Ping's anger. It was as if every

beautiful thing in the empire had suddenly ceased to exist. She turned her head the other way. The necromancer was climbing the stairs from below decks. He was wearing a magnificent black cape woven with red. Beneath it she glimpsed the jade vest. On his head he wore a ministerial cap. He had a red-raw burn on one side of his face. Ping lunged towards him, ready to strangle him, to gouge out his one eye for what he had done to Kai. Four imperial guards grabbed her and held her back. The necromancer sat down on a carved chair.

'What is he doing here? You don't know what he's done!' Ping tried to free herself from the guards.

'He killed the Dragon Attendant. He tried to kill me. He hurt Kai.'

'The necromancer was following my orders,' said the Emperor. His voice was as cold and sharp as icicles.

'But you captured him, I saw him in chains.'

The Emperor laughed. 'A little performance for your benefit, Ping. To stop you from prying where you weren't supposed to.'

Ping's brain stopped trying to make sense of the illogical world. There was a line of ants crossing the deck. She watched them hurrying along one after the other.

'I have appointed physicians to monitor the dragon's health,' the Emperor said calmly. 'They are devising a special blood-restoring diet, so that he can be bled but stay alive.'

A sneer disfigured Liu Che's handsome face. He smoothed a crease from his yellow gown.

'When the Touching Heaven Tower fell, I knew that there was disorder in the universe. I did not need my seers to tell me that Heaven was unhappy with some aspect of my reign. But no one could tell me what it was. I had to discover the truth myself.'

Liu Che looked at her as if she was as insignificant as the ants.

'It is you, Ping. *You* are what has disrupted the order of the universe. *You* have offended Heaven.'

'Me?'

'There has never been a female Dragonkeeper,' the Emperor continued. 'It is against the laws of nature. There is no prophecy in the bamboo books, no omens predicted such an unnatural event.'

Ping looked at Kai, limp and wounded, without the strength to stand. Her tears dried up. The misery and betrayal that filled her were replaced with rage.

'That's not true,' she said. 'Danzi believed I was his Dragonkeeper. He chose *me* to care for Kai.'

'Do you think I would trust the word of one senile old dragon against the advice of all my ministers and the wisdom contained in the bamboo books handed down for generations?' the Emperor said. 'The grain crops are failing, silkworm moths aren't laying eggs, there are floods in the south. It's all your fault, Ping.'

Ping was too stunned to speak.

No one had the right to disrespect Danzi. Not even the Emperor. Ping pushed the guards aside, and stood eye to eye with the Emperor.

'It isn't me who has disturbed the harmony of the world!' Ping shouted.

The Emperor rose.

'Ever since you took the role of Dragonkeeper upon yourself, things have gone wrong,' he said. 'The old dragon escaped. My father was struck by a fatal illness. The Touching Heaven Tower fell. I knew I had to restore the balance to the universe, but I couldn't leave the dragon without a keeper. You helped me solve that problem, Ping, when you suggested I look for another Dragonkeeper. As soon as I heard that a boy had been found, I ordered your execution.'

'It's your obsession that has disrupted the harmony of the universe,' she shouted.

She didn't care if Liu Che was the Son of Heaven. 'At first you just wanted to stay young. Then you wanted to live for a thousand years. Now you want to live forever! *You're* the one who has offended Heaven!'

The Emperor's gaunt face was red with rage, his eyes full of hatred. He stepped towards her. Ping flinched, thinking he was going to hit her, but instead he reached for the seal hanging from her waist. He gave it a sharp tug. The ribbon snapped. He looked at the chipped and grubby seal lying in his hand.

'You are no longer entitled to wear this seal,' he said. 'I have made another new appointment – the new Imperial Dragonkeeper.'

The ministers stepped aside. A small figure moved nervously towards the Emperor. It was Jun. Instead of his ragged clothes, he wore a pale green robe. The Emperor held out the seal to him. Jun took the seal from the Emperor with shaking hands, almost dropping it, and bowed.

'I will serve you well, Your Imperial Majesty,' Jun said.

The boy took his place next to Kai, resting his hand on the dragon's scaly back. He had something in his other hand. Something flat and round, which caught the sunlight. It was the Dragonkeeper's mirror. Kai moved closer to Jun.

'Boy is Kai's friend,' he said. He was making happy flute sounds. 'Fatso has plan for Ping. Kai help Fatso.'

The little dragon's words seared Ping's heart like red-hot coals. Her legs gave way and she collapsed to her knees.

'Now order has been restored to the universe,' the Emperor announced.

'But the necromancer . . .' Ping stammered.

'The necromancer understands that uncommon steps must be taken to achieve great things. The Longevity Council was wasting time quibbling over ingredients like women in a kitchen, just as the scientists did. When I heard about the necromancer, I knew he had to be in my service. I have you to thank for that, Ping,' the Emperor said. 'In the end, I didn't have to find the necromancer. He presented me with an offer.'

The necromancer looked down at Dong Fang Suo, who was still crouching on the deck. 'You are weak, Dong. You and your council only offered the Emperor long life. I guaranteed him immortality.'

'He bled Kai,' Ping said, but even her voice had lost its strength.

'This is why I had to replace you,' the Emperor sneered. 'Your first allegiance should have been to me, not the dragon. The necromancer bled the dragon on my orders.'

Ping's head was reeling. She couldn't believe what she was hearing.

The Emperor's voice was growing impatient.

'Kai isn't just a spoilt pet to amuse the imperial household. His purpose is to serve the Emperor. If you were really the Imperial Dragonkeeper, Ping, you would have realized long ago that dragons' blood is the key ingredient in the elixir of immortality. Kai will be revered as the last imperial dragon. He will live in luxury for a thousand years or more in my service and give his blood to me. That is his duty as imperial dragon.'

'You can't,' said Ping feebly. 'It's not right.'

He waved his hand as if brushing away a fly. 'I don't have to justify my actions to a slave girl. The necromancer says that to ensure that Heaven forgives me for my error in appointing you as Dragonkeeper, you must be sacrificed.'

Liu Che's eyes were shining with a sort of madness. Ping could no longer see any trace of her friend. The ribbon of friendship between them had always been a fragile thing. It had frayed before and been mended, but Ping realized now that nothing she could say would heal the rift between them. The Emperor was willing to risk Kai's life, to make him suffer centuries of pain in his foolish pursuit of immortality. She could never be his friend.

Dong Fang Suo was looking at her, moving his caterpillar eyebrows up and down alternately. His mouth moved. Ping had no idea what he could possibly want to say to her. If he was trying to apologize, it was too late. A guard brought a spear down across his back.

The sound of several trumpets repeating the same short refrain came from the river bank. No one on board seemed surprised to hear it. The music stopped and was replaced by the sound of horses' hooves. Six men wearing blue and gold tunics came riding down the north road on black horses. Each man held a trumpet to his lips. They sounded the refrain again. Soldiers on foot followed behind them. Blue and gold pennants fluttered from the butts of their spears. Behind them were dark, foreign men leading strange creatures, which were bigger than horses and had long, curved necks and two humps on their backs. They were ugly beasts that made unpleasant grunting noises. Ping had never seen anything like them before. The soldiers on the river bank parted to make way for another man on horseback. He was about six-times-ten years and his winged headdress was similar to those worn by imperial ministers. His horse wore a blue plume on its head. The man looked up at the Emperor with an unsmiling face. He got down from his horse, dusted off his tunic and strode up the gangplank.

The Emperor stood up. 'Welcome, Duke of Yan.'

'Your Imperial Majesty,' the Duke said, without bowing.

The Emperor ignored this discourtesy and turned to Minister Ji. 'Tell Princess Yangxin that the Duke has arrived.'

The minister bowed and went below decks. Ping realized that the baskets and chests on the dock were those that she had seen in the Princess's chambers. Princess Yangxin herself appeared. Her gown was made of fine hemp, the same shade of blue as the Duke's soldiers' tunics and trimmed with gold. Over it she wore a padded coat. A head scarf covered her lovely hair. Lady An and her other ladies-in-waiting were dressed in a similar way.

'I am ready to return to my husband and beg his forgiveness,' the Princess said in a calm voice as she bowed before the Duke.

She didn't look at Ping.

'If you can forgive my mistakes, my Lord,' she said, 'I will be an obedient wife.'

The Duke's stern face softened as he looked down at the top of Princess Yangxin's head.

'Do you have the treaty documents?' the Duke asked the Emperor.

Minister Ji sent a servant to get a table. He produced a scroll from his sleeve. The Duke read the document and held up the seal that was hanging around his waist. Minister Ji produced a pot of seal ink from his other sleeve. The Duke dipped his seal into the ink and pressed it on to the scroll. The Emperor and the Duke bowed stiffly to each other. Minister Ji shouted an order and servants brought tables up from below decks and set them ready for a banquet. The Emperor gestured for the Duke to sit on one side of him, the necromancer to sit on the other.

Guards dragged Ping below deck to a hold stacked with sacks of grain and jars of wine. They bound her hands and feet and left her.

The Emperor's words echoed in Ping's head. The old Emperor had died soon after he ate the dragon pickle that she had helped to make. Danzi had not been happy at Huangling, but after she helped him escape he became so sick and injured that he had to leave the Empire and fly to the Isle of the Blest. The Touching Heaven Tower had fallen on the very night she was snooping around against the Emperor's wishes.

She tried to think of what she could have done that would have made things turn out differently. Should she have tried to sail after Danzi? Should she have stayed on Tai Shan? Should she have drunk the star dew so she could live for a thousand years?

The sounds of music and voices came from the deck

above. The smells of the banquet found their way to the hold. No one brought her food or water. Time crept by with the slow steps of a tortoise. The banquet lasted until the light faded. The sacks and jars grew indistinct and then disappeared into blackness. The sounds of movement on the deck above her gradually stopped. More time passed and a bar of silvery moonlight crept down into the depths of the hull.

Ping heard the quick, scratchy scurrying of a rat. She was aware that Hua was no longer in the folds of her gown.

'Is that you, Hua?'

There were more ratty footsteps. The moonlight provided enough light for Ping to see that there were several rats — the ordinary-sized ones that lived in the small, dark places between the barge's timbers. None of them were Hua.

The band of moonlight made its unhurried way towards her as if determined to illuminate her in all her misery. When the light reached her torn and stained gown, she could see the faintest glow coming from her pouch. She could just reach in it with her stiff, bound hands. She pulled something from the inner pocket of her pouch. It was the size of a large leaf, but thicker and with a rough, scratchy surface. In the moonlight it glowed a soft green. She brought her hands up to her face so that she could smell it. It had the faintest aroma of overripe plums and fish brine. It was the dragon's scale.

Her arm was throbbing from the knife wound. There was

a searing pain in her chest. It felt as if someone were jabbing her cramped legs all over with sewing needles. What would Danzi think if he could see her now? She had failed completely to care for his son. She felt sleep come for her. Shouldn't she be trying to get free? Shouldn't she be thinking of a plan to rescue Kai? She just didn't know any more.

CHAPTER TWENTY-SEVEN

THE POWER OF FIVE

The dragon was standing in a circle of moonlight. He was glowing, full of the moon's brightness. He turned towards her. His red lips smiled.

'Danzi, you told me I was the true Dragonkeeper and I'm not.'

Are.

'But everything's gone wrong and now I have no one.'

Not alone.

'Yes I am, I'm totally alone. Even Hua has left me.'

The dragon's head moved slowly from side to side.

The world is made up of five elements – earth, water, fire, metal, wood – there are five directions, five colours. There is power and strength in five.

Ping reached out to touch the dragon. She felt his scales beneath her fingers. Despite their moon-brightness, they were still hard and rough to touch, but she loved the feel of them. They were as comforting as a sheepskin rug. She climbed on to the dragon's back easily, even though her hands were bound. He waited until she was safely seated and holding on tightly to one of his horns before he opened his wings and took off.

The air rushed past, making her hair rustle like leaves in the wind. She could see nothing but dark star-sprinkled sky. So many stars, it would be impossible to count them. The glowing dragon was beneath her. She didn't have to hold on. She felt calm.

'It's so peaceful up here, Danzi,' Ping said. 'I want to drift through the night sky forever. With you.'

Heaven decides the time to live and die.

The black sky turned the colour of a storm cloud, but there were no spots of rain, there was no rumbling thunder. The stars were growing dim. The sky was now the colour of doves' wings. There were no stars. It was dawn. She looked beneath her. The moonlight dragon was fading.

The sun rose above the horizon. Ping had to shade her eyes from its glare. Now there was nothing solid beneath her. Nothing but sunlit air. The dragon had disappeared. But Ping didn't fall. She smiled to herself, as she continued to fly through the sky. On her own.

Light seeped through her eyelids. She opened her eyes. It wasn't sunlight – it was light from a lamp. The necromancer was leaning over her. She could smell wine, garlic and the stench of decay.

'Get up, slave girl.'

Ping couldn't feel her legs. Even if her ankles weren't bound, she couldn't have moved. The necromancer picked her up impatiently by the back of her gown, threw her over his shoulder and hauled her up the ladder on to the deck.

It was still night. Guards were on duty, but they took no notice as the necromancer carried her ashore. Tents had been erected on the river bank to house the Duke and his men. Flags fluttered in the freezing night air. Some of the Duke's soldiers were gathered around a fire. They weren't interested in the plight of an insignificant girl either.

The necromancer soon tired of carrying her. He dropped Ping on the ground and then dragged her by the collar. She couldn't make any part of her body work. She could only look up at the patches of starlit sky between the clouds and allow herself to be bumped along the ground like a sack of grain. The necromancer dragged her into a bamboo grove, zigzagging through the canes. Ping's body banged against the bamboo canes. The sharp young shoots speared her flesh.

He stopped where the bamboo canes reached up into the cloudy night sky in a perfect circle around a clearing. He hammered two stakes into the ground. The full moon appeared in a gap in the clouds. In the moonlight the necromancer's skin was a sickly grey. It etched dark lines on his forehead and around his nose. He looked like a living corpse.

He tied her hands above her head to one of the stakes, her feet to the other. She was stretched out like a pig ready for slaughter.

The necromancer let his cape fall from his shoulders, revealing the jade vest underneath. Then he unlaced the vest and removed that as well. He gave off a smell like rotten meat. He stood before Ping, wearing only loose trousers. She shuddered at the sight of his bare, grey skin.

He held his knife in both hands so that it pointed towards the sky. He closed his eyes and muttered words in a strange language. It was a spell or it might have been a prayer – not to the eight Immortals in Heaven, Ping was sure of that, but to some demon in the worst regions of Hell.

Ping remembered Saggypants, the poor dead Dragon Attendant, and the horrible cavity hacked in his belly. She realized what the necromancer was about to do. He was going to cut out her liver too. It must have been a ritual that was part of one of his enchantments. Strangely, Ping wasn't afraid. The dream of Danzi had left her calm. The feeling was returning to her arms and legs, but she didn't strain against the ropes.

She could make out four marks on the necromancer's stomach – straight lines, radiating out like dark rays from his navel. They were evenly spaced and all the same length. At first she thought they were tattoos like the marks on his face, but the skin around them was puckered. She realized they were wounds cut into his flesh, arranged with care and precision. One was healed to a scar. Two others were not well healed, but swollen and bruised, as if some poison beneath was trying to find its way out. The fourth was a raw wound with fresh blood still drying around it. The edges of this wound were held together with silk thread. Ping remembered the needle and thread that the necromancer had held in his hand back in the lodge. Just as she had mended the rip in Danzi's wing with a needle and thread, the necromancer had mended a cut in his own flesh. There was space on his belly for one more scar to complete a five-pointed pattern.

The dragon's dream words came back to her. *Heaven decides the time to live and die.* If this was her time to die, she was ready. Danzi had also said something about the power of five. She didn't understand what he'd meant by that, but the old dragon's words were often a mystery to her.

At least she wouldn't give the necromancer the satisfaction of watching her die in agony. She had to increase her *qi* power so that she could suffer the pain without screaming. The full moon appeared between the clouds again. She breathed in the moonlight. It had low levels of *qi* compared to sunlight, but it was better than nothing. She thought of Kai. The little dragon was the one creature she couldn't bear to leave. Jun would try to fill the role of Dragonkeeper, but he had never known Danzi. He didn't have the knowledge the old dragon had given her. She started counting the silvery bamboo leaves that surrounded her.

The necromancer turned the knife in his hands so the tip was pointing down at her, still muttering his spells. Ping pictured all the beautiful and wonderful things she had seen in her life – Danzi in flight in the moonlight, Tai Shan, Kai when he was new-born, the Garden of the Purple Dragon before it was ruined, the smiling face of her little brother. Her life had been short, but it had been exceptional. She had no desire to exchange it for the life of someone who would live to old age without experiencing those things.

The necromancer raised the knife above her. The blade shone in the moonlight. Then the silence of the night was broken by shouting voices, the clashing of metal and a high-pitched tuneless whistle, like someone blowing hard on a flute without placing their fingers over the holes. Lowering his knife, the necromancer turned to see where the noise was coming from. Flashes of light appeared among the bamboo. Bright orange balls of flame arched high over the clearing. In another direction, an eerie purple glow moved through the bamboo. The necromancer peered into the darkness.

'Who's there?' he called.

There was no answer and the racket continued. A white mist was drifting from the bamboo. The mist cloud grew quickly until it filled the clearing. The noise stopped. There was silence for a moment and then a whooping and yelling, a screeching and a squawking. Dark shapes rushed out of the bamboo, attacking the necromancer from behind and from both sides. The ground seemed to be seething with small black shapes. Through the mist, Ping saw the point of a spear, a sword, balls of flame. She heard the necromancer scream.

Hope filled Ping's heart. Someone had come to her rescue. She felt her strength return.

But the necromancer blocked the spear with his arm, he met the sword blade with his knife, the fireballs fell short of their mark. The necromancer passed his hand through the air and the mist evaporated. He laughed when his attackers were revealed. Dong Fang Suo and Jun were sprawled on the ground, half of Hua's tail was missing. Kai was crouched among the bamboo canes, looking small and frightened, a wisp of mist trailing from his mouth.

Ping's hope had evaporated as quickly as the mist. So this was Danzi's power of five – a girl with her hands tied, an old man, a boy, a rat and a small dragon. The old dragon had had no idea how powerful the necromancer had become.

Dong Fang Suo stood up.

'Take my liver instead,' he said.

'Why would I want your feeble old liver,' the necromancer sneered, 'when I can have the liver of a young Dragonkeeper?'

Ping could hear small movements around her head. Fur and whiskers brushed against her bound hands. The ropes around her wrists began to loosen. Rats were nibbling through them. The last wisps of mist hid them from the necromancer, but Ping could see them. They were ordinary-sized rats, like the ones she'd seen on the barge.

'She doesn't deserve to die,' Dong Fang Suo said.

'Yes she does.' There was bitter hatred in the necromancer's voice. 'She stole the dragon stone from me. She humiliated me at Wucheng.'

'This power that you get from the livers of the dead,' Dong Fang Suo said, 'it is only short-lived.'

The rats were now gnawing through the ropes that tied Ping's ankles.

'There are plenty more livers in the empire,' the necromancer snarled. 'Leave, old man. Your day is over.'

'I know the source of your power,' Dong Fang Suo said. 'The liver is the house of the eternal soul – the soul that flies to Heaven when someone dies.'

The old magician wasn't just stalling so that the rats could free her, Ping realized, he was trying to tell her something.

'When you cut the livers from living men and sew them into your own body . . .'

'I've heard enough of your prattle,' the necromancer said.

He turned abruptly, raised his knife again and plunged it towards Ping. She rolled out of the way and the blade dug deep into the earth.

Jun had the mirror in his hand. He angled it so that a beam of bright, white moonlight shone in the necromancer's eye. He turned to attack the boy, but Dong Fang Suo tripped him with the shaft of the spear. Hua ran up the necromancer's back. The necromancer let out a scream. He dropped the knife and tried to pull the rat off. Hua jumped down with the man's ear lobe between his sharp yellow teeth. The necromancer grabbed what remained of his ear, blood pouring through his fingers.

The necromancer turned with fury in his one eye and glared at Jun. The boy was transfixed by his stare, unable to move. The necromancer raised his hand and blasted Dong Fang Suo into the air like a leaf. The old man crashed back down to earth like a sack of bones. The necromancer was stronger than the power of five. Ping knew that she would have to face him alone, but she needed something to shield her from his awesome power. The jade vest was lying at her feet. She picked it up and slipped it on.

The necromancer turned to face Ping.

'Cut him,' Dong Fang Suo gasped, struggling to his knees. 'Cut the scars.'

Ping dived for the knife, grasped it in her hand. She understood what she had to do. The necromancer focused his gaze on the knife in Ping's hand. It turned red hot and she was forced to drop it.

'Iron hurt Kai,' said a voice in Ping's head.

The little dragon, still glowing in the light of the full moon, was at her feet. Ping kicked the knife away.

'Don't need knife. Have Kai.'

She remembered how she had cut her own flesh. She had just the tool she needed. As she bent to pick up Kai, the necromancer grabbed hold of the glowing knife and hurled it at her. Dong Fang Suo lunged forward. The red-hot knife pierced the old man's chest and he fell.

Ping took hold of the dragon's left forepaw. She ran at the necromancer and with Kai's longest talon sliced open one of the healed scars on the necromancer's belly. The necromancer roared with pain and anger. Black blood and pus spurted from the scar. A putrid smell filled the air. He directed his power at her. It knocked her off her feet, but it had weakened and the vest protected her. He picked up Jun's sword and swung it at her. Ping focused her own power and knocked it aside.

'The other scars, Ping,' Dong Fang Suo gasped.

Ping slashed another scar on his belly and another. The stench was terrible. The necromancer sank to his knees as lumps of greenish, rotten liver oozed out of the cuts and slid to the ground.

Ping saw the glint form in his eye. She crouched down to avoid his stare, scraped up a handful of dirt and threw it into his face. His arms lashed out blindly and tried to push her aside, but his power was fading and Ping had the strength to resist. The air around him distorted as he tried to shape-change, but he couldn't do it. Kai's black talon cut the thread that held together the edges of the newest wound. A piece of fresh liver was wedged in the cut. Ping hooked it out with the talon. The necromancer slumped forward on his hands and knees.

A sudden unnatural gust of icy wind spiralled around Ping, blowing dirt and leaves into her eyes. The wind blew around her and through her, chilling her heart. A sound like a screech of anger filled the air.

Dong Fang Suo was weak, but he was still alive.

'Dig a hole, Ping,' he whispered. 'Quickly. Souls that have been denied a place in Heaven create the angriest ghosts. Bury the pieces of liver.'

Ping put Kai down at a safe distance and gouged a hole in the earth, scraped the grizzly meat into it and covered it over.

Dong Fang Suo muttered a prayer, asking the eternal souls of the angry ghosts to find their way to Heaven.

The screech trailed off into a sigh of relief and then faded away completely. The wind died but the air remained icy. Ping didn't know who the necromancer's other three victims were, but she prayed they had an easy journey to Heaven.

Heavy clouds blotted out the night sky completely. With the moonlight gone, Kai no longer glowed.

Ping hugged him close. 'Are you all right?'

He nodded.

'Fatso not all right,' he said.

Ping went over to the broken body of the old magician. Blood soaked the front of his gown. She looked into his eyes and knew he wouldn't live.

The necromancer was still on his hands and knees. Jun looked at him with disgust.

'You must kill him,' Jun said. 'He will always be evil.'

Ping shook her head. 'No. Heaven decides the time to live and die.'

Dong Fang Suo nodded slowly.

'What will we do with him?' Ping asked.

'Let him go,' the Imperial Magician said. 'He has sealed his fate with his own hands. The rotting flesh has poisoned his body. He will die soon enough without your assistance.'

The necromancer struggled to his feet. Ping could see now that it wasn't the moonlight that was responsible for the grey pallor of his skin. That was its actual colour. The rotten smell wafted from his poisoned body with every movement. When he looked at Ping, there was no magical glint in his one eye, just fear and defeat. He limped off into the bamboo grove, bent and broken, like an old man.

Ping crouched down beside Dong Fang Suo.

'He is losing his life's blood,' she said to Jun. 'See if you can find some moss to staunch the bleeding.'

Jun hurried off into the darkness.

'Don't concern yourself with me,' Dong Fang Suo whispered.

Ping took his hand. 'I misjudged you,' she said. 'I blamed you for everything.'

'I made many mistakes. I was too afraid of losing my imperial position to oppose the Emperor and his scheme to gain immortality. I didn't try to stop him when he wanted to kill you, when he started bleeding Kai. It did me no good. He still turned against me.'

Jun knelt beside Ping and handed her some moss. She placed it over the wound.

'On the barge, I heard the necromancer tell the Emperor that he intended to cut out your liver.' Ping had to lean close to hear what the old man was saying. 'I had to try and put things right. Jun wanted to help.'

Ping turned to Jun.

'I thought you wanted to be Dragonkeeper.'

The boy shook his head.

'Not when I saw what the necromancer had done to Kai,' Jun said. 'I knew I couldn't defeat him, but I hoped you could, Ping.'

'And you told Kai what you were planning?'

'No. I can't speak to Kai in my head like you do.'

Jun hung his head and wouldn't look at her.

'But . . .'

'I lied when I said I could understand him. In the carriage, I pretended I understood what he said. My mother made up the stories about me having second sight.' He finally looked up, peeping at Ping through his fringe. 'I'm not even naturally left-handed. My parents wanted me to have the position of Dragonkeeper. When I was small, they tied my right hand behind my back to force me to use my left hand. Don't blame them. They are poor and have many daughters.'

'But Kai knew you were a Dragonkeeper.' She turned to the dragon. 'Didn't you?'

He shook his head. 'Boy play games better than Ping,' he said. 'And have sweeties.'

'Sweeties?'

Jun pulled something out of his sleeve. He opened out his hand. Three red berries lay in his palm.

'It's a trick passed down from my great-grandfather,' Jun said, his head hanging lower. 'Dragons can't resist these berries. They will always come to you if you have some up your sleeve. I'm sorry, Ping.'

'When Jun and I discussed what we could do, we realized that Kai understood us and could help. Hua too.'

Ping had to lean close to hear Dong Fang Suo.

'We told Kai to tell you what the plan was.'

'I misunderstood,' Ping said. 'I thought everyone had turned against me, even Kai.'

She stroked the little dragon. 'I was wrong. You were very brave. It was your idea to cut the scars with your talons.'

'Father said use talons,' Kai replied. 'In dream.'

It had never occurred to Ping that Danzi visited Kai in dreams as well.

'I was ready to go with you, Ping, wherever your path lay, but that isn't possible now.' Dong Fang Suo's voice was faint, his breathing difficult. 'I should have tried to stop the necromancer at Twisting Snake Ravine. I followed the Emperor's orders blindly.'

'You gave help when it was most needed,' Ping said. 'You gave your life. I'll never forget your part in the power of five.'

Dong Fang Suo's shallow breathing stopped.

'Bye bye, Fatso,' said Kai.

Ping closed the old man's blank eyes. He'd died with a smile on his face. She wished she knew a prayer to help guide his soul to Heaven.

Jun held out the Dragonkeeper's seal to Ping.

'I don't want it,' she said. 'I'm not the Imperial Dragon-keeper. There is no imperial dragon. I'm keeper of a dragon born in the wild, who will live in freedom, not in captivity. You keep the seal – as a souvenir. It's the mirror I want.'

Jun handed her the mirror. 'I'll take Dong Fang Suo's body back and tell the Emperor that you have defeated the necromancer. Perhaps he'll realize that his plans to gain immortality will bring nothing but misery.'

'Tell him that Heaven decides the time to live and die,' Ping said.

Jun nodded. 'I'll stay hidden as long as possible, to allow you time to escape.'

He lifted the Imperial Magician's body. Jun was small and skinny, but Ping realized he had strength within that she hadn't given him credit for. He adjusted his grip on the old man, and then walked off into the bamboo.

'Bye bye, Boy,' said Kai.

The sky was growing light, though heavy clouds kept the

sun hidden. Ping felt tired and weak. She had forgotten about her injuries while she was battling with the necromancer, but now she realized that she hurt all over.

She heard squeaking. The rats who had chewed through her bonds had gathered together. Ping didn't understand why they didn't just run back to their home. Then she realized they were waiting – waiting for Hua.

She picked up Hua and buried her face in his soft warm fur. She wanted to tell him not to go, to beg him to stay and help her on the next part of her journey. But she didn't.

'Danzi sent you back to help me,' she said. 'You've saved me many times, Hua. You've done your job.'

She gently put Hua down on the ground.

'I don't know how I'll manage without you, but you should live a proper rat life,' she said. 'Go with them.'

Hua ran over and joined the other rats. He looked back at Ping.

'Goodbye, old friend,' she said.

The rats scurried off and Hua followed.

Sadness threatened to overpower her, but she didn't have time to begin grieving for everyone she had lost. Not yet. She had to decide what to do next.

Ping tried to remember all the times she'd dreamed of Danzi. Was there anything in his messages that would help her decide where she should go?

'Kai, in your dreams, did Danzi tell you anything else?'

'Eat worms,' the dragon said.

'Worms?'

'Good for eyesight.'

'Anything else?'

'Not too many. Too many worms make Kai fart.'

The little dragon made tinkling flute sounds. The sound made Ping's heart soar. It was good to hear the sounds of a happy dragon again.

'Also said five.'

'Five what? Power of five?'

'No. Five upside-down.'

Kai's dreams of the old dragon were as unfathomable as hers. Kai raised his head so that Ping could scratch him under the chin.

'But you don't like being tickled under the chin.'

'Do now.'

She scratched the little dragon, but her fingers caught in his scales. Beneath his chin he had five reverse scales, just as his father had.

'Five upside-down scales. Is that what he said?'

Kai nodded. Ping looked closer. His reverse scales were much smaller than Danzi's.

'Is there anything behind your reverse scales?'

'Maybe.'

The reverse scales were so small that Ping wouldn't have been able to fit a finger behind them, but she could see that they were all bulging a little.

'Show me what's behind your scales, Kai.'

'Not showing.' The little dragon looked guilty.

'Please, Kai. I won't get cross, I promise.'

The little dragon inserted two talons behind the first of his reverse scales. He pulled out a dead caterpillar and a half-eaten jujube.

'Snacks,' said Kai.

From behind the second scale Kai produced the jade pendant that Wang Cao had given Ping.

'I thought I'd lost that!' Ping exclaimed.

Behind the third was a gold earring in the shape of a lotus flower.

'Pretty,' said Kai.

'Did you steal that from the Princess? You're a bad dragon.'

From behind the fourth scale he produced a dragon talon.

'Father's,' the little dragon said. 'For dreams.'

Ping wasn't sure what he meant.

'What's behind the last scale, Kai?' Ping asked.

He pulled out a folded piece of undyed silk cloth.

'What's that?' Ping asked.

'Don't know.'

'Did you put it there?'

Kai shook his head.

'Who did then?'

'Rat.'

'Hua?'

The little dragon nodded. 'Red bird carried it across Ocean from Father.'

With trembling fingers, Ping took the piece of silk from the little dragon's talons. It was a message from Danzi. Not a dream riddle, but something she could hold in her hand. She unfolded it. In the growing light, she examined it closely. It was blank. She turned it over. The silk square didn't have a single mark on it.

CHAPTER TWENTY-EIGHT

A SILK SQUARE

Ping's happiness plummeted like a ripe peach falling from a tree. Just a short while earlier she'd had the power of five. She and her friends had defeated the necromancer using the five elements. She had deciphered Kai's dream. She had found a message from Danzi. Her heart had soared. Things were finally going right. But her band of companions had disintegrated, and the message from the old dragon had proved to be meaningless. The peach of her happiness splattered and turned to pulp.

Ping didn't need a magician, a homesick boy or a dragon to tell her. She knew what she had to do. She had to take Kai to a place where no one would ever find him.

The Emperor would send out guards to scour the empire for the little dragon. Once word spread, greedy people would be willing to hand Kai over for a reward, or else sell him for his value in gold. No matter where she went, if there were people near, Kai would never be safe. The neglect of incompetent Dragonkeepers and selfish Emperors had combined to reduce the number of dragons to one. People had lost their chance to have dragons live among them.

She and Kai would have to creep through the empire, hiding in forests, travelling at night until they found a deserted place where no one would disturb them. Ping suddenly pictured the desolate hills around Huangling Palace. That was a place where no one chose to live. And the Emperor would never think to look for her there. She and Kai could survive on lizards and birds. She could build a shelter of branches and bundles of grass. The winters would be cold and bleak; they would have to hibernate like animals. It would be a miserable life, but it was the only plan she could think of.

She remembered what Danzi had said in her dream. *Those who do not leave their beds are not always safe.* She had tried to seek safety – on Tai Shan, at Ming Yang Lodge, with her family – but Heaven had always guided her back to her true path. She vowed she would never stray from it again – if she could just work out which way it lay.

She wanted to get Kai as far away from the Emperor as possible. For the moment she would risk travelling by day and hope that the Emperor and his guards were too busy with Princess Yangxin's departure to notice her.

'You'll have to shape-change during the day, Kai,' she said. 'What shape do you want to take?'

The little dragon turned into a bucket, then a pot plant and finally settled on a basket.

Ping was weak, but so was Kai. She picked him up. Ping's chest hurt with every breath. Her left arm hung limp. The wound on the side of her head was bleeding again. She was weak and exhausted. She didn't know if she could carry her own weight, let alone the dragon's.

Heavy clouds hung low over the countryside. It was still early, but there was a great deal of activity on the north road near the river. Word had spread about the arrival of the Duke of Yan's camel caravan, and people were arriving from nearby villages to see the creatures. Stalls had sprung up on the dock to sell food and drinks to the spectators. Ping watched from the cover of the bamboo grove as imperial guards kept back the crowd while bearers finished loading the Princess's baggage, piling each camel with chests, baskets and bags. There were also two sedan chairs that would carry Princess Yangxin and her ladies, draped with hangings to conceal the occupants.

No one was looking for her yet. As Ping stepped out on to the road, Lady An emerged from one of the tents. Their eyes met, but Lady An looked away and went on with her business.

Ping had no money, no food, not even a water bag. She had lost all her belongings apart from the dragon scale and her mirror. Kai didn't ask where they were going.

Ping asked a farmer with a covered wagon if he would take her to the next town. He looked suspiciously at the grubby girl with a ripped gown and blood on what remained of her sleeve. He shook his head.

Ping walked slowly. She wished she felt stronger. At any moment Kai could grow tired of being a basket and turn into his proper shape. As soon as the Emperor found out that she had escaped with Kai, a reward would be posted for her capture. Soon everyone would be on the lookout for her.

Every step took them further away from the Emperor. Ping had never imagined that she would be so pleased to leave Liu Che behind her, happy that she would never have to see him again.

The silk square was scrunched up in her hand. She was angry with Danzi for raising her hopes. For a moment she'd thought she would learn something new and valuable from it. She threw the silk square on to the road.

'Keep silk!' cried a voice in Ping's head.

'What for?' said Ping. 'It's useless.'

A merchant pulling a hand cart passed them. One of the cart's wheels rolled over the silk square. The cart rumbled on with the silk stuck to the wheel.

Kai suddenly turned into a goat. Ping dropped him. She looked around. Fortunately no one had seen the transformation.

'Must get silk,' Kai said.

He started to run after it.

'No!' Ping grabbed him around his goat neck. He struggled to get away from her.

'You must stay with me, Kai,' Ping said. 'Promise me you won't run off.'

He stopped struggling. 'Promise.'

Kai stayed in his goat shape. After no more than twice-ten paces, Ping had to stop to get her breath back. She wondered how long she could walk without food or water.

Then she heard voices shouting. The alarm had been raised already. She glanced back. Imperial guards were dividing into search parties.

Pulling the goat with her, Ping ducked into the cover of the bamboo grove, but it was no safer there. Guards were moving through the bamboo grove as well, fanning out in all directions. Ping crouched behind a thick clump of bamboo.

'It doesn't matter if the girl is killed!' a voice shouted. 'But the dragon mustn't be harmed. And remember that it can take on disguises. It could be a bucket, a jar or a soup ladle.'

A guard strode past. He thrust his spear into the canes where Ping and Kai were hiding. The point came to rest less than a hand-width from Kai's nose. The little dragon didn't make a sound.

'Good boy, Kai,' she said.

She could hear imperial guards on all sides, slashing down canes with their swords, thrusting their spears into the dens-est growth. Ping was beginning to think that the road might be safer after all. She was just about to turn towards it, when a hand clamped over her mouth. Ping tried to free herself.

'There is no need to be afraid,' said a gentle voice behind her.

Ping stopped struggling. She recognized the voice. It was Lady An.

'Put this on,' she said, taking off the blue and gold cloak and head scarf that she was wearing.

Underneath she was wearing a reddish gown similar to Ping's. Ping draped the cape around her shoulders and put the head scarf over her hair.

'Tell Kai to turn into something you can carry,' Lady An said.

Kai understood her words. He changed back into a basket.

'More imperial guards are coming,' Lady An said. 'Go to Princess Yangxin.'

Before Ping had a chance to say anything, Lady An started to run through the bamboo grove, slipping through the narrow spaces between the canes, darting this way and that like a startled animal. Guards came crashing past. Ignoring the girl wearing the Duke's colours and carrying a basket, they chased after the running figure.

Ping stepped out into the road again, glad that the cloak and head scarf concealed her. Guards were everywhere, searching every wagon, prodding and poking every bucket and jar. She walked towards the sedan chairs and the camels that were loaded with the Princess's baggage.

She had to stop to rest. She put the basket-shaped dragon down for a moment near a stall selling hot food.

'I've found it!'

An imperial guard appeared at the stall. He had discovered a soup ladle with a handle carved in the shape of a dragon. He poked the ladle with his sword but didn't dare pick it up.

Ping couldn't see Kai anywhere.

She heard sweet flute notes. Ping looked around trying to find their source. There were people and animals everywhere, but her eyes fell on one little boy. He was about four years old. It was her own half-brother. He looked up at her with a gap-toothed smile. Ping reached out to stroke his hair. She felt a strange sensation as her hand rested, not on silky hair, but on the rough scales of a dragon.

Ping stared at the boy.

'But you didn't come to my family's house. How do you know what Liang looks like?'

'Kai see in Ping's mind.'

The curtains of one of the sedan chairs were drawn aside.

'Get in, Ping.' It was the Princess. 'Where is Kai?'

Ping pointed to the child beside her. Just as Ping and Kai climbed up, the camel drivers flicked their beasts with whips. The camels set off, groaning and complaining.

The bearers lifted the sedan chair. They were moving.

Ping slumped back in her seat, suddenly overcome by weariness and relief. She looked across at the Princess, who looked as cool and calm as ever.

'Thank you, Your Imperial Majesty,' she said.

Kai was sniffing a basket.

'Would Kai like something to eat?'

'He hasn't had any food since yesterday and he's very weak.'

'I heard what my brother did to him,' the Princess said. She opened the basket and the smell of roasted meat wafted out.

'Birdies!' said Kai, popping back into his dragon shape again.

The basket contained a number of roasted quails.

'Eat all you like,' the Princess said.

Kai didn't need further encouragement. He stuck his head in the basket and ate the quails, bones and all.

'I'm afraid you will have to wait until we stop for the midday meal to eat and change your clothes, Ping.'

'I don't want to cause you any trouble,' Ping said. 'Once we are away from the river, we'll make our own way.'

'You won't get far,' the Princess replied. 'You have serious injuries and the weather is worsening. Come all the way to Yan with us.'

'I've allowed the promise of safety and comfort to lure me away from my true path too often.'

'You mustn't punish yourself, Ping. You have saved Kai.

Heal yourself before you start on your journey. You haven't had time to decide where you are going. And, believe me, Yan is not always safe or comfortable.'

'But what about the Duke?'

'You can pose as one of my servants. Kai can be an orphan boy who I have taken on to train as a bodyguard. The Duke will have no interest in either of you.'

Through a gap in the hangings, Ping could see the bamboo canes march by without her having to lift a toe. She was willing to be carried wherever the sedan chair was going.

'You have been so kind to me, Princess Yangxin,' Ping said.

'My brother has treated you and Kai shamefully,' the Princess said. 'If he hadn't been blinded by his obsession, he would know you are the true Dragonkeeper.'

'You believe I am?'

'I know you are,' the Princess replied. 'I have watched you with Kai. I have seen your devotion to him. You are injured, bleeding, but your first thought is for him.'

'The Emperor doesn't think I'm the true Dragonkeeper.'

'I have to confess that I wasn't sure at first.'

'What convinced you?'

The Princess pulled something from the sleeve of her gown. It was a strip of bamboo with characters written on it. It was the same strip that Hua had brought to her. Ping looked at the characters. To her surprise she could read almost all of them. It was a prediction.

'In the second year of Emperor Wu a new Dragonkeeper will appear. She will be shunned but she is the true Dragonkeeper.'

Ping stared at the strip. 'It says "she".'

'Yes.'

'It could be a mistake.'

The Princess shook her head.

'How did you get this?'

'Your rat brought it to me.'

'But I thought you hated rats.'

'I do, but this one was so persistent. After he had brought it to me for the third time, I read it. It is the last strip of a book. Someone untied it, so it couldn't be read.'

Ping remembered when she had burst in on the Emperor and Dong Fang Suo when the bamboo books about dragons had first arrived from Chang'an. The Imperial Magician had been retying the strings of a book then. She looked at the strip in her hand. All the books would have been destroyed in the fire. This one strip was all that remained of them. Now there was no doubting it. All of the knowledge about dragons in the empire was contained in her head.

'You have had your doubts, Ping,' Princess Yangxin said. 'Are you now convinced you are the true Dragonkeeper?'

'I know I am,' she said. 'I didn't need a bamboo book to tell me. In my heart, I knew.'

She stroked Kai's rough scales. 'I just didn't believe I could do the job properly.'

Ping didn't know whether Danzi had withheld knowledge from her on purpose, or whether the old dragon had just forgotten what he was supposed to tell her. It didn't matter. No set of rules could help her. She had to teach herself. And Danzi trusted her to do that. She was the last Dragonkeeper, that's what he'd said. With that he had actually told her all she needed to know. She had to end dragons' reliance on people. She had to teach Kai how to take care of himself. Accepting the imperial seal had been a mistake. She had allowed her affection for the Emperor to cloud her judgement. She wasn't a slave girl, but she wasn't an imperial courtier either. She was the Dragonkeeper. The last one. She had to find a place where Kai could live in freedom.

'Liu Che said there was nothing that prophesised a female Dragonkeeper,' Ping said. 'He lied to me.'

The Princess's eyes filled with tears. 'His true character is good and honest. I pray that it is not lost forever.'

'Aren't you angry that he is sending you back to Yan?' Ping asked.

The Princess shook her head. 'I begged the Duke to take me back.'

Ping turned to the Princess in surprise.

'The Duke was ready to enlist the barbarians beyond the Great Wall and preparing to wage war on the empire. Liu

Che ignored this threat. You were right, Ping. My brother is obsessed with his search for immortality.'

'But he's going back to Chang'an now, isn't he? The Grand Counsellor will bring him to his senses.'

The Princess shook her head sadly.

'He is not going to Chang'an. He plans to sail to the source of the Yellow River, where he has heard the peaches of immortality grow. The empire is weak already, war would bring it to its knees. It is within my power to prevent this from happening. The Duke was fond of me before my indiscretion.'

The sedan chair slowed down and stopped.

'What's wrong?' Ping said anxiously.

The hangings were pulled aside and Lady An stepped in. There were beads of perspiration on her forehead.

'One of the boxes has come loose. The camel drivers are securing it.'

'You lost your pursuers?' the Princess asked.

Lady An smiled. 'They are chasing a deer.'

Urgent flute notes rang out. 'Kai need to pee.'

'No, Kai,' said Ping anxiously. 'You can't.' She remembered what had happened the last time they were travelling and Kai had wanted to pee.

'Must go now!'

Ping couldn't bear the thought of the Princess's sedan chair flooded with foul-smelling dragon urine.

'We won't be long,' she said to the Princess.

Princess Yangxin looked puzzled. 'But the camels will start moving again at any moment. We must keep up with them.'

'Quick, Kai,' Ping said. 'Take on the shape of Liang.'

The little dragon shook his head. 'Only pee in dragon shape.'

Kai jumped out of the sedan chair. Ping followed him. They had travelled no more than two or three *li*. The road was still crowded with people who had come to see the camel caravan from Yan. Ping held out her cloak to hide the dragon.

'Hurry up!' she said.

'Won't come,' Kai said sadly.

The Princess peeped through the curtains to see what the delay was.

'Trying,' said Kai.

'Your Majesty,' Ping said. 'Do you have a wine jar?'

The Princess nodded. She handed Ping a lovely alabaster wine jar. Ping tipped the jar and let the wine dribble out on to the road. The trickling sound did the trick.

'Peeing,' said Kai triumphantly.

A pool of dark green dragon urine formed on the road. Ping looked around anxiously, sure that the awful smell would attract attention. The camel drivers called out in a strange language. The camels answered with their grunting, groaning cry and set off again.

'Hurry up!'

'Not finished.'

The bearers picked up the sedan chair.

There was a sudden gust of icy wind. Leaves swirled in the air. Something else was blown along by the wind. It fluttered and turned, billowing in the breeze like a miniature sail on a boat. It fluttered down and settled on a tuft of grass poking up between two stone slabs. It was the silk square. The dragon repositioned himself. A new stream of urine splashed on to the tuft of grass, soaking the silk square.

'Wet,' said Kai cheerfully.

Ping peered at the silk. It was changing. Faint marks were appearing on it. Despite the terrible smell, she picked up the silk by one corner. She could see pale characters on it. The marks were getting darker.

The sedan chair had moved ahead. Ping picked up Kai and tried to catch up with it. Every step sent pain shooting through her body. The bearers increased their pace. The Princess held back the curtains. With a huge effort, Ping managed to lift the little dragon into the sedan chair. She ran, despite the pain, but she couldn't climb up herself. Her last *shu* of energy had been used up.

Snowflakes started to fall. The clouds that had been threatening for over a week decided to release their burden. Princess Yangxin reached out and took Ping's outstretched hand. She pulled Ping inside. The Princess had more strength than Ping had ever imagined.

Ping collapsed on the floor, gasping with pain and exhaustion. She lifted herself on to the seat next to the Princess and stared at the dripping silk, which was still clutched in her hand. The marks were now dark brown. The silk square was covered with lines and curves. There were some characters too, written scratchily with a shaky hand. Ping could read many of them. They were the names of roads, rivers and a mountain.

'What do these other two characters say?' she asked.

The Princess held a fold of her head scarf over her nose and looked at the silk. 'Kun-lun,' she answered. 'The Kunlun Mountains. It's a map.'

Kai was perched on the seat between her and the Princess, making high and happy flute notes.

'Message from Father,' he said.

'Yes,' said Ping. 'It's a message from Danzi. Hidden behind your reverse scale. Now I know where our path lies.'

'Not just yet though,' the Princess said. 'Allow yourself some time to rest and recover.'

The snow was falling heavily. The countryside had turned white.

'The Kun-lun Mountains are impassable in winter. You must spend the winter months in Yan.'

'Travel with Prissy,' Kai said, happily snuffling about in the basket to see if there was any food he had missed.

It took Ping a moment to work out who Kai meant.

The little dragon looked up at the Princess. 'Prissy play ball?'

'No, Kai!' Ping exclaimed.

'Prissy tell story?'

'No! You'll have to sit still and behave yourself all the way to Yan.'

Kai belched.

'OK.'

He walked round in a circle in the space between Ping and the Princess. Finally, he settled down. He coiled his scaly body into a tight knot with his nose under his back paws and his tail pulled up through the middle.

The Princess smiled. So did Ping. She settled back to enjoy the peace and quiet. She knew it wouldn't last long.

GLOSSARY

CHANG

A measure of distance equal to about 2.3 metres.

CINNABAR

A bright red mineral whose chemical name is mercuric sulphide.

HAN DYNASTY

A period in Chinese history when the Emperors all belonged to a particular family. It lasted from 202 BCE to 220 CE.

HAN FOOT

A measure of length equal to about 23 centimetres.

JADE

A semiprecious stone also known as nephrite. Its colour varies from green to white.

JIN

The measure of weight for gold.

JUJUBE

A name for the fruit known as the Chinese date.

LI

A measure of distance equal to about half a kilometre.

QI

According to traditional Chinese beliefs, *qi* is the life energy that flows through us and controls the workings of the body.

SHU

A measure of weight equal to about half a gram.

GUIDE TO PRONUNCIATION

The Chinese words in this book are written in *pinyin,* which is the official way of writing the sound of Chinese characters using the English alphabet. These words aren't always pronounced the way you might think. Here is a guide to help you pronounce them correctly.

Dong Fang Suo	Dung (u as in *butcher*), Fang Swar (as in swarm)
Hua	Hw-ar (rhymes with *far*)
Huan	Hwan
Huangling	Hwang-ling
Jun	Jun (u as in *butcher*)
Long Kai Duan	Lung (u as in *butcher*), Kai (rhymes with *buy*), Dw-aan
Lao Ma	L-ow (rhymes with *now*), Ma (rhymes with *far*)
Liu Che	Lee-oo (oo as in *loop*), Chur (as in *church*)
Lu-lin	Loo (rhymes with *shoe*), lin
Danzi	Dan-za
Ming Yang	Sounds just like it looks
Ping	Sounds just like it looks
Tai Shan	Tai (pronounced as *tie*), Shan

Xiao Zheng	Show (as in *shower*), Jung (u as in *butcher*)
Xiu-xin	Shee-oo (oo as in *loop*), shin (rhymes with *bin*)
Yangxin	Yang Shin (rhymes with *bin*)

ACKNOWLEDGEMENTS

I am indebted to all those researchers who have written about the Han Dynasty and scholars who have translated ancient Chinese books, and made all their knowledge available to people like me. There is a full bibliography on my website at http://home.iprimus.com.au/carolew/

I'd like to make special mention of Marinus Willem de Visser, to whom I have dedicated this book. He was a Dutch academic who studied Chinese and Japanese religion and folklore – and dragons. His book *The Dragon in China and Japan*, published in 1913, contains translations of dragon mythology from ancient Chinese works and is the source of most of my knowledge of Chinese dragons.

I would also like to thank my husband, John, and my daughter, Lili, for their continual support, love and friendship.

Special thanks to everyone at black dog books, especially Alison Arnold and Andrew Kelly, for their unflagging enthusiasm and dedication in the creation of this book.

Read about how Ping's adventures began in:

CAROLE WILKINSON

Ping is a slave in a remote royal palace at Huangling Mountain. Her cruel master neglects his duties as Imperial Dragonkeeper, and under his watch the Emperor's dragons have dwindled from a magnificent dozen to a miserable two. Soon only the ancient and wise Long Danzi remains. Ping has always been wary of the strange creatures living in their dark pit – but in a moment of startling bravery she rescues Danzi and the mysterious and beautiful stone that he protects.

Now fugitives, Danzi and Ping race across the kingdom, fighting enemies at every turn. But as they come to the end of their journey, Ping must prepare for a heartbreaking loss – and a truly thrilling revelation . . .

An enthralling magical adventure set in the exciting and colourful world of ancient China.

Now available in paperback

A selected list of titles available from
Macmillan Children's Books

The prices shown below are correct at the time of going to press. However, Macmillan Publishers reserves the right to show new retail prices on covers, which may differ from those previously advertised.

Carole Wilkinson

Julie Bertagna

All Pan Macmillan titles can be ordered from our website, www.panmacmillan.com, or from your local bookshop and are also available by post from:

Bookpost, PO Box 29, Douglas, Isle of Man IM99 1BQ

Credit cards accepted. For details:
Telephone: 01624 677237
Fax: 01624 670923
Email: bookshop@enterprise.net
www.bookpost.co.uk

Free postage and packing in the United Kingdom